D0992955

Forbidden Fruits

"In *Forbidden Fruits,* Joscelyn Godwin and Guido Mina di Sospiro, authors of the acclaimed *The Forbidden Book,* return with more secrets and discoveries that the protectors of complacency would like to keep under wraps. Blending together the Atlantis myth, prehistoric civilizations, alchemy, postmodern politics, international intrigue, and just the right amount of esoteric eroticism, they've come up with a magical cocktail that keeps captivated readers turning the page. Take a bite of the forbidden fruit: expulsion from the garden was never so tasty."

GARY LACHMAN, AUTHOR OF *DARK STAR RISING*
AND *THE RETURN OF HOLY RUSSIA*

"*Forbidden Fruits* is an occult novel that weaves together a fictional murder thriller and decades of scholarship on actual esoteric traditions and historical practices, including—yes—the ingestion of psychedelic mushrooms and their religious revelations. This is the truth in the guise of the trick; the fact in the fiction; what may have actually happened in the guise of what did not happen. Such is the nature of the secret."

JEFFREY J. KRIPAL, AUTHOR OF *SECRET BODY:*
EROTIC AND ESOTERIC CURRENTS
IN THE HISTORY OF RELIGIONS

"*Forbidden Fruits* is a long-awaited follow-up to Godwin and Mina di Sospiro's first coauthorship, *The Forbidden Book*. Now, after eight years, they have released a novel that will be a favorite among readers of esotericism as scholarship.

Authentic insights into ancient and modern occult practices and suspense meet in the alchemical retort of the "Society of Harmony." With the entheogenic key as its focus, *Forbidden Fruits* provides insight into ancient practices and visions and, like its predecessor, is prophetic, with the island of Malta being the focal point of a near-Lovecraftian evil that is encircling the world.

Complete with psychedelic journeys, therapeutic blasphemy, and child seers, *Forbidden Fruits* is a journey into the unknown and one that will leave readers questioning the nature of reality—and how to know the real from the unreal—in their spiritual journey and the world around them."

MARK STAVISH, AUTHOR OF *EGREGORES: THE OCCULT ENTITIES THAT WATCH OVER HUMAN DESTINY*

Forbidden Fruits

An Occult Novel

JOSCELYN GODWIN
— AND —
GUIDO MINA DI SOSPIRO

St. John the Baptist Parish Library
2920 New Hwy. 51
LaPlace, LA 70068

Inner Traditions
Rochester, Vermont

Inner Traditions
One Park Street
Rochester, Vermont 05767
www.InnerTraditions.com

Text stock is SFI certified

Copyright © 2020 by Joscelyn Godwin and Guido Mina di Sospiro

All rights reserved. No part of this book may be reproduced or utilized in any form or by any means, electronic or mechanical, including photocopying, recording, or by any information storage and retrieval system, without permission in writing from the publisher.

Cataloging-in-Publication Data for this title is available from the Library of Congress

ISBN 978-1-64411-157-4 (print)
ISBN 978-1-64411-158-1 (ebook)

Printed and bound in the United States by Lake Book Manufacturing, Inc. The text stock is SFI certified. The Sustainable Forestry Initiative® program promotes sustainable forest management.

10 9 8 7 6 5 4 3 2 1

Text design and layout by Priscilla Baker
This book was typeset in Garamond Premier Pro with Belda and Futura used as display typefaces

The two engravings are from Johann Georg Gichtel's 1682 edition of the works of Jacob Boehme.

To send correspondence to the authors of this book, mail a first-class letter to the authors c/o Inner Traditions • Bear & Company, One Park Street, Rochester, VT 05767, and we will forward the communication, or contact the authors directly at (Joscelyn Godwin) **https://sites.google.com/a/colgate.edu/jgodwin** (Guido Mina di Sospiro) **http://guido-mina-di-sospiro.com**.

For Stenie

—GMdS

For Ariel and Annie

—JG

PREFATORY NOTE

The authors wish to point out that they
neither advocate nor encourage the ancient
rites and practices to which some
of the characters resort in the narrative,
but rather caution the readers against them.

1

Hunting, for once, was a pretext. He just wanted to be alone with his dogs. Since daybreak they had been roving on whatever hilly ground his small island had to offer. Sebastian Pinto was frustrated. After two dedicated years, all he had to show for his pet project was lack of progress, and he had never imagined how infuriating that could be.

The September heat and his three hundred pounds were taking their toll. Sebastian paused at the foot of a hillock, his bloodhounds waiting by him. Beyond it, he knew, was the sea. He did not look forward to climbing, but the view would be worth it. As he wiped his bald head, unbuttoned his shirt, and took a deep breath, his dogs sprang forward and up the hill. Once at the top, they started barking furiously. If their master had been hunting, that would have been unforgivable, but they must have noticed that he hadn't fired a single shot.

He followed, panting. The sea, dancing under the dazzling sun, was as marvelous as expected. Lowering his eyes, right along the coast, a few hundred yards away, he saw a car and, close by, a small group of people. That was all his naked eye could see.

He laid down his shotgun, dropped his backpack and took out the spotting scope. He aimed it in the direction of the car but because of the magnifying power, the image would be too shaky to make out anything. Should he bother at all, he wondered? The dogs kept barking. Were they telling him something?

"Oh, what the hell," Sebastian said as he reached for the tripod. Once stabilized, the spotting scope would provide him with a clear picture. The problem was that the tripod was small and low, made for ground use. He mounted the scope on the tripod and then crouched down till he lay on his belly. Letting out a sigh, he finally rested his eye on the eyepiece. A blur.

His fingers fidgeted with the focus ring as his dogs kept barking. Finally, a scene presented itself with crystal-clear sharpness.

There were five people by a car. An African man, tall and skinny, his back to the sea, was hemmed in by four shaven-headed youths. He was shifting from one foot to the other and gesticulating, as if he were trying to build an invisible shield. The youths imitated his gestures in mockery as they closed in on him.

The bloodhounds must have sensed that evil was in the air. Animus yelped and came to lie down by his master, lapping his cheek. Sebastian moved away from the eyepiece and looked at his dog, and then at the sea in the distance. All he could hear was the wind and the croaking of the cicadas. Then he looked back into the spotting scope.

The black man now lay sprawled on the ground, while the four youths raged against him. In sharp detail Sebastian saw them kick him savagely, in the ribs, in the head, in the back, driving the points of their boots deep into his body. The magnification made all details come to the fore, including blood, from the man's head.

Sebastian panted, his head throbbing. The first impulse was to yell, but he wouldn't have been heard. Should he get involved at all, he wondered? What for? How could he stop those beasts? And why would they want to stop? There was lucidity in cowardice, the same cowardice that was making him look away again. But not for long.

The scope revealed that the youths had picked up their victim, one grabbing each limb as if to wrench him apart. Something stirred in Sebastians's bowels: this was too much to stomach.

The shotgun, of course!

But he was hopelessly out of range, and birdshot would not kill them.

Kill them? Had he just thought that?

The youths suddenly paused, looked at each other, and dropped the man on the ground.

The poor wretch must be finished, Sebastian thought, and his killers would be leaving in a hurry. He felt sick with revulsion, and with relief, but still lay prone, his eye to the scope.

The horrible fascination of the scene had closed his ears to the dogs, but now their staccato barks changed to a high-pitched baying, a sound that he had never heard from them before. At that, all four youths looked toward him. They were so clear in the scope that he felt he had made eye contact with each in turn. To all his emotions of horror, pity, and fear there came a sense of injustice that such subhuman beings should intrude upon him, of all people.

They started up the slope toward him.

Sebastian rose to his feet but kept his cool, trying to appraise the situation. Running was not an option; besides, his car was miles away. The dogs looked questioningly at him as he picked up his shotgun.

The youths hesitated, the leader nodded, and they quickened their pace. Two of them made gestures like children pretending to shoot.

Sebastian looked all around, his eyes searching the scorched landscape for an improbable rescuer. In a confused way, he wondered if he could offer them money.

They were now eighty, sixty yards away, their shaved heads shining under the sun. He leveled his shotgun at them and was answered with obscene gestures. Threats, obviously, were not going to suffice. He raised the gun and fired in the air.

The shot stopped them in their tracks. As they looked at each other to see if anyone was wounded, he shouted at the top of his voice: "Go away! I have no business with you. Let me be!"

The only response was laughter and jeers in some foreign language. The heftiest of the youths, older than the rest and evidently the leader, reached behind his hip and drew out a hunting knife. He turned to the others, and two of them also drew knives, while the third produced a straight razor and made as though to draw it across this throat.

Sebastian wondered for one irrational moment whether he was in a nightmare, and would wake up in bed; his imagination obliged with scenes of stabbing, cutting, and dismemberment. At a sign from the leader, the four youths started up the slope—at a run.

There was only one thing to do. He aimed in the middle of the group; held still for a few more seconds; then fired the second barrel.

One seemed to have been hit, in the knee. He fell and rolled over, screaming in pain.

A second clapped his hand to his face.

Their companions huddled around them. Sebastian could hear them jabbering, but paid no attention: what he had to do now was reload. He broke open the gun and felt for his cartridge belt.

It was not there.

Of course: with hunting merely a pretext, he had not bothered to strap it on. He dropped the gun and patted all his pockets, feeling for spares.

Nothing.

He then felt in the backpack that carried the scope, the tripod, and a bottle of water. There was nothing in it but water.

Without cartridges, his side-by-side Purdey was nothing more than an expensive five-foot club.

The dogs had been silent since their baying had drawn the attention of the youths, and Sebastian looked helplessly around for them. The leader and the youth with the razor were staring at him curiously, watching him with his gun still broken, feeling desperately in his pockets, purple and pouring with sweat. There was no mistaking his predicament. The youth who had grabbed at his face couldn't have been badly hurt: he too was staring. With razor and knives at the ready, the three youths grinned at each other. They were coming for him.

A club was better than nothing, thought Sebastian with the contentment of desperation. As he bent to pick up his gun, the blood pulsed in his ears and his heart pounded like a jackhammer. He thought he heard the roaring of an engine as he tottered, lost his footing, and fell.

For a moment everything turned crimson, and he was conscious only of the roaring in his ears. When he came to and staggered to his feet, his eyes registered a new scene.

A man on a motorcycle was standing between him and the aggressors, twenty yards away from both. He dismounted and stood still, short and sinewy. Two of the youths, each a foot taller than he, approached him, still cautiously. Time seemed suspended.

The biker took off his helmet slowly, and walked up to them casually. "Hello, mates," he said, "do you happen to have a cigarette?" As the two looked at him and each other, he flung the helmet against the leader.

"Bull's-eye!" he shouted as the young man, hit smack in the stomach, folded up. The biker jumped on him, seized his knife, and kicked him in the stomach, then in the back. The youth with the razor stood pale-faced and staring. He looked about seventeen and very nervous.

The biker, now armed, made a lunge at him, then another, and as the youth recoiled, followed through with a kick to the elbow. The razor sailed harmlessly into the air, landing by Sebastian's feet. The third youth had now climbed the hill, blood already congealing from a pellet wound on his forehead. He shouted to the younger one, evidently to hem the biker in from both sides.

But his companion dared not come within range again. The biker scooped up his helmet and held it as a buckler in his left hand. Sebastian watched with a sense of unreality as the two faced off against each other. The youth was hopelessly outclassed: it took half a minute to disarm him and send him down the hill with a wound to the left forearm. It was obvious that the biker could have disemboweled or castrated him, had he felt so inclined.

The leader struggled up, and with one look at the scene, he too limped away to regroup with his battered companions.

"Joe! I should have known it was you."

"Always present and correct, Cavalier Pinto!" said Joe Dagenham, exaggerating his Cockney accent. "I think we've seen the last of those bastards," he added, looking down the hill as they hauled their wounded friend up, dragged him to the car, and dashed off with a screeching of tires.

The bloodhounds reappeared, their tails between their legs. Sebastian, his heart still pounding, knelt down and put his great arms around their necks. "Oh, Animus, Anima! A fine pair you are, no good at pointing or retrieving, let alone protecting your master; what are you good at?"

"Cavalier Pinto," Joe said, "there seems to be another detail."

Sebastian came out of his daze. "My God, yes, the wretch those beasts were killing! I totally forgot."

The two men hurried down the hill and approached him, still lying on the ground, motionless.

"Is he dead?" asked Sebastian as Joe kneeled down and placed his forefinger on the man's neck.

"No, he's still breathing."

"Have you got your cell phone? Good. Call the police. They'll need an ambulance, too. I'm not moving him: it might make matters worse."

Joe did as he was told.

"What brought you here?" Sebastian asked. He was in a state of shock; unlike Joe, he had no experience of warfare or even street violence. Small talk, he thought, might help.

"I came looking 'round your favorite stomping grounds. Dr. Bettlheim sent me."

"Monica?"

"She wanted you to know soonest that the Newt Suits, you know, for the exploration of the seabed, just arrived from Canada."

"The Newt Suit? Oh, good," he said. It had been his chief preoccupation for the last five weeks. "You've probably saved two lives today. That's *very* good. Listen—"

Animus suddenly jumped on Sebastian, and Anima, too. "What now?"

The dogs were springing, capering, frisking about; then one of them would dart off in a specific direction; stop; look back. There was urgency in their actions. "They want me to follow them."

Joe nodded, intrigued.

"I'll tell you what we'll do," Sebastian said. "You talk to the police and the paramedics and hand over this man to them. Ask them to drive you back, then take a taxi. You'll have my car recovered tomorrow; there's no hurry."

"And you?"

"I'm done walking for the day. I'll ride your bike and follow my dogs."

"Shouldn't you call it a day, Sir?"

Yes, it was enough excitement for the day, and following his dogs had already been risky. But he hated to look scared, no, terrified, as he had been, in front of a servant. And he didn't want to stay there any longer.

2

Within the week, Dr. Monica Bettlheim had set up the new suits on Sebastian's yacht *Thetis*. For two years, the pair had been searching the coast of Malta, along with Joe. Seismographic studies, sediment corings, and remote-control cameras had been tantalizingly suggesting the presence of man-made structures on the seabed. But concrete evidence was still lacking, and Monica feared that if they failed to find any this time, Sebastian would lose patience and abort the project.

Then, just recently, she had located a rock formation that, for all the accretions of sediment and sea growths, she could no longer dismiss as natural. At 110 meters it was beyond scuba-diving depth, but the new atmospheric diving suit, virtually a man-shaped submarine, allowed Joe to dive deeper without needing decompression, and to work in wired communication with the control center on the yacht.

The suit's twin thrusters wafted him slowly among the immense stones jutting up out of the bedrock, while Monica followed his progress through a camera attached to his diving helmet. She strained to resolve the shapes that loomed through the sediment-heavy water. Could this be a monumental gateway? Was that a collapsed roof, or a solitary monolith? The voice of reason cautioned her imagination. The prehistoric temples on Malta and its daughter island of Gozo had indeed sprung up, fully formed in style and technique, a thousand or more years before Stonehenge or the Pyramids of Egypt, but this seabed had not been dry land for ten thousand years before that.

When Joe surfaced from his fourth descent, he had not been empty-handed. Now, in one of the *Thetis's* cabins, adapted as a laboratory, Monica and Sebastian were working on Joe's astonishing discovery: three rounded jars made of black basalt, a stone harder than steel but nonetheless favored and worked by Stone-Age peoples. Wearing surgical gloves, Sebastian focused the halogen lamp on the first vase and gently inserted a circular blade around its stopper. With a screwing motion, he loosened the basalt plug, breaking its resin seal.

"Nothing but mud in it," observed Joe.

"Prehistoric mud has many tales to tell," replied Sebastian, gently emptying it into a laboratory dish, then turning to the next vase.

"Hold it a moment," said Monica, setting aside the brush and scoop she had been using. "I heard something outside."

The three people in the cabin listened.

"What sort of sound was it?" asked Sebastian.

"It sounded like," she paused, "screaming." She held her mane of black hair away from her ears and turned to and fro. "There it is again. Listen." Another pause, then, "Did you hear that?"

After another silence, Joe shrugged. "Seagulls."

"No," Monica insisted. "I'm sure it's human voices. Come up on deck, Joe, Sebastian."

"You go, Joe," said Sebastian to the wiry ex-Royal Marine. "I'll keep working on these vases; then we can all turn in for the night."

"If you say so, guv," said Joe. He put down the helmet that he was cleaning and preceded Monica up the companionway.

Sebastian's eyes followed them, and he paused a moment in thought. He passed a hand over his bald head, pulled at his nose, bit his lip, and took a deep breath. Then he turned back to the workbench and the day's findings.

Joe, once on deck, made straight for the captain's bridge and asked him to shut the engines down.

"Sorry to trouble you, mate, but Monica thinks she heard noises outside. You'd better come and listen, to calm her down."

The captain was reluctant. It was difficult sailing, as a thick fog had descended and he was steering blind, relying on radar and the GPS. At this rate they were an hour from their dock in Marsaxlokk Bay, and he had counted on spending the night at home in his own bed. Still, he stopped the propellers and came outside. Two sailors joined him. Leaning over the rail, they could hear the waves slapping as the ship slowed down but could see nothing. Monica shivered.

"There! Did you hear it this time?"

The others were silent, straining their ears. Monica spoke again, almost in a whisper: "Those aren't birds. They're human voices. Can you shine a fog light or something? We should tell Sebastian."

"I heard it just then," said Joe. There was no mistaking it this time: a distant wailing which the fog seemed to amplify, but also made it difficult to tell the direction.

"Sounds like someone's having a noisy party," said one of the crew, but the captain hushed him. He returned to the bridge and swiveled the powerful searchlights around. But they revealed nothing, their beams dying into the mist before even reaching the waves.

Monica had been moving nervously around the deck, following the beams and trying to focus her hearing in this direction and that. She joined the captain on the bridge. "It couldn't be coming from the coast, could it? How far out are we?"

"Six kilometers," said the captain. "Too far to hear any noises from land."

"What should we do? Someone's in distress, somewhere."

"I'm afraid someone's always in distress, somewhere," the captain said, "but there's little that mortals can do about it. You can ask

Cavalier Pinto if you like, but I'd strongly advise him against changing our course. Not on such vague suspicion. Do you realize that I'm navigating blind? I have a good fix on the harbor through the GPS, but if I leave that and start wandering around in circles looking for a shipwreck—you get the point. Can we start her up again now?"

Joe had now joined them. "There's no point cruising around in this pea soup looking for bother," he said. "Whatever you heard, there's nothing we can do about it."

"You make me feel as though I'm imagining things," said Monica. "But I suppose you're right. Go back to the cabin, and yes, do start the engines."

As Joe disappeared down the companionway, Monica hesitated, then turned and stayed a while at the rail, looking into the impenetrable mist. The eerie voices had stopped now, and the interrupted business down below was clamoring for her attention, but she needed a moment to collect her thoughts.

This discovery was going to drop a bombshell on the complacent world of the prehistorians. The seabed on which the jars were found had been dry land during the Ice Age, when Malta, Sicily, and Italy were a single landmass. Then, beginning about sixteen thousand years ago, the European icecap had melted and poured into the Mediterranean basin. Over five or six millennia, the sea level had risen in a series of catastrophic floods, submerging whole civilizations.

It had taken Sebastian's faith in her, and his money, to make this breakthrough. And now that objects were coming up, what further secrets would be revealed? Under the specialist's microscopes, three basalt vases full of dirt could change everything.

Monica descended the stairs and entered the cabin. The light of the halogen lamps dazzled her vision, and through a subtler sense she could tell instantly that the atmosphere was charged. Sebastian was beaming, leaning forward on his arms over the workbench. Joe was looking from one to the other with an expectant expression.

"Monica, my dear," said Sebastian, "I think you should sit down."

"Why, what's happened?"

"It's time to break out the champagne."

"What do you mean?" said Monica. She felt her heart beginning to pound and sat down on the long sofa that lined the cabin's wall.

"I'm sorry that I was the one to open the last vase. It should have been yours to discover, instead of hunting for ghosts outside. But now, look—we've found the forbidden fruit!"

"I don't know what you're talking about," said Monica unsteadily.

"Then come here," said Sebastian, indicating a stainless steel tray, "and take a look at it."

In size and shape, it resembled an apple—no, a pomegranate, for it had five rounded sides and a calyx on top. To judge by its weight, it was made of solid gold.

3

Monica climbed out of the bathtub, wiped the mist off the full-length mirror, and took an appraising look at herself and, as one admiring journalist had written in the *New Yorker,* "blessed with the lineaments of a callipygian Venus." Was it this that had allured Sebastian?

She started making a mental list of grant-making institutions. With these specimens in hand, it should be possible to raise the huge grant necessary for a proper underwater excavation of the site; unless Sebastian himself decided to fund the excavations personally. At last, she felt, she had justified the confidence that he had placed in her intuitions. It would put her own career back on track, and finally erase her humiliation by academia.

Two senior colleagues at an American university, undistinguished in their own careers, had been moved by spite and jealousy to have her denied tenure. Rather than reentering the academic rat race, she had returned to her native New York City and pulled every possible string. It had worked. At the ends of the strings had been several research grants. Thanks to them, and her grueling work and intuitions in Peru, she had managed to discover an Inca citadel. Touted as the "second Macchu Picchu," it had landed her lectures at the big universities, radio shows, TV appearances, a fat contract for a book, and she had made the cover of *Time* magazine as the "archaeologist extraordinaire." In passing, she also made another discovery, this time about herself: she delighted in fame, and all that came with it. But much as she enjoyed it, interest in her waned and with it her modicum of fame and fortune.

Some doors had remained open into high society, where her looks and vivacity still made her a welcome spare dinner guest, and she had rushed in. At one such dinner, the spare man had been this Maltese grandee, Sebastian Pinto de Fonseca, with his own ideas about prehistory. He had persuaded her to turn her attention from the Americas to his own coast, and was providing for her more generously than all her previous patrons combined. For almost twenty-five months now, his palace in Malta's former capital of Mdina had been her home.

For her former patrons, she had been a pretext to jump on the bandwagon, and a prestigious tax write-off. She would only see them at social functions or sporadic meetings. Other than that, she had had carte blanche. With Sebastian it was different. He was genuinely interested in archaeology and, surprisingly, vastly learned.

During their first formal meeting—for which he had flown her to London first class to meet "halfway and conspiratorially away from our liaisons"—he had told her that if she accepted his patronage, she would be his "sixtieth birthday gift, along with two dogs— bloodhounds." He liked her for her accomplishments but also, he had stated with candor, because she was "so beautiful *in spite* of your profession. You redeem the entire category. Let me kiss your hand." Amused at the squirming discomfort that his comments had created in her, he had concluded the meeting and committed to supporting her research in Malta by saying: "Don't worry: though I'm temperamentally lecherous, I'll try hard not to forget myself." Her astonishment made him burst into laughter. "Besides," he added, "I'm married to a stunner, so you've got to wait your turn before you get lucky!"

His hands-on approach had thankfully limited itself to archaeology, except for the occasional patting of her backside. There was no end to his flattering remarks—some full of feeling, others marred by innuendo—and to his mock-wooing. Or was it genuine? She could never tell, and therein lay both the obnoxiousness and the charm of a man who in every way seemed more than life-size. But she put up with the occasional pats; they would not get in the way of her attempt to recapture fame.

And now she had fulfilled his true desire: to give Malta its rightful place in the human story. What he aptly called the "forbidden fruit" would force mankind to rethink its origins. Everything taught about early civilization would have to be rewritten. Established archaeology might scream blue murder at the discovery, in a location that had not been dry land for perhaps eighteen thousand years. But why not? The Ice Age was then at its maximum; the future Mediterranean Sea, ideal territory for hunting and habitation. Over in France, the Magdalenian cave painters were busy, preparing their paints through ingenious high-temperature processes and creating the wonders of Lascaux. All over Europe, Paleolithic sculptors were making figures out of mammoth ivory and playing bone flutes. Who had the right to set limits to the capability of early man?

As soon as she was dressed, she decided, she would see if he was ready to talk about the next step of the project. Before she had a chance, her telephone rang. She knew it would not be the man himself; he was very formal in some regards, and communication between the palace and her apartment always came via the servants. When she heard the old butler's greeting, she guessed that it would be an invitation, perhaps to dine and spend the evening exulting in their finds.

"The cavalier sends his compliments and regrets that he cannot meet with Madam this evening."

Monica was taken aback. "I hope nothing's wrong?"

"Not at all, Madam. He has business to attend to but expects to see you tomorrow in the Wunderkammer," the palace's cabinet of curiosities.

"Thank you, Dingli," said Monica, quite disconcerted. "Thank you for telling me."

She moved distractedly from the dressing room to her book-lined study and rang for the maid to bring her tea. When it arrived, she sat down at her desk and looked up the numbers of all the contacts she had in the media in New York. She would talk their ears off about the forbidden fruit, starting with a producer at the Discovery Channel.

As Monica was on the phone, Sebastian, three floors down, was fuming: he was being detained, and in his own study to boot, by "Platitude incarnate: a civil servant!"

Inspector Soldanis sat comfortably in an armchair across from Sebastian's desk. He had the devil-may-care expression which had been his life's vade mecum. Perhaps he was enjoying his interviewee's mounting anger.

"I told you already and I'll tell you again: you're wasting your time, which doesn't concern me at all. However, you're wasting *my* time, in *my* home, when *I* have urgent business to attend to—that is *in-tol-er-a-ble*!" Sebastian had now turned purple with rage.

The Inspector took out his cigarette pack and offered him one, saying: "You might as well overstress your coronaries. Don't care for one? That's all right. Don't mind some good old secondhand smoke?" Without waiting for a reply, he lit a cigarette and looked around the room, with its mahogany and ormolu furniture, terrestrial and celestial globes, and French windows opening onto a garden. Between the tall book presses and the coffered ceiling was a row of battle paintings, some on land and others a turmoil of galleons and galleys. "Couldn't help noticing your paintings," he added, changing the subject.

"That's the kind of reaction all paintings hope to elicit."

"I mean, their subject matter. Do they all depict the Great Siege of Malta?"

"Only about half of them," said Sebastian. "The other half, since you'll ask, the Battle of Lepanto."

"Both . . . how can I put it? Seminal dates in European history."

"Absolutely: we repelled the Ottoman galleys twice, and both times against all odds. I can't think of a better sport than driving away Muslims."

"Oh really? Is that what you did on Friday night with your yacht?"

"I told you already: the fog was so thick we couldn't see anything. We heard some faint screams, true, but water carries sounds a long way off. Will you leave me alone now?"

"I'd love to, but you see, it's the biggest immigrant shipwreck in Malta's recent history: thirty-eight victims. Since we joined the European Union, illegal immigrants from Africa come to our shores, too. It's a national emergency; I guess belonging to an exclusive club has its drawbacks, too."

The two men stared at each other for some time. Then Sebastian said: "Whatever you say, Inspector. . . . For the last time I tell you: there was nothing we could do about them; you see, my yacht has no cannons aboard!"

Sebastian expected an explosion of righteous anger, but Soldanis said nothing and seemed content to puff on his cigarette. He was neither tall nor short, neither slim nor fat, neither young nor old, neither handsome nor ugly, neither elegant nor shabby in his gray suit. His hair was graying and, to a lesser degree, so was his moustache, not very well groomed, with some nose hair mingling with it. His face was pale. The only note of color was in his eyes: green, and alert.

It was Sebastian who broke the silence: "Here, have a cigar." He offered the Inspector a big box of Cuban robustos. "Your cigarette is ghastly."

Soldanis took a cigar, lit it, and inhaled. "All right, Cavalier Pinto, just out of curiosity: why did you fire your *captain*?"

"It's entirely within my rights to fire an employee of mine."

"I knew that already. Why did you fire your captain?"

"He reported the incident to the authorities without running it by me. That's unacceptable. As for what he saw, you should ask him."

"I already have."

"Bravo!"

"And spoken to Mr. Dagenham."

"Joe? What for?"

"I wanted to hear firsthand the details of your heroism."

Sebastian gave him a puzzled look, and then let out a burst of laughter fit to shake the battle paintings.

"Why," resumed the Inspector when Sebastian had calmed down, "there's talk of decorating you for it."

"It's more than talk," Sebastian said when he finally stopped laughing. "I got a letter from the prime minister, that meddlesome mouse—"

"He's a friend of mine, I mean, we went to school together."

"Really? I'm sorry to hear that. Anyway," he resumed, "about these infernal politicos: usually they want me to donate something for this or that. No sooner I do than another request comes in. This time," he started laughing again, "this time," he reprised between laughs, "they want to award me the Medal for Bravery for—wait," more laughter, "for an 'act of exceptional valor!'"

"The Midalja ghall-Qlubija? Then it's official. Congratulations!" The two men were enjoying themselves, and, oddly, for the same reason. "In the current social climate, the fact that the most famous Maltese citizen, and a Knight of Malta at that, would save the life of an African illegal immigrant is—"

"But Inspector: I was only trying to save my skin!"

"Intentionally or not, I'm sure he's happy to be alive."

"That's true, and good for him. And whatever happened to those bastards who attacked us?"

"The Russians? Another problem we're trying to deal with. There seems to be a colony of them, white supremacists, apparently, all from St. Petersburg, making trouble here in Malta."

"Well, what are you waiting for? Kick them back to Mother Russia."

"Easier said than done. They have regular visas, and they all look alike, which makes identification problematic. Above all, we haven't managed to catch them red-handed, so they can't be charged without any evidence against them."

"What can I say? Go bug *them*."

"I won't; a colleague is handling the case. He lent me your file."

"Oh yes, must be the other one who came around with more tedious questions."

The Inspector had finished his cigar. Before the smoke of the last puff settled, Sebastian said: "Well, Inspector, that's all I can tell you. Satisfied now?"

"Yes. The paintings are impressive, and so is your cigar."

4

Sebastian had stopped for lunch at his club in Malta's capital, Valletta. He needed the ear of the one person who was privy to his inmost concerns: his uncle Sophocles. After listening without comment, the old man shook his head. "A *golden* pomegranate? Aurum non vulgi, sed philosophorum! That's the real quest, Sebastian: for the Gold of the Philosophers, not the common gold." While he busied himself with his pipe, Sebastian looked affectionately at his uncle, who always brought the conversation around to his esoteric preoccupations. "I know, I know," he replied, "and you know I've tried it, but I'm not cut out to be an alchemist."

The older man smiled and took a sip of his anisette liqueur. The great room could hardly have been more hospitable, with its gracefully laid tables and its aura of ancient books, leather, and Latakia tobacco.

After a pause, Sebastian continued: "Let me tell you of another thought I'm playing with, Uncle. To put it in your favorite language, Visita interiorem terrae: rectificando invenies occultum lapidem. 'Visit the interior of the earth: by rectification you will find the hidden stone.' How does your Society understand that?"

"Ah, the celebrated acronym of VITRIOL. It can have many meanings."

"How about starting with the literal one? You recall our spelunking expeditions when we were both a lot younger, and a trifle more subtle about the waistline?"

"How could I forget those?" Sophocles smiled in reminiscence.

"I feel a tremendous nostalgia for those caving days, and after so much underwater archaeology, I want my next project to be on our mainland again, and to hell with the prohibitions of the nanny state."

"Ah, Sebastian! Always some project!"

"How could one live otherwise?"

Their exchange was interrupted as two old friends came over to greet uncle and nephew; they were not initiates and the conversation changed its tone.

After the group broke up, Sebastian had a few private words with his uncle. He was keenly aware that every meeting with this venerable and beloved old man might be the last.

"Sebastian, do be careful. You're the master of your universe— nobody in Malta more so—but as uncle to nephew," he hesitated.

"What is it, Uncle?"

"There are dark clouds on your horizon. This finding you've told me about has an odd taint to it; I don't like it. When I get home, I must look up your horoscope and check your transits for the coming months."

Sebastian wrinkled his brow.

"Yes," Sophocles hastened to add, "vir sapiens dominabitur astris; is that what you're thinking?"

"Of course, Uncle," he managed to say rather than snort in deference to the old man. "'The wise man rules the stars.' Think of the ancient Roman generals who confuted their augurs by winning the very battles they were foretold they would lose."

"But to do so," Sophocles countered: "they had to resort to many anti-karmic measures: send for reinforcements, employ different strategies, and apply a high degree of conviction and cunning. I prefer to translate it as, 'The wise man is ruled by the stars.' It takes so much less work to align oneself with one's destiny."

A brief pause followed.

"Anyway," Sophocles resumed, "after I've consulted how your future is constellated, we must have the pleasure of luncheon again. Goodbye."

There was solemnity in both men's eyes as they embraced and parted.

The next morning, Monica was astonished to discover that Sebastian had gone to his club in Valletta and would not be back until late in the evening. Moreover, Dingli, the butler, wouldn't give her the key to the Wunderkammer, in which the new discoveries had been temporarily stored. Much as she ached to examine them, she could not. It was so infuriating; she could have slapped both the butler and Sebastian. But that was how her patron was, and he ran the show. Perhaps this was his way of reminding her.

Undaunted, she tried Sebastian's cell phone; it was not switched on. Then she obtained the phone number of his club. A very old man answered in a tremulous voice. When he finally understood who Monica was asking to speak to, he announced that the cavalier had left word not be disturbed by anyone except by his wife, and only in case of an emergency.

That left only one course open: she asked Dingli where Sebastian's wife might be found.

Monica's resolve waned as she approached the breakfast room. She remembered vividly the first time she had met Lady Penelope. Monica, just in from New York, had been sipping lemonade in one of the palace's many halls when Penelope had entered the room unannounced. Monica had looked up incuriously and then rose to her feet and demurely shook hands. There was something about Penelope's presence that awed her despite her democratic principles and being of the same age. Not only was she a classic English thoroughbred of the Princess Diana type: she had also mastered the royal technique of apparent empathy with any and everyone.

There she sat in a pool of dappled sunlight, in a flowery empire waist dress that accentuated her breasts. *"An Impressionist master-piece,"* thought Monica as Penelope looked up from the daily papers, then gracefully unfolded herself. "Monica!" she said, as though this visit crowned a secret dream. "Good morning. Did you have a good night's rest?"

"Yes, thank you."

"Have you had breakfast?"

The smile was infectious, hard to resist. "Actually, I was wondering if you knew where your husband is?"

"Oh, busy somewhere, I'm sure."

"Would you call him, please?" she asked awkwardly.

"What for?"

Monica explained, and Penelope said: "It's not an emergency, my dear. I don't wish to upset him. But don't worry, he'll be back soon. He's just relaxing, I'm sure. Why don't you join me? I'll be going out on our other yacht shortly."

Monica declined the invitation, appreciatively. If her patron was unpredictable—at times kind, at times saucy—his wife was unfailingly considerate. Exasperated but knowing that all she could do was wait for Sebastian to return, rather than simmering in her own resentment, Monica went back upstairs. She pulled on a pair of tight-fitting cotton pants that made the most of her slim hips and a linen shirt. Canvas sneakers seemed a sensible choice. Then she went down to fetch the Fiat that he had put at her disposal.

At the garage door she met Joe Dagenham, who was holding Animus and Anima on leashes.

"Morning, Joe. It's such a gorgeous day, I'm going to take a ramble on the Victoria Lines."

"Would you like some company?" He relished Monica's hesitation in replying. Eventually he added, "Company of the canine species, that is."

"Oh yes, I'd love to take them with me."

The dogs were enthusiastic; they clambered into the back seat and stuck their heads out of the windows, tongues and ears flapping expectantly. She drove fast, the wind on her face helping her to calm down. Why would the butler not give her the key to the Wunderkammer? What did Sebastian fear she'd do in there? Certainly, the place *was* weird. In a room the size of a museum gallery, cabinets displayed nacreous shells and objects made from amber; Roman and Venetian glass; ivories, ranging from Byzantine reliquaries to prehistoric Venus figurines; Mannerist vessels of jasper and lapis lazuli; and, more disturbingly, a display of the skulls of freaks born with occluded eyes, overshot jaws, or vestigial horns. Among all these objects, and many more, there now was also the forbidden fruit—under lock. Why? And where the hell was Sebastian?

She turned off the busy road toward the Great Fault, the geological divider of the north from the more populous south.

It was a region she knew well, but it never ceased to fascinate her. Its precipitous slopes were a haven of solitude in a seething, overpopulated island. The meager garigue vegetation waited breathlessly for the November rains, beguiling the walker with aromas of crushed thyme and rosemary. Whenever the wall snaked uphill, she would pause at the summit for the panoramic view. The northern vista ended with the island of Gozo, where she had the keys to Sebastian's lodge; to west and south was the cliff line of Malta's tilted tabletop and the shimmering sea. The eye-catcher to the east was the Mosta Dome, an example of the Maltese passion for building gigantic churches. The Stone Age inhabitants had built equally grandiose temples, piling twenty-ton megaliths on one another and hollowing out three-story underground sanctuaries.

Beneath the surface: that was the mystery land. In her early days, Sebastian had guided her into natural fissures and caves where the bones of extinct fauna, pygmy elephants and giant dormice, still lay undisturbed. Human industry had converted some of these into prehistoric tombs, enlarged them into Roman catacombs, reservoirs and cisterns for the sparse rainwater, and finally air-raid shelters and stores for military matériel. All disused now, it was sometimes hard to tell one from another, and most of them had been closed off to protect the public from its own curiosity.

Monica was now less than a mile from Fommir Rih Bay, "The Mouth of the Wind." The path that the hounds had chosen continued down one of the steep little watercourses, well grown with tamarisk and prickly pear that pierced the cliff of the Great Fault. She remembered the stony track from her early explorations. Where it reached the bottom, there had been a broad cave entrance, shut by a rusty iron grille. It had seemed promising, as perhaps giving access to the honeycombed cliffs, and Monica had resolved to return and investigate it properly someday.

After a breathless scramble down the cliff path, Monica was delighted to see that she and the dogs had the bay to themselves. As they nosed around its rocky shoreline, she was less pleased to see plastic bottles and Styrofoam in abundance, a used condom, a cache of disposable syringes, even a Chinese cigarette package.

Having found a clean spot, she ate her picnic lunch in the shade of the overhanging cliff while the dogs frolicked in the surf. Then she took a careful look around, stripped to her underwear, and prepared to go for a swim. Before doing so, she walked further out along the bay, to read a sign standing in perfect solitude. "No bathing— Sharks!" It boasted a stylized image of a shark, in case the would-be bather spoke no English. "Oh well," she thought, and put her clothes back on.

After the strenuous hike back up the cliff, Monica asserted her authority over the dogs and chose the Mosta Road, with its less interesting smells. She reached the car within an hour and found that someone had unlocked it during her absence.

5

Monica spent the strangest and most anxiety-ridden two weeks in her life. Sebastian continued to avoid her, and the forbidden fruit remained locked in the Wunderkammer. This while she was receiving pressing calls from all the American media she had contacted. More than embarrassing, the situation was becoming unbearable.

Then one morning she was finally granted access to the Wunderkammer, but not to Sebastian. She wasted no time to take the bull by the horns and, to answer a few of the questions that kept her awake at night, she made an appointment with a metallurgist at the University of Malta.

When she knocked on the laboratory door, Professor Gara opened it himself. He had the short, muscular physique of the islanders, with an olive complexion and a well-groomed cap of prematurely silver hair. "Ah, Dr. Bettlheim," he said, with the lilt of those Maltese for whom English is a second or third language. "Good morning to you. I am sorry that I can give you so little time, but I leave on Tuesday for a geological expedition in the Pacific Islands and will be abroad at least until April."

"That sounds wonderful."

"In some ways, yes. But now to this object that you have discovered."

Monica took the golden pomegranate out of its wrappings and handed it to the professor.

"A valuable piece," he said immediately, hefting it in his hand and turning it over. "As one would expect from Sebastian Pinto," he added. He took it to the window and examined it under a strong magnifying glass. "Please have a seat while I weigh it, ascertain the purity of the metal, and do a specific gravity test."

Monica watched him deftly at work.

"Purity of twenty-two carats," he announced, "probably compounded from native nuggets rather than an artificial alloy." Ten minutes later he turned to her again: "The specific gravity test reveals that if the object, weighing 1753 grams, is gold, 37.2 percent of its volume must be void. Ergo, it is hollow."

"Hollow? But there's no way in."

"Excuse me. You may not have noticed a seam around the calyx."

Monica looked through the loupe. Feeling uncharacteristically amateurish, she said, "You're right. I haven't had the chance to do a proper examination of it, because it's been in Cavalier Pinto's private museum."

"Shall we open it for him?"

"If it can be done gently, yes. Perhaps by heating the outside of the seam?"

"Very gentle heat, I promise you," said Professor Gara. He returned the pomegranate to the laboratory bench and drew on a pair of gloves.

After a few minutes, he spoke again: "It's loosening." He kept working, "Careful, now." He continued working, then spoke. "Look, here it comes."

He held up the pomegranate in one hand, and in the other the calyx. "A simple stopper, very precisely ground, sealed with a microscopic layer of resin. Simple, yet clever. Now what is inside?"

"Careful!" said Monica.

"Have no fear," Gara reassured her. "Please pass me that glass tray." He reversed the pomegranate over it, and a brown, granular substance poured out.

"Can we," Monica began, but the professor was already at his binocular microscope. She waited impatiently while he prepared a sample and fiddled with the controls.

After a quarter of an hour, which seemed interminable to Monica, he rose and gestured for her to look for herself, saying as he did so: "The substance is exclusively of organic origin. Its long inclusion has preserved it from oxygen and other hazards. A proper analysis lies outside my field of expertise, but it's easy to discern vegetable tissue, possibly cereal, and a number of fungal spores. Now, if the substance is indeed coeval with the container, you have the opportunity of carbon 14 dating."

"There's no lab on Malta that can do C-14 testing," said Monica.

"You'll have to apply to one somewhere else in Europe or the U.S. They all have long waiting lists. But you can try. If you think it's worth your while," he added.

Monica looked at him questioningly.

"I know that it was *officially* picked up on the seabed," he elaborated, "where someone carelessly dropped it when that was dry land. Sure, gold occurs naturally, it's easy to work, and this *could* have been made with Stone Age tools over a charcoal fire. But if I were you, I would scrutinize every detail of its discovery."

"But I was there!" Monica retorted.

"On the seabed?" said Gara, with a cold smile.

"No. To tell the truth, I was up on deck when Sebastian opened the jar that contained it."

"A-ha! To me, that spells a rather awkward gap in its history. Then there is the question of when it was sealed, and by whom."

Monica was speechless. Eventually, she said: "I'll have to think this over. It's a great shock. I have to thank you for your time, but it's thrown me into a sticky situation."

"Cavalier Pinto may be disappointed, too," said Gara. The ensuing silence was eloquent as he poured the dirt into a fresh jar, sealed it, and handed her the specimens.

By the time she reached Sebastian's palace, Monica no longer knew what to think. It was not a terribly curvy road, but she had been sick twice already, barely making it in time to screech to a halt, open her door, and vomit.

As the afternoon hours went by, each of the five rooms in her apartment felt claustrophobic. The more she racked her brains, the less they produced viable answers. She finally decided that a walk might distract her, and at the same time help her find a solution. She walked down the grand stairway, the wrapped pomegranate in her arms. Entering the Wunderkammer, she restored the treasure, now somewhat devalued in her eyes, to its case. As she left, she noticed that the library's door was open. Could Sebastian be in there at long last, sipping one of his colorful aperitifs? She paused for a moment. Should she go out, as planned, for a breath of fresh air, or step inside and confront him? Sooner or later, that had to happen, and seeing him had become almost impossible. This was her chance. Trying to steady her nerves, she took a deep breath and entered the library.

"And who is this?" she wondered in her mind, caught by surprise.

Sitting on an armchair by the window, his eyes intent on an old book he held in his hands, was a man she'd never met. He was beautiful in an ancient way, she couldn't help noticing, as if he had walked out of a Caravaggio—no, a Mantegna painting. Yes, that painting that had made such an impression on her in a Milanese museum. *The Lamentation over the Dead Christ.* In the man's chiseled features, his long hair, his short beard, she could trace the same lineaments of the painting's figure, though this man looked even thinner.

"Hello?" she said.

"Yes?" he replied, looking at her with a fixed gaze. The sun streaming through the window revealed the room's fine dust as if it were suspended in midair; he seemed enthroned amid the floating particles.

"I'm sorry, I was looking for Cavalier Pinto."

"So was I," he said at length, closing his book.

"And who are you?" was the question on her lips, but this wasn't her house. She'd better go find Dingli and tell him about this possible intruder.

"Why are you leaving?" came his voice, deep, every word pronounced precisely yet in an unplaceable accent. Before she could answer, he stood up and walked up to her, slowly, smiling. It was a surprisingly charming smile, she noticed, as the stranger got so near to her that he could kiss her. He did. Twice, on her cheeks. Then he moved back, just a few inches, and said: "You've been very good to my father; thank you."

"Oh, I see," she said, "you must be—"

"Rafael. I'm sorry, I should have introduced myself."

They looked into each other's eyes, then she looked away. Monica finally entered the room, but rather than sitting she waited for his invitation to make herself comfortable. Rafael said, "Don't expect me to say 'make yourself at home'; you're more at home here than I am!"

Even if the situation was now explained and it was perfectly natural for Sebastian's son to behave as he had, somehow there remained a tension in the air that she could not quite explain. But as he smiled again the tension quickly metamorphosed into its opposite. She now felt relaxed in his presence, and rather silly, too. What did she care about exchanging pleasantries with Sebastian's son when she had such problems to sort out?

The strange thing was that he didn't promote any conversation, but was seemingly content to smile at her without saying a word. He closed his eyes, his smile gone, the very image of Mantegna's dead Christ.

Eventually he broke the silence and her train of thought. "Anything you could show me from your search?"

"Sure, our greatest find so far: the golden pomegranate, or the forbidden fruit, as your father calls it."

"Would you show it to me?"

Did he feel obliged to pretend interest? Or was he genuinely intrigued? She couldn't tell as she led him to the Wunderkammer.

There it was again, shining in her hands, the source of so much hope and worry alike. Rafael, standing tall beside her, observed it keenly, and then asked permission to hold it.

As he scrutinized it, Monica found herself traveling back in her mind a few hours, to her journey back from the university. On her second stop she had felt compelled to unwrap the golden pomegranate. *"Could this really be a modern fake?"* she had asked herself. Surely no one would have thought of filling it with dirt! More likely it had been found somewhere else, and Sebastian had bought it on the antiquarian black market. She had hefted it in her hand, thinking, *"Crazy, generous Sebastian, spending who knows how much, and sure that he was doing me a favor."*

"Was Rafael impressed?" wondered Monica, coming back to the present. She had no clue if he had enough historical and archaeological knowledge to grasp the implications, if the thing were genuine.

He had removed the stopper. "What was inside?"

"Some organic matter."

His enquiring glance invited her to elaborate.

"Fungal spores, apparently."

"Really? So that opens up the possibility of a carbon 14 test, to establish its age."

"Well, at least the age of the contents. The thing itself seems to be undatable."

"Or timeless. But anyway, let me guess, Malta has no facility for C-14 testing?"

"Unfortunately not." Rafael seemed very knowledgeable. She should have known better; with a father like Sebastian, he had grown up surrounded by antiquities and curiosities.

"A friend of mine teaches physics at the Università della Sapienza in Rome," he added. "Through him, you may get a C-14 on your specimens fairly quickly. It won't be cheap, but Father won't care. I know he's used his expertise other times."

That was good news, thought Monica—or was it? She no longer knew what to believe and was reluctant to put her find to such a conclusive test. Still, she thanked him and put the sphere back in its case. They left the Wunderkammer and walked back to the library, absorbed in their own thoughts.

The sound of footsteps distracted them. Monica knew the gait well but still wondered how she had managed the art of walking so sure-footedly on high heels.

Penelope saw the two of them and said: "Rafael? What a surprise!"

Rafael was up on his feet and now beside her. Penelope, too, was kissed lightly on both cheeks.

"When did you arrive?" Penelope asked welcomingly.

"Today."

"Does Sebastian know you're here?"

"No, I wanted to surprise him."

"How sweet of you. It's been ages since you've been here, hasn't it?"

He nodded.

"Let me call Dingli; we must—" she brought her index finger to her mouth as she heard an unmistakably heavy tread approaching.

Sebastian entered the library. He glanced at the women, then at Rafael. "And who are you?" he said, recovering quickly from the surprise. "Jesus Christ? Then I must be your father, God Almighty. Come here, my son!"

Sebastian hugged him tightly. "Now, sit down, sit down everybody." He seemed uncommonly moved. "Dingli! Dingli?" The butler turned up soon after. "Dingli, master Rafael is here." The butler had been in their service for over thirty years; he looked at him and bowed, smiling.

"Bring some champagne," Penelope continued, "we trust your choice."

"Now, Rafael," Sebastian said, "to what do we owe the honor of your visit?"

"I heard you'll be awarded the Medal for Bravery, and I wanted to be here, with you."

"Why, isn't that something?" Sebastian didn't know if he should believe his son but was happy to see him nonetheless. "You've met Dr. Bettlheim, haven't you?"

Rafael nodded.

"And isn't *she* something?" giving Monica a mischievous look.

A titter from Penelope seemed to encourage Rafael to stare at Monica all the more.

Dingli was back with the bubbles, and three of them were soon toasting and making light talk. Not Rafael, though. He was content to look at the others, his glass in his hand, hardly drinking.

Penelope eventually told Dingli to go and fetch the chambermaid. Master Rafael's room needed tending. Penelope herself would choose the linens and towels. "Rafael, won't you join us? Surely you have some luggage?"

Sebastian and Monica were left in the library. *"Well, wasn't this the perfect opportunity for confronting him?"* Monica wondered. Indeed it was, and yet she hesitated.

"Strange chap, isn't he?" Sebastian asked eventually.

That was it, she knew it. She wanted to know more about Rafael. Her worries, her doubts could wait. Sebastian was back in the palace; she'd confront him tomorrow.

"He didn't always look like Jesus Christ Superstar."

Monica sat down, close to him.

"Yes," he continued, looking not at her, "he was a nice child, and then a nice boy, full of life and whatnot."

As Rafael had been conspicuously absent during her entire stay in Malta, Monica had tactfully never broached the subject.

"Spelunking, rock climbing, scuba diving, waterskiing, swimming, motocross—he did it all. But he was no jock. He learned easily, too, and quickly. He grew into a good-looking boy; girls fell at his feet. So I was told, anyway—he was at a boarding school, close to Geneva. Then the accident happened."

Monica looked at him wonderingly. He elaborated. "His mother. Agata was a Sicilian beauty, by the way. Small nobility, you know, but ancient. She was wonderful in many ways, but marrying her had been—how shall I put it?—a gentleman's obligation. Anyway, I eventually managed to get our marriage annulled by the Tribunal of the Rota Romana. For the Catholic legal system, it was the only way to get out of it and preserve my prerogatives to become a Knight of Malta and marry again in church."

"So, the annulment was the accident?"

"What? Oh no, not that. Besides, Rafael was a little child when we separated. No, it was a scuba-diving accident. An embolus when she resurfaced from deep diving—too hastily, it turned out; she was always so impulsive, dear Agata. Rafael hardly knew her, yet her death changed him. It must have been that; I know of nothing else. Since then, he dropped out from many schools. There are all sorts of idlers in that milieu, heroin addicts being the commonest pest. He did dally with heroin, and God knows what else."

Dingli asked if the cavalier wished for more champagne; he declined.

"But he's done with that now. I hardly ever see him here," he resumed. "He's become tall and skinny and . . . unattainably hand-some. Unattainable is the word. He's got an apartment in Rome. When I eventually visited him, the place was filled with so many books that I didn't ask, 'Have you read all of these?' because I dreaded both a yes and a no. Why are you looking at me like that?"

She was lost in vicarious contemplation, but he couldn't know that.

"Overall," he added, "I suspect Rafael finds the world uninterest-ing, and its dwellers, too. But who is he? He himself wouldn't know: sleepwalkers have a better sense of self."

6

If Rafael's presence in Malta was rare, his attendance at the monthly rites of the Society of Harmony was unprecedented. But there had been great urgency in his great-uncle Sophocles' summons, and *this* was the true reason for his coming at long last to the island.

Ever since its foundation in 1785, the Society had met in the Ambini Palace in Valletta. Over two centuries it had developed a vast metaphysical system that explained the workings of the elemental spirits, the daemons of the intermediate zone, the planetary and angelic hierarchies, even the sephirothic hypostases of Kabbalah. Worldly matters, too, were not neglected. The Superior Intelligences with whom the Society was in contact had much to say about the fate of nations and the astrological cycles governing them, which had resulted in some astonishing predictions.

It was Rafael's position in the Order of Misraïm—a Rite imbued with occult, alchemical, and Egyptian references—that authorized his great-uncle to introduce him to this very secretive lodge, in which few of the members were a day under seventy. Rafael hoped that he could hide his discomfort from them. He knew only that they worked with child mediums, whose purity acted as a channel, so they believed, for the Intelligences.

Like many hard-up mothers before her, the widowed Mrs. Vassallo had made no objection to her daughter's participation in well-paid "psychological experiments," stipulating only that "Miss Despott must be present." Mary Despott, an Anglo-Maltese lady in her sixties, was crippled with polio, but blessed with a stentorian voice and the manner of a natural hierophant. It was she who greeted the young girl, Honoria, as Mrs. Smyth, the housekeeper, ushered her into the drawing room of the Ambini Palace.

Honoria was ten years old, with frizzy hair in plaits and big brown eyes. "Bonswa, Miss Despott," the child said in her native Maltese.

"Merħba, Honoria," replied the lady courteously from her wheelchair. "Has Mrs. Smyth given you your hot milk and honey?"

"Yes, thanks, Ma'am."

"Good. Come and make yourself comfortable on the sofa, and close your eyes."

Honoria wriggled happily into the cushions. Sophocles drew up a straight chair and sat facing her. He began a mesmeric lullaby in his old melodious voice, holding his open hands toward her as if conferring a blessing. After singing it three times, he resumed his speaking voice: "When you hear the bell ring, you will rise, and come through to the chapel." With these words, Sophocles rose and joined the waiting initiates.

The chapel was an oval chamber adjoining the drawing room, some thirty feet long, hung with tapestries in Egyptian style. At one end was a small chamber organ; at the other, the instrument of Mesmer's séances: a glass harmonica. Twenty-two high-backed chairs, more of them empty than occupied in these days of the Society's decline, were arranged around a great oval table. This bore a magic mirror on a stand and eight silver candelabra, each made in the image of one of the planetary sirens. Like the founders of the Society, Miss Despott spoke in French.

"In the name of Ananke," she began, "the Necessity to whom even the Gods submit; in the names of her daughters Lachesis, remembrancer of the past; Clotho, knower of the present; and Atropos, foreseer of the future; and in the names of the Sirens, the divine souls of the celestial Spheres, who incline all things through celestial motion to their ruling Gods; I declare this lodge of the Society of Harmony open."

"Amen. Ainsi soit-il," said the others.

Miss Despott summoned Honoria with a silver bell attached to her wheelchair. The girl drifted in, her eyes open like a sleepwalker's, and took her seat at the head of the table, facing the magic mirror.

Unearthly sounds now filled the air. Adeodatus Ambini, hereditary owner of the palace, played on the organ, while the moistened fingers of Monsignor Buttigieg, priest and magus, wandered over the gold-rimmed glasses. Their music, like nothing ever heard outside this chapel, consisted of long, sustained chords, sometimes blending, sometimes conflicting, calling from one instrument to another like angelic voices across the abyss of time and space. As it plunged Honoria deeper into her trance, her expression changed from that of a child to something more ancient.

The music died, giving way to the shuffle of slippered feet as the two players crept back to their appointed chairs.

Miss Despott began the scrying session, speaking clearly in Maltese.

"Guiding spirits, what news of evil and of good?"

There was a pause, then in a voice slower and lower than her own, the child replied:

"Little good—much evil."

A shudder ran through the company. The ritual question was not meant literally: it was a stock opening, like "How are you?" which generally led to a conversation with some notable figure from the annals of occultism. An elevated discourse would follow, often wandering off into languages the child had never learned. Seldom had the answer been so literal and succinct as this.

Miss Despott swallowed and spoke: "Tell us of this evil."

The old initiates waited, knowing better than to break the silence, during which the medium peered more closely into the mirror, as though reading a difficult script.

"Tas-Santi. Tas-Santi. Tas-Santi."

"But you spoke of evil, not of saints. Saints do no evil, surely?"

Honoria stared into the void without replying.

"What manner of evil?" asked Miss Despott.

In a growl: "Cut-ting. Kil-ling."

The old people were startled by the things the little girl was saying, and by her voice, so raspy, unnatural, and unlike a girl's voice.

The Monsignor kept his cool and intervened. "Do we really want to hear about this? There's always some horror going on in the world."

Miss Despott quieted him with a look and pressed on: "Is the evil in these islands of Malta, Gozo, and Comino?"

"Tas-Santi. Tas-Santi. Blood. Guts." The child's face twisted in horror, as though she were seeing what she spoke of. She gasped, then turned pale. Her whole body shook and trembled while she frothed at the mouth.

The initiates looked at each other. "I think we should stop this," said Rafael. The Monsignor was now clutching his jeweled cross.

Honoria gasped, wiped the spume off her mouth with the back of her trembling hand, and continued, shaking like a leaf in the wind although no other question had been asked. "Blood. Guts." It was a throaty, low-pitched growl: "Blood. Guts." Her face was pale green, now, her eyes staring in unspeakable terror.

Visibly altered, Miss Despott was inwardly torn between curiosity and foreboding. Ambini leaned forward, likewise fascinated. Eventually she asked: "Who is doing this evil?"

The answer came in another growl, as if from a distant, ultra-mundane place: "Tar-tars."

"Is that someone's name?" asked the Monsignor, no longer cool as he still tried to appear outwardly.

"Who is, or who are, Tar-tars?" said Miss Despott.

A stream of incomprehensible words followed. There seemed no stopping it. Now, however, the medium spoke in a high pitch, every syllable a shrill, nasal oddity, as if calling a roll of outlandish names.

"Enough!" screamed Miss Despott.

It was at that moment that Honoria fell off her chair.

"Adeodatus, get some water!"

"Loosen her clothes!"

"Honoria, Honoria, can you hear me?!"

"Rafael, help me lift her up!"

The octogenarians were beside themselves. Their child medium had suddenly become cataleptic with one leg straight, one bent, one hand behind her head, the other behind her back, and her head drawn to one side, staring.

"Oh, Rafael, that it should come to this!" said Sophocles, bustling around the table and forcing his creaky legs into a kneeling position. "We've had trouble with the girls before, but never," he trailed off as he knelt beside her. Rafael stooped and deftly lifted the child, gro-tesquely twisted but stiff as a corpse, onto the table, then helped his grand-uncle to his feet. Quietly he asked him "What sort of trouble? And what did you do then?"

"Fainting fits, hysteria; but after the dismissal of the spirits they remembered nothing."

While the old gentlemen fussed over the girl and debated calling a doctor, Miss Despott pronounced the closing conjuration, tracing a pentacle in the air:

"In the name of Ananke; of her daughters Lachesis, Clotho, and

Atropos; and of the sirens, I command all spirits who have been summoned by this ceremony to depart with blessing unto their abodes and habitations, and I declare this temple closed. Amen, so mote it be. Rafael, please cover up the mirror."

"What are we to do now?" said Buttigieg. As there was no reply, he reached out a plump hand and shook the little body, but to no avail. "Pass me the water, please."

Sophocles handed him the carafe, and the priest sprinkled some over the girl's face. Not a stir. He made the sign of the cross over the carafe and sprinkled more water. Nothing.

"What could be wrong with her? Oh, our Lady of Help: cast out the demon from this child," invoked Monsignor Buttigieg.

"We may have to call an ambulance."

"But what would we tell them?" asked Ambini. "Anyway, they couldn't set foot in here," he added, protective of the secrecy of the Society and its activities.

"Let's send for her mother," said Sophocles.

Mary Despott took charge of the dithering ancients. Her square jaw was set, her steel-gray hair bristled. "First get the child out of the chapel. Rafael, please carry her into the drawing room, put her on a sofa, dry her, and cover her with my shawl. Take it." She followed in her wheelchair, then: "Hand me the phone," she said, pushing herself over to the desk. She dialed 196, the emergency number. "This is Miss Mary Despott. I am at the Ambini residence on Merchant Street. A young girl has had an accident. She is unconscious. . . . Thank you." She put the phone down. "They'll be here in ten minutes. Now what *are* we going to tell them?" Then she added, as an afterthought: "Honoria Vassallo, I command you to forget all that you have heard and seen since you fell asleep. I shall count up to ten, and when I reach ten, you will wake up." Trying to keep calm and not to rush the procedure, she counted to ten, then commanded, "Wake up!"

Honoria didn't come to.

"Wake up, wake up!"

She continued to lie, motionless.

The housekeeper knocked, and Ambini opened the door. "An ambulance has arrived, Sir, asking for Miss Despott. Is something wrong?"

"Tell the men to come up to this room, with a stretcher."

"A stretcher? Oh, Mother of God, what's happened?"

Ambini ignored the question and gave the housekeeper a wintry look.

When the emergency team entered, the ambulance driver gasped as he lifted the blanket and saw the contorted body. Blood and gore were his daily fare, but this was plainly uncanny. "Are you her grandparents, or what?"

"No, she's the daughter of a former servant. She came here for a birthday treat."

The driver's assistants, who were also staring dumbfounded, jolted into action and busied themselves with the stretcher. Mrs. Smyth was hovering in the doorway.

When the stretcher reached the ambulance, a crowd had already gathered around it. "Someone must come to the hospital with her," said the driver.

"I'll go," said Rafael.

7

Asking Dagenham had been even more unpleasant than she had thought. Sitting on a boulder overlooking Calypso's Cave, Monica shivered at the recollection of their conversation: the factotum undressing her with his slippery eyes as he spoke to her. Though he had not done anything inappropriate, it had felt to her as if the coldest snake had been slithering all over her bare skin. But it had been necessary. Sebastian had been playing the vanishing act for three weeks, and the one time she had come across him she was too busy thinking about Rafael. *"And a fat lot of good that's done me!"* she said to herself in anger. No, Dagenham might be the only one who knew Sebastian's whereabouts. And that is what she had asked.

Enjoying his importance, he had taken the longest time to reply but had seemed informed and accurate. Now she sat by the sea, a favorite hunting ground of Sebastian's, waiting to create a chance encounter. Or was Dagenham joking? How many hours had she been sitting there, by the signpost to Calypso's Cave? Was Sebastian ever going to materialize? And if he did, what would she do? Jump out from behind a boulder and say "Hello!"? A chance meeting in one of the most desolate spots of Gozo, Malta's sister island? But it had come to this: Sebastian had suddenly become completely inaccessible to her, right after their great discovery, and after over two years of working together. It was inconceivable, and the more he made himself scarce, the less she could silence her questions and doubts. "Why are you doing this?" she asked out loud and looked around as though for an answer. But only the wind replied, ruffling the dry grass and tourist litter at her feet.

She had become a mere guest in the palace, one who could never see her host. Penelope was all smiles, but she, too, didn't have a clue about her husband's strange behavior, or maybe she did, but was not supposed to say anything. And Rafael was never home, though Dingli had assured her that he had not left Malta. Really, the whole family was impossible. Meanwhile, in the real world, the Discovery Channel wanted to come all the way to Malta to film the forbidden fruit and its discoverers. Inevitably, she had been temporizing, and they weren't the only members in the media concretely interested. Monica could hardly invite them to the palace without Sebastian's approval. She had contemplated doing it on the sly, on her own. But that would weaken the credibility of the whole story. It needed her patron to be on camera, too. Why was the most prominent citizen in Malta not eager to be seen by the world next to his discovery? Was two years' obsessive work of no consequence to him? It was all very depressing.

Leaning her back on a boulder, Monica tried to find a comfortable position, pulled her hat over her eyes, and closed them. All she could hear was the wind and the tireless cicadas. Resentment, frustration, and fear had exhausted her. Her career, which she thought had finally revived, was going down the drain as steadily as the wind kept blowing and the cicadas croaking. *"Must stay awake,"* she said to herself, still afraid, against all odds, that Sebastian would pass by and miss her. She drifted in and out of consciousness until she trailed into sleep.

She slept for some time and then began to dream. Something wet and cold was touching her arm. Now her other arm, too. *"I must be dreaming,"* she thought as she woke, her eyes still shut. Then the wet and cold feeling on her arm gave way to something hard and pointy. She suddenly realized that she was no longer dreaming or sleeping; her eyes snapped open, and she let out a scream. In an instant she was up on her feet, ready to run for her life. But she stopped: Animus and Anima, their tails wagging, were giving her an affectionate welcome. They weren't barking, but were delighted to have tracked her down. She caressed them and said: "You two, what are you doing here?" They replied by wagging their tails even more vigorously.

"Hello, stranger!" the unmistakable voice boomed from the crag behind her. She turned around and saw Sebastian approach, a smile on his face. Dressed in linen, a shotgun dangling from his shoulder, he looked as cool as a cucumber despite the heat.

"Sebastian! *I* am not the stranger. How are you?"

"Well, thank you. And you? Enjoying the great outdoors? Animus, Anima: did I ask you to hunt her down?"

She had so many questions, she didn't know where to begin. And yet, she was hesitant. At that point she didn't even know if he cared for her contribution any longer. The last thing she wanted was to put him off. He stood in front of her, smiling expectantly. He knew what was coming and stood his ground. She simply said, "Why, Sebastian?"

"Why? My birds were missing me." He indicated his gun. "I realized I had been neglecting them for far too long."

He seemed to be in a good mood. Monica dared to say: "Come on, Sebastian, what about our findings, the forbidden fruit?"

"Oh yes, that. Let's see, the media have begun to pester me. My secretaries have been barraged by phone calls, emails, faxes, express mail. I suspect I owe it to you if the media know about this?"

She looked him in the eye, without answering.

"And then there is your taking it to that intractable boor, that Professor Gara, without asking permission."

"But that's just standard procedure, for the finding to be analyzed."

"Yes, but not by that . . . whatever he is. I know much better experts; shall we say worldlier, too? At Oxford, for example. You should have consulted me before taking any such step."

"So this is what's made you vanish?" she asked, but only in her mind; then: "Sebastian, you've known since you fished it out of the sea that this is an earth-shattering discovery. I'm sorry if you feel I've—what—usurped your authority? But we are a team; I just took the obvious steps. Besides, I couldn't find you, so how could I consult you?" She continued in her mind, "Come on, this doesn't make any sense: why, what have you been hiding?"

Sebastian didn't say a word. Other questions formed in Monica's mind: "Did you plant the forbidden fruit, Sebastian? Is this a scheme? Am I just a part of it? Did you hire me to lend credibility to it? Did you wait patiently until it was the right time to surprise the world with the artifact that you had gotten God knows how and where?"

Sebastian knelt down to pat his dogs. Monica's silent questions turned to silent reproaches: "And now that you've pulled your stunt, now what? You're afraid to be exposed and ridiculed? Couldn't you think about this before? You're much too intelligent for this."

Sebastian took Monica's hand. Then, with one arm around her shoulders and the other cradling the shotgun, he began to walk slowly along the path to the cliffside parking lot.

"My ancestral home," Sebastian finally said, "is not a circus. I won't have hacks and TV clowns desecrate it. When the time is ripe, we'll hold a press conference, or something of the sort, somewhere else."

"Of course, Sebastian, as you wish."

Sebastian removed his arm, to Monica's relief, then stopped and faced her.

"I've been thinking about this, lately, while hunting, mainly here on Gozo. The publicity, the fanfare—I thought it would be gratifying. Satisfaction deliciously mixed with vainglory; what could be wrong with that? And yet, now that the thing we both yearned for, the 'desideratum,' has been produced, we couldn't just tell the media how pleased we were and leave it at that.

"No, that would be just the beginning; the project would take on its own momentum. How? Two possible scenarios. What would the media, and in turn the world, think if you and I ceased exploring the seabed? The skeptics would find their suspicions of fraud confirmed, while the believers would be furious. To them, the golden pomegranate was the first stone in the temple of their faith in Atlantis.

"That leaves the second scenario: a huge enterprise involving UNESCO, foundations, museums, the state, maybe even the infernal European Union. It's not the money: you realize that. No, what I dread is the sheer tedium of the work involved. However many people I employed, every day would begin with bulletins and appeals for decisions. It would swallow up my whole life in paperwork and constant communication. Can you imagine the untiring petulance of my cell phone, solicitations, secretaries, and so on? The thought of the bureaucratic aggravation and overall nuisance still takes my breath away. And what, my dear Monica, if there is nothing more to be discovered? Do you understand?"

"Yes, but it can all be sorted out," she said, though mindful of a couple of hints he had dropped: "suspicions of fraud," and "what if there is nothing more to be discovered?"

"Oh," he continued, "you probably think I've been terribly rude in cutting off communication with you, but don't worry—I can get worse." He turned his attention to the dogs, who were getting bored by a conversation that excluded them, and continued along the path ahead of her.

Monica was not to be put off and caught up to walk beside him. "Sebastian," she said, "even a control freak would realize that sooner or later things such as these take on a life of their own, and it becomes impossible to control them." "Always assuming," she added in her mind, "that they are not a fraud to begin with. Because if they are, then your behavior makes a lot of sense. You thought you could get away with it, then realized you couldn't, so now instead of being eager to show off the—"

Sebastian turned and looked her straight in the eye: "To make the esoteric, exoteric:" he interrupted her thoughts, "that is the dilemma. We find proof of a civilization so ancient, one could say we have evidence that Atlantis was not a myth. So, you learn a secret, guarded for millennia. And what do you do? You divulge it to the whole world. There, it's a secret no longer." As they reached the parking lot, he plumped down on a bench and added, with a malicious smile: "Now if Jesus had kept to his small sect of followers, he would have never ended up on the cross. But wait a minute: you're Jewish; this may sound even more ambiguous than I intended it!"

"This is Sebastian all right," she thought but kept it to herself. "So," aloud, "what next? Are you out of quarantine, Sebastian?"

"I suppose I am. Besides, the Medal of Bravery farce is coming up, and that can't be missed."

"Of course not. But as far as our project?"

"We'll see to it, don't worry. Let's just coordinate our next moves. Are you here with the Fiat? Would you mind giving us a lift to the ferry?"

A festive atmosphere welcomed Sebastian Pinto, as a day later he walked into the Grand Council Chamber in Valletta. This investiture ceremony was nothing like the usual one held on Republic Day, in which awards would be handed out by the dozen. Conferring

the Medal for Bravery on Sebastian Pinto had strong political over-
tones. The president of the Republic, flanked by the secretary to the
cabinet and the prime minister, formally greeted him and then said:
"The Maltese nation cries out for tolerance of those who come to us
from different cultures and countries. That is why, Mr. Pinto, I have
received the prime minister's suggestion with enthusiasm."

Sebastian smiled back. He was enjoying the attention but already
planning his counterattack. The democratically correct president
could address as "Mr." just about anyone else; but he, Sebastian Pinto
de Fonseca, was a Knight of Malta. As a reminder to the world, he
was festooned with its insignia. A number of TV crews were present, broadcasting the ceremony in several European countries. Also
in attendance were all of Malta's ministers, assorted bigwigs, as well
as a number of foreign dignitaries and politicians. Penelope glowed
with elegance in her Chanel tailleur, her shoulder-length blonde hair
pulled back in conservative fashion. She sat in the first row, with
Rafael to her right. Monica, on whom Sebastian had pressed an invitation, watched from the back.

The president went on with his speech while Sebastian, all smiles
to match the minister's, was thinking of something else: that the
scene of his investiture had originally been the Magisterial Palace,
the official and private residence of the Grand Masters of the Order;
that its expansion had been commissioned by his very ancestor Grand
Master Pinto in the eighteenth century; and above all that, if this
was the Ivorian immigrant he had "saved," now alert and dressed in a
suit and tie, the emphasis should have been on *him,* and on what he
had come to represent.

The president's concluding words were about the latest threat.
"White supremacists from the Russian Federation have come to
our island. Malta has spoken to them, and spoken strongly, through
Mr. Pinto's heroic action. He, our most prominent citizen, has risked

his life to save that of an immigrant. In so doing, he has set an example to us all. Mr. Pinto, please approach."

Once bedecked with his shiny new medal, Sebastian shook hands with the man he had saved and congratulated him on his recovery.

At the reception that followed, Penelope and Sebastian faced the barrage of journalists and cameras as a couple. If only he had cared about power, thought Penelope, Malta certainly could have used a more enterprising political leadership.

"Paparazzi, enough already, be gone!" thundered Sebastian after a few minutes. Everybody laughed, thinking it a joke, and the couple was left in peace. Sebastian went looking for Monica and found her in a corner, by herself. "Monica, my dear," he said, "come with me; I want you to meet somebody." She followed him, and after some searching, he singled out two men. "Here we are," he said, addressing the three of them. "Gentlemen, meet Dr. Bettlheim, the mind behind our great discovery." Monica looked both pleased and puzzled while Sebastian continued with the introductions. "Monica, this is Jeff Bloom, from the *New York Times*, and this is Matthew Milton, from the *London Times*." Monica shook hands with them, wondering what this was about. Sebastian explained. "They'll meet us tomorrow morning on board the *Thetis,* for interviews and photos. The forbidden fruit will be on display, too. See you tomorrow, gentlemen."

Sebastian offered Monica his arm and dragged her away, explaining: "I thought those two would make for a good start. There will be more."

"That's wonderful, Sebastian, thank you. I think—"

"Here you are, my darling," Sebastian interrupted Monica as he addressed his wife. "How are you dealing with the consequences of my heroics?"

The prime minister shuffled up to them, arm in arm with his

horse-faced wife. "Congratulations, Cavalier," he had the good sense to address him, "I have no words to express—"

"That's all right: you can remain speechless." Sebastian said and then suppressed an *ouch,* as Penelope had pinched him.

"Prime Minister," she said, approaching with the broadest of smiles, "will you and Mrs. Missigonzo be attending our dinner party, two weeks from tomorrow?"

"Our RSVP is already in the mail," replied the minister's wife. "Thank you, we are very much looking forward to it."

"Oh dear," thought Sebastian.

"Cavalier," the prime minister said, "allow me to introduce you to Signor Altieri, former senator from Palermo and now Special Commissioner for Refugees of the European Union."

The two shook hands, but before that, Altieri had hand-kissed both the wives. "A politico with manners?" wondered Sebastian in his mind. Elegant, tall, blue-eyed, and with a moustache that was just beginning to turn from blond to gray, he did not fit the stereotype either of the Sicilian or of the troublemaking politician. Everyone knew that as a senator, Altieri had repeatedly threatened to upset the flimsy center-left coalition if it did not give in to his defense of immigrants' rights. In the process he had become somewhat of a celebrity.

"Dr. Altieri is in Malta on an official visit," added the prime minister. "If there is any hope for immigrants coming into the European Union from the south, it rests squarely on his shoulders."

"If you'll still be here, we'd love to have you, too, at our dinner party," said Penelope.

"Thank you, Lady Pinto," Altieri replied. "I'll have to check my schedule, but I might need to return to Malta soon; so I hope I can attend." He returned Sebastian's smile, then went to talk to the Ivorian— in fluent French, noticed Sebastian, who couldn't help eavesdropping.

Commissioner Altieri addressed the immigrant both respectfully and straightforwardly. "Monsieur, you have become a cause célèbre and will be treated fairly. But when the publicity fades, you may be more in trouble than ever. Believe me, I know how white men think. Don't wait for that to happen. Here," he handed over a visiting card to him. "Just call me and I'll help you. I mean it, you can count on me."

"What do you know?" thought Sebastian, as he moved away from the two, "the politico knows the languages, doesn't pontificate, even seems capable of being useful. . . ."

In the meantime, Sophocles was talking to Rafael in very hushed tones. "No improvement yet, I'm afraid; the girl is still in a coma."

Rafael made no reply. It was plain to see that the news troubled him deeply. Eventually, he said: "This goes beyond anything the medical profession understands. I know of only one person who might be able to help. He lives in Rome. . . ."

The tête-à-tête was interrupted by his father, dragging Monica by the hand. "What's going on? Are you relapsing into your reclusive habits, Rafael? Well, not now, this is a party! Come, both of you, we must immortalize this moment. And that includes you, Monica, yes, you."

"Please, Sebastian, I don't belong. It should be just your family," protested Monica. The photographers clustered around.

"Nonsense. You're honorary family today. And I find symmetry irresistible," he said, "especially when it comes in female form," taking Penelope with his other hand and drawing both women close to himself. "Now my beloved son, stand thou upon my right hand, and my dear uncle at my left." There was no resisting the command and Sophocles and Rafael moved into position. They certainly made for an interesting quintet: the doddery uncle exuding aristocratic distinction, the skinny yet handsome Rafael—rarely seen in Malta—his bigger-than-life father, framed by a pair of gorgeous women.

The photographers seized on a particular moment: when Rafael, with no preamble or paternal request of any sort, hugged his father.

8

Liveried footmen showed the guests to the salon and kept them busy with hors d'oeuvres and champagne. Penelope was wearing a crimson silk gown with a plunging V-neck, held at the waist with a crystal-encrusted bow-shaped buckle, and a generous opening in the front, showing off to perfection her long shapely legs. Before entering, she had lifted her dress in front of her husband enough to reveal a pair of high-heeled sandals with a pavé crystal chain resting on her gracious, milk-white feet. Monica was wearing a dress Penelope had lent her, looking very attractive in it, too. The Goddess and the Amazon, as Sebastian called them on this occasion, dazzled with their different beauties. On the other hand, when the prime minister and Mrs. Missigonzo came over to greet him, Sebastian mentally compared them to the pygmy elephants of prehistoric Malta and purred with delight at his own witticism. Giorgio Stilnovo, the Milanese fashion designer, had come with an entourage of anorexic models. Then there were old couples, all Knights or Donats and Dames of Malta, and sundry socialites. Sophocles and Rafael came unescorted, the latter soon striking up a conversation with the fashion guru.

Penelope and Sebastian were quick at making everyone feel at ease, introducing all the guests to one another and dropping in witty, or barbed, pleasantries. "Dr. Altieri, it's nice to see you again," said Penelope. The Commissioner, elegant in his old-fashioned smoking jacket, smiled back at her. "I would like you to meet the Baron and Baroness de la Richardière. You may be familiar with their wine—a Pauillac." Sebastian, who was greeting the prime minister and his wife, turned and interposed: "But what makes them so dear to me is that, come every July, they go into mourning for the whole month."

Baffled, the prime minister said, "I'm sorry to hear that."

"Aren't we all? You see, my dear politicos," looking from minister to commissioner, "14 July in France is the national holiday that celebrates . . ." he trailed off, waiting for an answer.

"The storming of the Bastille," Altieri eventually answered, as Sebastian insisted in getting the obvious reply.

"Yes, that, but also the official beginning of the rule by the rabble and state terrorism."

Altieri clearly resented this interpretation, but at a glance from the prime minister he controlled himself.

When the sorbet was served between courses, Sebastian got up and wandered to the other tables. As he reached the models, he looked at them appraisingly and said: "Tell me, are you enjoying the food so far?"

They were, thank you.

"Good. Now, you're all very pretty, but to be prettier still, you must eat to your heart's content!" They giggled. "No, I mean it." He leaned forward, resting his giant arms on the shoulders of two of the models, and confidentially whispered: "Your friend the designer— the maker or unmaker of your destiny—is *not* your friend. Shush, hear me out. He doesn't like women, doesn't care for them at all; it's as simple as that, so he'll only pick anorexic, flat-chested girls that look like boys." Loudly again: "Put on thirty pounds, each of you! A woman's body is a temple of voluptuousness, not a plank. Eat up! Waiter, over here!"

Monica and Stilnovo sat across from Rafael, a few seats up toward Sebastian. As Rafael had been casting glances diagonally in her direction, Monica, gorgeous in her black gown of flowing Italian silk chiffon, had initially returned them only to realize, to her disappointment, that his focus was Stilnovo. He was now looking almost fixedly at the designer. "What's going on?" Monica wondered in her mind. "Why does Rafael stare at Stilnovo so much?"

Mrs. Missigonzo broke the lull following Sebastian's remarks by congratulating him again on his Medal for Bravery.

"Please, don't start," the topic invariably made him want to laugh. Controlling himself, he added: "What can I say? It's a nuisance."

"I'm sorry, did I miss something?" asked Mrs. Missigonzo. "What's the nuisance?"

"The instinct of self-preservation. Those punks were coming after me; I panicked and shot at them; then my factotum arrived and solved the situation. Yes, we saved the immigrant's life, but it was fortuitous."

Sophocles looked alarmed as he waited for the prime minister's reaction. He had heard as much from his nephew, but such self-deprecation, however honest, seemed to devalue the award.

"Anyway," Sebastian resumed, "I'll be more careful from now on, both here in Malta and when I travel to South America."

"Which countries do you go to?" Stilnovo inquired.

"Just to Venezuela, to change my blood. Please, Commissioner, don't look so disapproving. Rock stars do it all the time; in fact, it was a rock star who told me about it, on St. Kitts. Total blood transfusions: out with one's stale old blood, in with something fresh and ruttish."

"Cool," said Stilnovo.

"And therein lies the proof of my democratic convictions: I welcome into my veins the blood of street urchins, none of them white, let alone blue-blooded."

Altieri looked dumbfounded. As Sebastian met his blank stare, he burst into laughter, a long, Homeric laugh. The two disconcerted politicians interpreted it as the end of a prank.

"For a moment there, Cavalier," said the prime minister, "I thought you were being serious. I should have known you were pulling our legs."

"Was I?"

After dinner all the guests adjourned to the salon for more champagne or coffee, Marsala, and cigars. Here, as in the dining room, the usual electric light fixtures had been removed for the occasion. In ancient chandeliers and sconces of Venetian glass, a myriad of candles dripped carelessly on the Caucasian rugs.

Altieri, standing tall and handsome in the middle of the room while the old Dames eyed him languorously, exuded sobriety as he spoke: "My dear Cavalier, I think I'm beginning to appreciate your personality—in fact, to appreciate who you are." He took a breath and, raising his voice so that everyone in the salon would hear, said: "You sound off your Neanderthal opinions, but in fact you risk your life to save an African illegal immigrant from certain death. Facts speak louder than words. I toast to you, a true Knight of Honor and Devotion!" He raised his champagne flute, inviting everyone to join in.

Sophocles had been trying to get his nephew's attention for some time. When he succeeded, he said in a low voice: "I've consulted your horoscope, Sebastian."

"And?" his nephew said impatiently, as Sophocles seemed hesitant.

"Perhaps we should meet somewhere in private and discuss this; I'm afraid it doesn't bode well."

"Uncle," said Sebastian with a spark in his eyes, "you're lucky I don't have my shotgun handy—I know of no better target than birds of ill omen!" He laughed loudly, but then, seeing Sophocles's grave expression, he added, in a sober tone, "We believe in different cosmologies, that's all. You think we're dominated by the stars; I think we can outwit them. Wasn't I supposed to be going through a bad patch already? Look at me: I'm sitting on top of the world! Come, come, have some champagne, it's the magic potion; don't you agree?"

For the whole evening Monica had been feeling ill at ease. Her confrontation with Sebastian, first, and the many interviews they had given together since had not entirely silenced her doubts about the authenticity of their discovery, now trumpeted the world over by the media. How could she follow it up if it were a fraud? Might it be just a matter of time before she was exposed, discredited, and ruined? She could have used Rafael's company, but he seemed immersed in a ponderous conversation with his great-uncle. So she found a comfortable spot on a sofa, and very soon an oldish Italian socialite sat beside her, pretending to be greatly interested in archaeology while scrutinizing her torso with his pointed, piercing eyes.

Sophocles' voice trembled as he confided to Rafael: "Honoria snapped out of the coma. The doctors are puzzled, but relieved. And so are we all, of course."

"Thank Heavens!" said Rafael. "How is she now?"

"She's well and remembers nothing about the incident. So there are no consequences for anyone. That said, we've decided that we will never again employ a medium of . . . that age. But," he added, "what was revealed through Honoria stands, Rafael."

"I'm sorry, great-uncle, but I have to be honest about this. I'm amazed that you can take that poor girl's ravings seriously. It was clearly garbage from the unconscious. I would pay no attention to it whatever."

Sophocles had always considered Rafael his spiritual son, and his disbelief hurt him. "I'm sorry," Rafael repeated and then walked out of the salon.

Stilnovo saw Rafael's exit out of the corner of his eye and was disappointed. Sitting at the piano, he was singing some retro tunes with both models and Dames of Malta hanging around his neck, though he was certainly not serenading *them*.

Then something unexpected happened. Rafael now stood in front of Monica and her Italian ogler and stared at him so long and so brazenly that eventually the guest got up and walked away.

When Rafael sat beside her, he didn't say a word. He just lingered there for endless minutes, adding to the awkwardness by looking her in the eye. Then he grabbed her hand and held it tightly. The situation was becoming strange and mildly embarrassing; some of the guests were looking at them. "Wonderful party," Monica said, "isn't it? I'm so happy for your father."

Rafael looked away. He let go of her hand and left her wondering on the sofa. As if on cue, Stilnovo stopped singing and followed him into the library.

The prime minister, meanwhile, had trapped Sebastian in a prolonged tête-à-tête. Suddenly he left the minister in the lurch, in the middle of a sentence, and with great bearlike strides reached the center of the salon. All eyes were on him. In a loud voice, he said: "Our prime minister has been telling me of a project that may need my wallet, just for a change: a hospital to be built right next to the Ħal-Far detention center. Yes, a hospital for the immigrants."

The guests, all back in the salon now, were paying attention.

"That's his new project," Sebastian resumed. "I, too, have a new one; it's time I announced it, and since I see a link with the minister's, why not tonight?" Penelope and Altieri came closer, and so did Monica and Rafael. "As you know, our recent discovery," Sebastian elaborated, "has the potential of changing humanity's view of the world and of history. Such a challenge cannot be met by Dr. Bettlheim and myself alone. It's time to turn it over to an official organization. I've tossed the golden ball into the wedding feast: it's up to others now.

"In the meantime, something else has caught our attention. Come here, Monica." The guests made room for her to pass. "We were recently both led by my dogs, independently from each other, to a place along the Victoria Lines, not far from Fommir Rih Bay. I know from casual explorations in my youth that there, beneath the surface, is an archaeological and paleontological treasure trove. But now we find to our dismay," he cast a reproachful glance on the prime minister, "that the authorities have sealed it from the public, and from researchers such as ourselves."

Altieri and the prime minister were already on to what was coming. "So," Sebastian continued, "I was thinking, while speaking with our prime minister, that it's time the ban was lifted." He addressed him directly. "If that could be done, just for Dr. Bettlheim and myself, I believe Lady Penelope might persuade me to fund the construction of the hospital in its entirety. Don't you think, darling?"

The prime minister looked stunned. "The motion will have to go through Parliament, of course. I'll let you have the details as soon as possible. As for the hospital—"

"You'll get the check the moment the ban is lifted."

A few minutes later, Monica spoke to Sebastian in private, in the library. She fully realized what was expected of her: to fight for the right to lead the new, expanded phase of the research. Without revealing the source of her disquiet, she protested until Sebastian said: "Calm down, calm down—I'll do what I can, my dear, and see how far my influence goes, once the new organization's set up. But I have a hunch that the two of us, working on our own and on the mainland, might find something just as exciting. It's something I've been meaning to do since I was a young man. I just never had somebody as lucky and clever as you as a partner."

A knock on the door was regarded by both as a welcome interruption: neither one wanted to add anything to their exchange, but neither would admit as much.

"Cavalier Pinto," Altieri said, walking up to him, "I've been looking for you. Thank you very much for having me; I've already thanked Lady Penelope. I'm afraid I must go."

"But Commissioner," Sebastian protested, "you'd be the first to leave."

"I'm sorry, Cavalier; we'll meet again. But for now, I'm needed elsewhere; in fact, I'm going directly to the airport. Good night."

"Not so soon!" exclaimed Sebastian. With unexpected agility he relocated his bulk right in front of the door, making it impossible for Altieri to leave. "When a politico needs to go somewhere in a hurry, I become both suspicious and titillated."

While Monica wondered if Sebastian was doing this to distract her, Altieri frowned.

"So," he continued, as the commissioner stood his ground three feet away from him, "I will not let you through this door until you come clean. Tell me, my handsome Norman Communist—you *are* a Communist, aren't you?—might it be a romantic rendezvous? Better? An illicit tryst? Monica, quick: call the paparazzi, tell them to follow him!"

"Cavalier, please!" Altieri said in a controlled tone. "My time is not my own, and now I must leave; please, move out of the way." The commissioner was in a quandary: on the one hand, he hated to be detained and ridiculed; on the other, he was trying not to make too much of this, lest he fuel his host's histrionics.

Monica had appreciated how Sebastian had seized the chance to distract her; she herself didn't know how to get out of their tête-à-tête. But she now felt this was enough: Altieri might erupt, insult her patron, even come to blows. "Sebastian," she said, preceding the commissioner, "I didn't know you were a prohibitionist."

Her remark surprised both men, who looked at her quizzically. "Yes," she elaborated, "by prohibiting me from going back into the salon, you're condemning me to an empty flute. It's time to refill it."

Sebastian looked at the glass in her hand and burst into laughter. Next, he stepped into the salon, clamoring for "champagne for my Amazon!" while Altieri made a hasty escape.

The party had splintered into small groups, gravitating around the piano, various sofas, the huge balconied windows open to the cool breeze of the night. It was time to showcase Sebastian's final surprise of the evening. The prime minister and his wife were close by, and so was Monica with the baron and baroness. Rafael and a bony model were also within earshot, but both seemed to be dozing. "Monica, are you ready for a surprise?"

"Only if it's a pleasant one."

"Yes, this one is just a curiosity, but a very intriguing one. It arrived a few days ago from Florence. As the guest of honor, Monica, I promise you'll see it first. And you, would you like to see it, too?"

The small group said yes.

"Very well, then: follow me."

Sebastian led the way out of the salon, arm in arm with Monica and with the two couples trailing behind. As he went, he explained: "I have recently converted a small *salotto* into a camera obscura by piercing a hole through the wall of my Wunderkammer. There are many interesting experiments one can make with it, but I am currently using it to display a remarkable panel in *pietra dura* work."

"Florentine inlay, using jasper, onyx, lapis, and so on?" asked the baron. "I also collect it. May we see it?"

"It's more a question of *can* you see it," said Sebastian mysteriously, enjoying his guests' puzzlement. "You can't just go in and gawp."

"Why not?" wondered the baroness.

"I will tell you. This panel is made entirely from phosphorescent minerals, which can be made to glow in the dark. By daylight, it presents one image: that of the Penitent Magdalene in all her naked splendor. In darkness, a different image appears, carrying a moral lesson." Looking at the baroness, he winked cheekily. "But it is very faint," he added. "You have to accustom your eyes to the darkness before you can see it."

He opened the door. Those who had not seen the Wunderkammer before gazed around in astonishment. As they milled around, Sebastian pointed to the curtain at the far end of the chamber. "You'll go behind there," he said, "and look intently through the opening into the camera obscura. Be patient: it'll take at least five minutes for the pupils to dilate. Then, gradually, you'll see this masterpiece of *magia naturalis* emerge. Go on, Monica, you first. Meanwhile, I'll show the rest of you some things of interest in here."

Monica smiled her assent and disappeared behind the curtain. Once behind it, she stood facing an adjustable viewer set into the wall at eye level, like the diaphragm of an old camera. She peered through the slit; it gave a view into a small drawing room. It was entirely dark except for the panel above the mantel, lit by a dim bulb. This showed the Magdalene as a voluptuous figure, rolling her eyes heavenward. Monica put her head around the curtain and called out: "Sebastian, I've seen the fat lady, but shouldn't you turn the light off in there?"

He was busy taking ivories out of the cabinets for his visitors to admire. "It's on a timer," he shouted. "Be patient. Just keep watching."

As he spoke, the light on the picture faded out and the darkness was absolute. After a few more minutes, she began to see areas of gray, with the bluish cast caused by black light. The room loomed dimly into focus and with it a sight that sent shivers down her spine.

Ten feet in front of her, facing the mantel, there was a large black sofa, and two people were on it. One must have been a man in evening dress, for she could see the flash of a white shirt collar, moving rhythmically to and fro. The other person was concealed by the back of the sofa, except for her feet, raised on the man's shoulders. The sandals with their glinting straps were unmistakably Penelope's. As Monica recognized the man, she gave an audible gasp.

"Quite impressive, eh?" came Sebastian's voice, muffled by the curtain.

"Ye . . . es," she called back, trying to keep her voice steady. Her urge was to leave at once, yet wasn't she supposed to wait for the allotted time for her eyes to adjust? No, she could not move from there, however much she wanted to. She could have closed her eyes, but somehow, she looked on, not knowing why.

The panel above the couple finally began to mutate. The luscious pink body had become a livid green skeleton, like an X-ray. It followed the lineaments of the living portrait, but instead of hair, bluish snakes crawled out of its skull and between its thighs. When she looked back at the sofa, Rafael had turned his head toward her, facing full into the black light. His teeth shone in a smile, and he winked.

9

Salvatore had started on an early morning run from Lampedusa's only town to the sanctuary on Cala Madonna, a cove with turquoise waters well loved by snorkelers and scuba divers. A plump man in his fifties, he had been an energetic youth and still displayed impressive biceps under his taut, tanned skin. A gold cross and a medal of Our Lady gleamed over his T-shirt. The late October dawn was cloudless; the full moon was setting in the west, but the faint breeze was tainted with a disagreeable smell. It became stronger as he approached the sanctuary, some fifty feet above the beach. Once there he paused, panting, sniffed the air with increasing displeasure, then looked down.

An inflatable rubber raft had run aground on the sparkling white sand. On it was a confused heap of bodies. Not a living soul was to be seen, either on the raft or on the beach. Mastering his revulsion, Salvatore took the steep path down and stood a few feet away, a folded handkerchief clutched to his face, his stomach churning. After taking stock of the situation, he turned his back on the wreck and ran back into town. Once there, sweating profusely and with his heart racing, he alerted his colleagues, managing to find coherent words.

In the course of the morning the local carabinieri, and many more who had flown in from Agrigento, reconstructed the dynamics of the tragedy. The strong sunlight revealed the details that had escaped Salvatore. From the bow of the raft dangled a tattered remnant of tow rope. There were six bodies: those of a woman and five children. They had apparently died of thirst, but there was worse to come. When the forensic unit arrived from Palermo, it took them a mere glance at the mangled bodies to state that they had been bitten, even gnawed to the bone, by human jaws and teeth.

Salvatore had not only informed the carabinieri *and* the police, but the Ministry of the Interior, Amnesty International, the European Council on Refugees and Exiles, Italy's main press agency, and even Commissioner Altieri. It was he who had promoted him from humble policeman from Altieri's own neighborhood in Palermo to the task of inspecting all Sicilian Temporary Residence Centers and reporting to the government, and to various human rights organizations.

Malta's authorities had liaised with their counterparts in Sicily after the shipwreck off their shores. Inspector Soldanis was informed of the tragedy by Malta's commissioner of refugees, who had been alerted by his Italian equivalent. So well before the news had leaked, Soldanis found himself on a plane bound to the island.

A tiny rock in the Mediterranean between Malta and Tunisia, Lampedusa belongs to Sicily and Italy politically, but geologically to Africa. Once a sunbather's paradise, during the last few years it had become the gateway to most illegal immigration from North Africa into Italy and the European Union.

"Thankfully," thought Soldanis inside the police car that was escorting him to Cala Madonna, "this is outside my jurisdiction."

The raft, still untouched and unmoved, was being photographed and analyzed by a crowd of policemen and technicians, all under the supervision of a public magistrate and an investigator. Soldanis introduced himself, and they greeted him gruffly. They clearly had no patience for outsiders, but he didn't care; he was trying to hold his breath. After one look at the mangled corpses, he wondered if he couldn't leave right now. But even if his Italian colleagues were ignoring him, his departure would be noticed and get back to the Maltese authorities. He had no choice.

"Have some of this," said a technician in yellow overalls, offering a jar. "It's an olfactory suppressant: daub it under your nose. Put these on, too." He held out a pair of latex gloves.

"I don't plan to be touching anything," said Soldanis.

"Still, cover up your skin as much as you can. This whole place is a bacteria festival."

After about an hour, the chief investigator relented and came up to Soldanis. The mustached Sicilian laid a hand on his colleague's shoulder and said, "So what do you think happened here?"

"You tell me; it's your investigation."

"Very well," said the investigator. "It looks as though a family of illegal immigrants set off from Tunisia early in the week. Their towboat abandoned them, God knows why. The *scafista* might have sighted the coast guard, or whatever, and they were left adrift to die of thirst. Then," he hesitated, looking Soldanis in the eye, "the odontologist says the bites were all inflicted by a male African in his thirties. I think the father began to," he hesitated and continued: "eat them."

The two men stared at each other in silence. Then the Sicilian added: "But where is he now, the father, I mean?"

"Maybe he threw himself overboard?" put in Soldanis.

"One possibility of many. Your guess is as good as mine. Also, this is the first time a boatload of immigrants has stayed adrift for so long. Maybe six, seven days. Usually they're sighted earlier. But who cares? What's done is done. Those who ferry them across, the *scafisti*, are the culprits, and there's nothing new there; but a cannibal father, man. . . ."

Shortly before sundown, the corpses were stuffed into body bags, ready to be removed by ambulance to the airport. There were no adequate facilities on the tiny island, so the authorities had decided to store the bodies temporarily in Palermo's main morgue.

Soldanis checked back into his hotel room and took a shower that lasted a precious twenty minutes on a very droughty island. He could not scrub the stench off his body, and in his mind's eye he kept seeing the mangled corpses, the gnawed limbs, the bare bones, the gorging maggots, accompanied by the ceaseless buzzing of the flies. He went to bed without supper and smoked himself to sleep.

"Monica? Hello, it's Rafael. How are you?"

She was taken aback. How did he get her cell number? Why was he calling her? She was sure that he had winked at her that night, from inside the camera obscura. She was no prude, far from it, but she was still shocked by what she had witnessed. All this went through Monica's mind as she eventually heard herself reply flatly: "I'm OK, Rafael."

"Listen, I'm in Rome." He ignored the long time she had taken to reply. "I was calling to invite you to come here. The laboratory at the Sapienza has finished the carbon 14 test. You could meet my friend there, hear the results in person, ask questions, and so on. Oh, if you don't want to bother with a hotel, I have a large apartment with separate guest quarters."

"Thanks, Rafael," said Monica, her mind full of reservations. "I'll get back to you tomorrow."

She would see Sebastian that evening, she decided, and settle this business once and for all: if he had pulled a hoax on her, she could forgive him, but she could no longer deal with the uncertainty. She went downstairs to the main house and found out from Dingli that the master would be available later in the day. In the meantime, she would be taking the old Fiat out for a few hours.

She badly needed a change of scenery and thought of a brisk walk along the fortifications of Valletta, to inhale the sea air and feel the spray of the breaking waves. She started toward the capital, then another idea struck her, and she left the main road for the narrow, shabby streets of Paola. She had a sudden urge to revisit the Hal Saflieni Hypogeum, that complex of underground chambers that, more than anywhere else, seemed to hold the secrets of prehistoric Malta. Uncharacteristically, in an almost superstitious way, she felt that its creators were summoning her, and she obeyed.

The staff knew her well and regularly allowed her to study the place on her own. She made her way past the small group of visitors in the Main Chamber. They were admiring the heavy-set doors and windows, the massive curved beams of the ceiling, all carved into the solid rock in imitation of the aboveground temples. She passed the spherical pit and the long room that must once have blazed in torchlight with its red, orange, and yellow ochre decorations. From there she clambered through an opening at window height and continued into the depths of the labyrinth. Here she settled in a small egg-shaped cavity, cross-legged on its stone floor, and faced the turmoil of her own thoughts.

First, she was famous again. To judge by the fallout from interviews and editorials published by prestigious newspapers and magazines, there would soon be invitations to speak at universities, she'd be interviewed on talk shows, would chair conference sessions. Now all archaeological eyes were on Malta, its underground mysteries and those of the surrounding seas. Whether or not those rock formations from which they had fished out the pomegranate had really been a sunken temple, her intuition had hit pay dirt.

Yet there were doubts. What *was* this golden pomegranate, this forbidden fruit? It had been crowned with approval, but only by members of the press handpicked by Sebastian. What would happen when her fellow archaeologists—*"Envious bastards,"* she thought with a shudder—got their hands on it? But would they be able to? It was Sebastian's treasure, and he kept it locked up in his precious Wunderkammer. One might never discover the truth of the matter. Then there were the contents, now sitting in a laboratory at the Università della Sapienza. This had not figured in the interviews, nor, she reminded herself uncomfortably, had she raised the matter with Sebastian. He seemed so preoccupied these days, the opportunity had never occurred, and the longer she left it, the more difficult it was going to be to say: "And by the way, the thing was full of garden dirt, which is now being analyzed in Rome."

Perhaps it was best to leave it like that: the forbidden fruit kept in secret in Mdina. If the C-14 test showed a modern date, she would put it behind her and concentrate on the real work ahead. There was no need to go to Rome or get any further involved with the impossible Rafael. The lab could send the results, and she would pay for them herself, publishing them or not as she saw fit.

She left the Hypogeum with a friendly word and a tip to the custodian. Her meditation in that womb-like space had cleared her mind better even than the salt spray. She felt doors opening in her life, vistas of new possibilities before her.

10

The brand-new helicopter bore Maltese police markings and was furnished in Spartan style, with ten seats for policemen and a cage for dogs or criminals. For now, it ferried only the pilot and co-pilot, Soldanis and the same officer who had summoned him from Lampedusa on orders from the chief of police. None of them had offered any small talk or explanation. The Inspector had not insisted; he did not know where he was going, but that did not bother him. In fact, everything about Lampedusa had been nauseating.

The helicopter was flying fast and at low altitude over the Mediterranean, an uninterrupted expanse of rippled, shimmering blue. It was hard to believe that it soon would be scarred for its whole width. Yet that was what Altieri, the commissioner for refugees of the European Union, had announced two hours before on a televised speech addressed to an auditorium in Palermo packed with heads of state, ambassadors, Eurocrats, a U.S. delegation, representatives from the United Nations, most of Italy's ministers, the prime minister, and the president of the Republic. International pop stars were also conspicuously in attendance. Soldanis had followed it on TV while drinking espresso and smoking in a bar close to his hotel in Lampedusa. At the end of his impassioned speech, Altieri had said:

"On the other side of the Mediterranean there are millions of desperately poor people waiting for fewer than one hundred scafisti to load them onto wrecks. The first thing we need is this: a massive naval blockade to prevent further ferrying of illegal immigrants into the European Union. We need the navies of all EU members to participate in this. This will temporarily stop the scafisti's slave trade. No one will die at sea.

"In the meantime, the Rome Conference will commence in earnest, and all members of the European Union will work together to put an end to twenty-first-century slavery. Our governments must start at once to give credit, incentives, and grants to entrepreneurs who open factories and all sorts of new business ventures in Africa and other developing countries. It's time to redistribute the world's wealth and improve the quality of life in these countries so dramatically that their citizens will no longer need to leave them out of desperation."

Soldanis smiled at the recollection of his reaction after these words: "Far outside my jurisdiction. . . ." "Was it?" he wondered suddenly. Were they taking him to Palermo, and in a hurry? For what reason? The fax from the chief of police handed over by the officer had merely said: "Come immediately. I'll meet you on your arrival." What on earth would the chief of the Maltese police be doing on Italian soil?

After half an hour's flight, the familiar south coast of Malta came into view, the Dingli cliffs pink in the setting sun. Next would be the brighter lights of Valletta, and the helipad in police HQ, thought Soldanis, relieved. But he had guessed wrong.

The helicopter was turning to the left, following the cliffs and almost skimming the gray sea. The western bays and the Marfa Peninsula flashed by in a matter of minutes. "Gozo?!" mouthed Soldanis over the roar of the twin rotors. The officer nodded.

"Whatever could be going on there?" thought Soldanis. The small island with its giant prehistoric temple was big on the tourist map, but on his it was negligible. The inhabitants were mostly farmers and second-home owners, disinclined to crime and immune to the immigrant problem.

They landed with a shudder near a lookout tower, a staunch, battlemented remnant of the imperial era. The same description might have fitted Chief of Police Crizzo, who stooped under the slowing blades and offered his hand as Soldanis descended. He motioned the inspector to follow him and marched briskly away from the helicopter. Soldanis caught up with him. As soon as words stood a chance of being heard over the din, Crizzo shouted: "I know you're assigned to the shipwreck investigation, but that's paralyzed while we await information from the Italians. I'm taking you off it because there's worse yet, at least for Malta."

"Please tell me what's going on!"

They were now walking along the rough path that led inland from the tower. Without breaking his stride, Crizzo turned and met his eyes. "You're our best investigator, and the country won't stand for less."

Flattery will get you nowhere, thought Soldanis: this is sheer evasion.

"Worse yet?" he said, but the chief held up his hand to quiet him, then pointed ahead.

They had reached a lodge, a substantial piece of rustic baroque carved out of the creamy local stone. Three police cars and an ambulance stood in the courtyard, screened from visibility by the outbuildings. "We're trying not to draw attention to it," Crizzo went on. Good God, he looks haggard, thought Soldanis.

"Chief," he said, his patience finally exhausted, "will you tell me what's going on?"

"No, I won't."

"Why not? What have you flown me in for, all the way from Lampedusa, if you keep me in the dark?"

"It won't be a minute now, and in the meantime, I don't want to influence your opinions with mine. Here, see for yourself," said

Crizzo in a growl. He buried his great nose in a handkerchief as the two constables on guard opened the front door. Soldanis caught a whiff of eau de cologne before he stepped inside and was immediately wafted with a sweet foul stench that he knew only too well.

Inside the house, the inspector noted the typical island decor of wrought iron and stucco, setting off an outrageous collection of big-game trophies: huge antlers, tusks, specimens of lion, tiger, buffalo. A junior detective, the photographer, and the police pathologist were in earnest conference beneath the whiskered head of a hippopotamus. The chief introduced them.

"Now we have to go upstairs. I'll let Constable Bondi lead the way. He was the first one here."

They followed the young constable to a broad landing, then through double doors into the principal bedroom. There were no trophies here, just plain whitewashed walls and black lacquered furniture. Black curtains covered the tall windows and framed an alcove containing the bed. Bondi stood at ease by the doorway, staring ahead, expressionless. Crizzo stood ramrod straight and silent, watching Soldanis. All three were trying not to breathe too deeply in the foul air.

What struck Soldanis first was the graffiti, spray-painted in black and red by inexpert hands: swastikas, mostly, but also the hammer and sickle, and an attempt to draw a medal with the words "FOR BRAVRY."

A white blanket covered the ominous heap on the bed.

"So let me guess: this is a murder scene." Soldanis turned to the constable. "Bondi, was that blanket there when you arrived?"

"No, sir. It was folded up on the chest. I didn't mean to disturb anything," said the young man, looking nervously at Crizzo, who gave him no comfort.

"But you thought it more decent to cover up the body," said

Soldanis. "You shouldn't have, but what's done is done. Now I think you'd better uncover it."

The constable hesitated, waiting for a signal from the chief. "Go ahead," he said gravely, and the constable drew the blanket aside, to reveal a head.

"All this fuss and mystery for another African immigrant?" thought Soldanis, seeing a black face. It was tragic, but nothing out of the ordinary lately. He went over to get a closer view. The man was bald, fleshy, the eyes closed. Soldanis recalled the bloated corpses of the drowned immigrants of the shipwreck on Malta and the mutilated bodies on Lampedusa; the air was impregnated by the same horror and stench. He reached over and drew the blanket down to chest level. Thank goodness, the corpse was dressed, in an open-necked white shirt and jacket. "Not your usual immigrant tailoring," he thought as he looked back at the face. Then something hit him.

Involuntarily he took a deep breath and felt his whole stomach churn, while a shudder ran down his spine. He spun around and faced Crizzo. "Christ, it's Pinto!" he let out.

The chief nodded once, then turned to Bondi. "Get the doctor."

Nothing was said as the constable's steps were heard hurrying down the stairs. Soldanis looked around the room again, at the crude graffiti and the calm tidiness of everything else. He had thought himself a seasoned professional, unshockable. But this was beyond imagination.

When the constable returned with the pathologist, Crizzo said, "Inspector Soldanis has identified the body. You can explain the details to him now."

The pathologist moved over to the corpse, on the opposite side of the bed from Soldanis. Crizzo came to stand at the foot, while Bondi resumed his station in the doorway. The three officers looked at one another. "You could start with the cause of death," said Soldanis.

The pathologist carefully raised the left lapel of the jacket.

"You see that there are three bullet holes, with powder burns, on the cavalier's clothes. Death occurred some three or four days ago. It is fortunate for us that the weather has been cool. We were reluctant to move the body before you'd studied the whole situation. Being obliged to establish the cause of death, I examined the three entrance wounds and found no corresponding exit wounds. That suggests a feeble weapon, probably a .22 caliber handgun, but fatal if the bullets are fired into the heart or ricochet in the body cavity."

"And the face?" asked Soldanis. Sebastian's face and bald crown were solid black.

"Spray paint," said the pathologist. He went on hastily, "Once we get the body to the mortuary, we'll perform an autopsy."

"Black spray paint," commented Soldanis in his mind, "talk about black humor." He was trying to appear collected and professional, but the enormity of the murder, and its consequences, were daunting.

"Cavalier Pinto owned this farmhouse." Crizzo had spoken at last, and as if to break the tension, he added a profusion of details: "It's only five kilometers from the Mġarr ferry, but as you've seen, it's quite isolated. He was only discovered around noon today. He left his principal residence in Mdina on Thursday morning and didn't return that night. His wife says that he likes to play the vanishing act from time to time but still calls her to let her know where he is. On Friday she rings around all his friends, his club in Valletta, and so on, and no one's seen hide nor hair of him. By Saturday she's worried silly and calls us. Well, we do the usual checks of ports and airports and conclude that he's not left Malta, at least not in the normal way. His two yachts are berthed for the winter. Then someone remembers that he uses this place for shooting parties in the migration season. That's how we found him. Anyway," he added, looking at the corpse, "no struggle took place here. It's as though someone came in and shot him while he was sleeping."

"On his back; in his clothes," mused Soldanis.

11

The whole Maltese nation was in shock, and thousands of them, dressed in their Sunday best, were thronging Mdina's Cathedral of Saint Peter and Saint Paul. They trod respectfully on the marble floor. One by one they paused, crossed themselves, and reverently touched the immense catafalque in the center of the nave. Ushers fussed around, leading some directly out of the church, others toward the altar, others yet to seats of lesser dignity. Monica was among the latter.

"It's like being the late king's mistress," she thought. "One day you're the most important person in his court, and the next day, a nobody."

She had been deeply shaken by the news. For all his eccentric opinions and insolent behavior, Sebastian had been a sincere companion on their shared quest, his enthusiasm matched by a knowledge that, in certain areas, surpassed her own. As she thought back over their two-year archaeological partnership, she could not withhold her tears.

If local attitudes to Sebastian had been mixed in the past, they now tended to reconciliation, even glorification. Some of the eulogies praised his bravery and the medal it had earned him; others, his promised benefaction to the immigrant hospital. It emerged for the first time that in his life he had donated a little over four hundred million dollars, mostly toward the building and upkeep of hospitals the world over. But his beloved Malta had always been the main beneficiary of his liberality. Then there was the fast-spreading news of an archaeological discovery that, in his home island, was by and large credited to him alone. But this funeral was not a coming together to celebrate a long life, with its well-anticipated sense of closure. His life had not been very long, and its end, sudden and brutal.

Monica dried her tears as the long Requiem Mass came to an end, and the coffin was lowered into the crypt. By now everyone in the Chapel of the Cross had turned their chairs around, and they had a fine view. To the sound of the "Dead March" from *Saul,* twenty-four mutes lowered the coffin on silver ropes, with military precision and infinite slowness. Then the mourners began to file out, one by one, and fifteen minutes later it was Monica's turn to step into the early November sunshine. She elbowed her way through the crowd on the short walk back to the palace, where Penelope had sent word that she was welcome to stay in her apartment as long as she needed to.

Soldanis, too, had attended the funeral, heavy with his own dark thoughts. For the first time in his career he felt overwhelmed, and not sure whether he was equal to the task. It was as if the island's unofficial but de facto king had been slain, and on Maltese soil. This was, indeed, inside his jurisdiction. Not that he and his colleagues had found much on the scene of the crime. Yes, there had been a clue: the graffiti spray-painted in black and red over the walls of the hunting lodge, and Sebastian's very face, grotesquely painted black. But that hadn't persuaded Soldanis; it seemed much too obvious. Nevertheless, to appease the authorities and the people, he and the inquiring magistrate had had all the Russians on Maltese soil arrested. Interrogating them was proving to be a circus, what with the interpreters flown in from Moscow who would rather be basking in the Mediterranean sun and the skinheads' insults, threats, screams, and sundry histrionics.

Once the last rites were over, Soldanis requested an interview with Lady Pinto. He began by stating the obvious, yet hoping that it would help: "Sorry to intrude at a time like this, but it's inevitable." He had been ushered by Dingli into Sebastian's study. Penelope was dressed in black, yet to his eyes her mourning outfit looked sexy. "That's going to be a distraction," he said to himself as he sat down across from her. Pale and worn out, her eyes reddened from crying, it was evident that she was deeply distressed. "How did you meet your husband?"

She didn't like the first question at all. "I'm sorry, what relevance does that have? Do you keep a gossip column on some tabloid? Inspector, I have suffered a great deal; I understand that you have to question me, so please get to the point."

Soldanis happened to be the only Maltese investigator still on duty who had solved, albeit early on in his career, not one but two murder cases. He remembered that back then he had talked his suspects silly, and eventually insignificant details had emerged between the lines. In the present case, it was emerging how little Penelope really knew about her husband's past, even his present life. Soldanis pressed on.

"What about his friends and business connections? Anyone who sticks out as being antagonistic?"

"I went to a lot of parties with him, in various European cities, but didn't take much notice. For the last two years, he mainly loved to talk about his research with professorial types—there was a serious side to my husband."

"And in the meantime, you enjoyed being admired by the more social types in attendance," Soldanis thought as he saw her bite her lip and fidget with her black pearl necklace. "Did your husband travel without you?"

"Every four months he went to Venezuela on his own, even before I married him."

Soldanis looked at her inquiringly.

"He had a quack doctor there," she elaborated, "who claims to cure impotence."

"I didn't know that," thought Soldanis, wondering whether or not he should be asking more about this particularly delicate subject.

"Yes," she volunteered, "Sebastian was not worried by his obesity but obsessed by his sexual impotence."

"I see," replied the inspector, looking for the right words to press more on the topic.

"It suited me fine, if that's what you were going to ask. I never really contemplated having sex with him."

A long, awkward pause followed. There was nothing artful about it on the inspector's side. What he had feared was happening: she was distracting him with her mere physical presence. All he could think was: "Well, what a mismatch!" Her lips, breasts, legs—intoxicating.

"Are we done, Inspector?"

"Not yet; your candor encourages me. Lady Pinto, do you have a lover?"

Her answer was an abrupt "No!" Then, as Soldanis raised an eyebrow, she added, "Not that it would have mattered. In our world, things that seem all-important to you are trivial."

"Yes," thought Soldanis, unable to repress a smile, "we plebeians are jealous savages, and we will stone our women to death if they cheat on us."

His strategy was working. She could not bear the silence and went on: "What many people don't know is that we accepted each other's weaknesses and loved each other. Yes, a sexless marriage can be full of love and happiness, but that may be beyond your comprehension."

"Of course," he thought, "I'm a plebeian swine."

"Oh, I'm also very wealthy," she added with the air of instructing a child, "though that wouldn't necessarily prevent me from wanting to become wealthier yet, would it?"

"If you say so."

"Money, sex, power: the only motives. It certainly must be appealing to simple minds. Would you like to know what else he did in Venezuela?"

"Change his blood?"

She nodded.

"I thought so. I had the pleasure of interviewing your husband some months ago, right in this study, and the background check on him produced a number of . . . curiosities."

"Now, Inspector, it has been a very trying time for me, and I don't expect it's going to improve any time soon." Soldanis shook his head in agreement. "I loved him," she added, "and I had no reason in the world to want him dead. I've reached the limit of my patience, and I shall ask you to leave me alone."

"Do you know if he had any enemies here?" he went on remorselessly.

Exasperated, she exploded, at the top of her lungs: "Obviously! Those hideous punks, the ones who were beating to death the man he saved. The graffiti on the walls of our hunting lodge, my husband's face painted black in mockery—aren't these a *hint,* inspector? Am *I* supposed to tell *you* how to conduct your investigation?"

Penelope took Soldanis by surprise: she covered her eyes with her hands and burst into tears. Sobbing helplessly, she got up and left the study.

He walked out himself and looked for Varranin, his assistant.

"See if you can get Mr. Pinto to come to the study."

Rafael looked dismally pale and emaciated. His appearance called to mind a bereaved son, but more than that—a junkie. Soldanis posed his first, astonishing question:

"Mr. Pinto, are you a drug addict?"

Rafael lifted his head and moved his long hair away from his face. He didn't reply.

"I know you've been a heroin addict both in Switzerland and in Italy," Soldanis continued, his cigarette hanging from his lips. "I also know you've been through rehab, but it's human to relapse, isn't it?"

Still Rafael didn't reply.

"Now, your father got you out of trouble a number of times. You need to tell me if you've been back at it, because that may give me a lead. Mind you: I'm not going to pass judgment. I'm an addict myself, you see," pointing at his cigarette stub, "except, for reasons that escape me, my drug is legal."

"I haven't bought or used any illicit substances since I got out of my second rehabilitation," he finally answered. "It's been a long time, Inspector."

"Are you sure about that?"

"Yes," he said and looked at the floor.

"Can you think of anyone who would want to kill your father?"

"I thought it was those skinheads."

"You did? Very well, and why would they want to kill him?"

"Why, he was awarded the Medal of Bravery for saving the immigrant; he ridiculed them, and then they were signaled out as Malta's new foes by the president himself and all the media. It didn't occur to any of us at the time, but in a sense, they were incited against him."

"Is that what you think?"

Rafael now looked the inspector in the eye. "Listen," he said, "I don't know what happened; *you* will find out. All I can say is that I didn't see it coming, and now I'll have to live with it."

This surprised Soldanis. Did the young man feel guilty for not having foreseen his father's violent death? "Look here, Mr. Pinto:

guilt feelings won't do you any good. What should the president say? And the media? It was they who put the blame on the Russian skinheads; are you saying they're guilty, too? Don't do this to yourself."

Soldanis dismissed him and moved on to his next interview.

"Dr. Bettlheim, what can you tell me about Cavalier Pinto? Anything that might have struck you as unusual about him lately?"

"No," she replied after thinking about it for a while, "on the contrary: he was at his happiest, with everything going his way."

"Now, here is another very fine specimen of a woman," Soldanis couldn't help thinking; "less distraught than Lady Pinto, of course, not stuck-up, and hopefully not as distracting." Out loud: "Were you aware of the fact that Cavalier Pinto was sexually impotent?"

Monica's discomfort was visible. "No! And . . ."

"Yes?"

"Well, I could never have guessed it; I mean, I was under the opposite impression, that he was . . . lecherous, he and his roving hands."

"I see." What if Lady Pinto had invented her late husband's impotence? But what for? As an extenuating circumstance to her having him killed? That seemed too crude—and too clumsy. Of course, there was another possibility: "And as far as you can tell, did Lady Pinto have a lover?"

It was the question she had feared.

"Even if you don't know it for a fact, did you suspect it, and if so, why?" Soldanis pressed on as she thought.

She could tell him what she had seen in the camera obscura. She had been reticent until then because it was none of her business, and because she didn't want to hurt Sebastian's feelings. But now he was dead, and the inspector was asking her. She could and should tell him. "I don't think so," she heard herself say, "Cavalier Pinto was a very outrageous man, but I think his wife loved him, and I don't believe she would cheat on him."

The interview continued for a few more minutes with some routine questions. The shock of Sebastian's death was now compounded, in Monica's mind, by the shock she had caused to herself by lying to the inspector. She knew that she didn't care enough about Penelope to lie for her; so she could only have done it for him, for Rafael. The conclusion was as unmistakable as it was astonishing to her. What had he ever done for her? Like a roguish child proud of his mischief, he had winked at her as he was having sex with his stepmother, for God's sake. Why was she covering up for such a man? This question would remain with her for a long time, she feared, as she took her leave from the inspector.

The interview with Aurelius Dingli brought something more tangible to light: Joe Dagenham's recent and unexpectedly brusque dismissal, and the rage it had occasioned both in Sebastian and in the factotum. With acute embarrassment, Dingli confessed that he had overheard their every word; he couldn't help it, they were shouting at each other.

"Do you think," Soldanis asked the old butler, "that your employer's murder might be Dagenham's doing? Think carefully before you reply."

Dingli's mind went blank for a moment. His master's death had not just shocked him: it had collapsed his entire system of reality. "I can't say, but there are a few things I don't like about Dagenham. First of all, I've been trying to reach him, on the cavalier's orders, to give him his severance pay, but he's left Malta, apparently, and left no forwarding address. I do hope you find him."

"You said you didn't like a few things. What else?"

"Oh, a few things I noticed during the twenty-five months he's worked for the cavalier. It's difficult to describe them one by one, but overall he seemed to me an unscrupulous man, or rather, a mercenary."

Further questions yielded less potentially interesting results, or so thought Soldanis. The interview over, the inspector asked Dingli to introduce him to all the staff. He would grill every single one.

12

During the following days, the palace was in chaos. Since Joe Dagenham's departure, the aged butler had taken over much of its day-to-day running. Courtly by nature, he did not have Joe's skill at repelling unwanted visitors, and soon a flock of lawyers, accountants, and bankers had convened there uninvited.

By the end of the week Monica could stand it no longer, and neither could Anima and Animus, who had been sorely neglected of late. She decided to take them out for a long walk. "Let's go to the Victoria Lines again," she said as she opened the car door for them.

Once out of the Fiat, the dogs were like prisoners released. They leaped around, snapping at the tall weeds, then putting their noses to the ground. They would follow some scent for a few yards, leap up again, bark, and set off on some other trail.

After half an hour of random pursuit, the hounds suddenly became more serious. They had picked up an interesting scent, it seemed, and announced it to Monica, standing and baying at her in chorus, running ahead, and looking back. She had no choice but to follow, as they led her—again—down the cliff path to Fommir Riħ Bay.

The sun was lower this time, but it was not cold. With dogs like these, a flashlight and a double leash in her anorak pocket, she had no fear of getting lost in the dark. The path, however, was harder to negotiate, for it had been raining and some of it was little more than a mudslide. At the worst point, with the beach already in sight, she slipped and had to sit down to break her descent.

The seas had been higher in the recent storms, and a large amount of flotsam had been washed up and strewn among the rocks. Animus and Anima, far from losing interest, were now going berserk. They had almost reached the end of the bay and were trying to draw her attention.

"What's the matter, you silly dogs?" she said as she neared them. They went on ahead, not on the pebbles now but on the large rocks at the foot of the cliff. Suddenly her eye caught a flash, reflecting the westering sun, and she paused. No, it was only another damned plastic bottle, caught in the rocks above the tide line. Something about it prodded her subconscious memory, though, and she went over, almost automatically, to look at it.

When she saw it, consciousness returned with a jolt. It was an oddly shaped half-liter plastic bottle. "Ty Nant," she said to herself aloud and picked it up. It was half full. The label had washed away, but the shape was unmistakable: it was Sebastian's favorite mineral water, its twisted form probably contributing to his whim. He imported it from its source in Wales, going to a degree of trouble and expense that no one else on Malta would dream of. And he religiously recycled his waste. Once on the *Thetis,* he had almost twisted the ear off a crewman whom he caught throwing a plastic bottle over the side.

At a time like the present, every anomaly deserved attention. She started to climb among the rocks, looking for further clues. The cliff was folded and pitted as it rounded the point of Il-Pellegrin, the footing treacherous with seaweed and rock pools. The sun sank into a belt of cloud, and the temperature seemed immediately to drop. The Gregale, a cold northeasterly wind, had begun to blow.

Monica turned back to reexamine the place in which she had

found the bottle. Could something have happened to him here?

Might he not have died on Gozo?

The thought sent shivers through her, and she felt the need for the comforting presence of the dogs. It was awhile since she had heard or seen them. "Anima! Animus!" she shouted, listened, and shouted again.

In the silence that followed, it struck her that the last thing she should be doing was to shout. She was now trembling, and it couldn't be the cold.

She headed for the cliff path, grabbing a stick of driftwood as she hurried along the shingle. It would have been a feeble weapon, but it served her well as she climbed the muddy path, her heart racing, looking back every now and again to see if the dogs were following her.

When she reached the cliff top, still alone and now panting, she discarded her walking stick and began to run. The sun must have set behind the clouds, for everything was in shades of gray, the shadows inky black. She didn't exceed a jogging pace, for fear of twisting an ankle on the uneven path. More than once she did slip and fall. What was she running away from? She didn't know, and that increased her anxiety.

When at last she reached the Fiat, she sat in the driving seat for a while with all the doors locked, trying to catch her breath.

She started the engine or, rather, she tried. The old, beat-up Fiat wasn't very reliable in the first place and had worsened since Dagenham had left. But this was no time to stall. She cranked it again and again as it grew darker and windier.

"Calm down," she said to herself, "calm down." She turned the key once more and the engine started.

Seconds later, it sputtered out, and the battery refused to make any further efforts. She got out of the car and noticed that she didn't slam the door in anger, but left it open. Why? she asked herself as she strained her eyes to scan her surroundings in the increasing darkness.

No one in sight.

Was the battery really dead? Or had the car been sabotaged? *Sabotaged?* The very question made her shudder: what was she thinking?

And if sabotaged, by whom?

In spite of herself, her probing mind was not relenting—or maybe it wasn't her mind asking those questions; they just arose of their own accord, logically.

She tried to brush them aside but found that she refrained from calling the dogs one last time, for the same reason she hadn't slammed the car's door.

As carefully as she could in the semidarkness, she started to jog again. Hopefully she'd soon reach the main road. Then she would have to hitchhike or stop a passing car outright. She could scarcely make out anything in front of her, but she was running now, breathlessly. Her luck wouldn't desert her, she said to herself as she ran; "Not now it won't."

Soldanis's investigation had continued at a frantic pace. The media, domestic and international, were having a field day with their speculations. No more pressure could have been heaped on the inspector, who had even been summoned by the prime minister for an "informal talk."

Shortly after that, Soldanis had met with Zecconi, the inquiring magistrate who was coordinating the investigation. Together, they had paid a visit to the attorney general and then the Court of Magistrates, which, in Malta, acts as a court of criminal inquiry.

Soldanis had hastily reviewed the code of penal law but wanted to know exactly where he stood, legally, and what he could and could not do. Since the prime minister had told him that he should treat Lady Penelope Pinto "with the highest regard," his intended plan of action needed a viable compromise.

As for other leads, Dagenham was nowhere to be found. Soldanis had consulted with Interpol on whether they could issue a warrant of arrest. Under normal circumstances, his being a mere suspect didn't entitle them to do so. But Cavalier Pinto was not just any victim. The warrant was issued, and now Interpol was looking for him. The angry young Russians continued to be questioned, now by a number of police officers with orders to pass the most suspicious ones on for interrogation by the inspector himself.

At the end of a grueling week, Soldanis had heard his share of alibis and bilingual insults; none of the skinheads he had questioned seemed any guiltier than the next one, or any more innocent. For that reason, he decided to keep them all under arrest.

Much against his wishes and convictions, Magistrate Zecconi found it necessary to sign the order for the Russians' continued detention. Then Soldanis hit him with another warm recommendation.

Meanwhile, the media besieged the old palace. Neither Rafael nor Penelope ventured out any longer, but rather spent a lot of time grieving together. That increased Monica's uneasiness, or was it jealousy? Jealousy? Why should she be jealous? And of whom? Somebody so morally corrupt that he wouldn't think twice about "flirting" with his stepmother only days after she had been widowed?

What was she thinking? Monica asked herself as she sipped tea in her apartment. These were assumptions, and anyway it was none of her business. Still, she felt there was something sick and twisted about Rafael and Penelope. Her patron had been shot dead; she had come to some alarming conclusions at the bay, when the dogs had disappeared; the Fiat had been recovered, but the dogs were still missing despite the promise of a reward to their finder; creepy Dagenham was on the loose. No, she wanted out of Malta.

In the salon below, Soldanis was speaking to the family's administrator. The old trusted employee was giving the inspector reluctant and convoluted answers, till the latter lost his patience and asked brusquely: "Where's the money now?"

"Let's say it's being transferred with bureaucratic efficiency to the rightful heirs, of which there are only two main ones: Lady Penelope and Mr. Pinto."

"No one else is to receive anything?"

"Well, I am in no position to reveal what Cavalier Pinto's last will and testament lays down and—"

"I have a copy of it in my office. I haven't had time to go through it all yet. Do tell me. Or do you intend to hamper the investigation?" The inspector did not have a copy of the document. He might be able to get it after a lot of red tape. This was a good shortcut, if it worked.

The administrator took a deep breath. "Very well, Inspector. All the contents of the Wunderkammer have already been conveyed to the Order of Malta, as the cavalier's legacy to it. He also left sums of money to some of his friends, collaborators, and staff. In addition to that, he set up a philanthropic foundation for the country of Malta."

"Is that all?"

"In a nutshell, yes."

The inspector now knew that he would have to find these "friends, collaborators, and staff" benefiting from Pinto's liberality. But first, he had someone else to meet in the palace.

When Soldanis was shown into the study, she was waiting for him. Standing proud and anguished like a wounded animal,

Penelope acknowledged his presence with the slightest gesture.

"What is it, Inspector?"

"Your prenuptial agreement, Lady Pinto."

"What of it?" She was furious already and not concealing it.

"I read it; it was published at the time of your wedding."

"Continue," she said, quivering.

Soldanis tried not to be distracted, though he had to admit to himself that he felt aroused. Smiling at his own unrepentant male nature, he took out a cigarette and lit it, then said, matter-of-factly: "It states that in case of separation or divorce, you could claim nothing of Pinto's fortune; but that, in case you should be widowed, you'd inherit half of it, the other half going to his son."

"Yes?"

"Lady Pinto," Soldanis was again in control of himself, "I have with me a warrant issued by Magistrate Zecconi. Please, read it yourself." He handed it over.

As she did, she turned pale. Before she could remonstrate, Soldanis added: "You are to surrender your passport today. Under normal circumstances it would have been house arrest, or even provisional detention, but in view—"

The loud thud of the door slamming behind her was her reply.

"Whatever," Soldanis thought. Shortly after that, he conferred with Rafael and then Monica. Both were free to leave the country if they wanted to but were to keep him informed of their whereabouts and be at his disposal at all times.

Leaving to his assistant the unenviable task of impounding Lady Pinto's passport, he left for the day.

Dinner in the palace was more spectral than ever. Penelope told Rafael and Monica that she was grounded in Malta indefinitely, "a necessary measure to prevent the escape of one of the suspects," the inspector's assistant had brutally explained to her. He had added that it was a symbolic gesture; she didn't really need a passport to travel within the European Union, but who wouldn't recognize her at the airport or at the harbor?

Then she hardly ate, much like her stepson. Monica tactfully emulated them, though she was hungry, at last. Above all, she felt relieved by not being held in Malta.

Penelope left immediately after dinner. Monica would have followed her, but Rafael planted himself between her and the door that led out of the dining room.

"What now?" she asked herself. He kissed her. On the lips. She didn't push him away; he didn't stop. Her eyes closed, she kissed him back. Then she snapped from it. "What on earth?" she should have asked, or something of the sort, but didn't say a word. They stared at each other for a long time, until she saw tears in his eyes. She was clueless: what was this? What was *he* all about?

"Come to Rome with me," he said at last. He took her hand into his and squeezed it. "Come and see the results. Say *yes,* say it."

They heard steps outside, perhaps Dingli. She wriggled away from him without giving him an answer. He didn't come after her.

Back in her apartment, Monica was more agitated than she had ever been in Malta. Rafael was an enigma, and Penelope, could she really be the killer? The authorities in Malta obviously suspected her enough to prevent her from leaving the country. And Rafael? What did *he* know? And why did she kiss him back, knowing what she knew about him?

She took a shower, hoping the water would soothe her. But it didn't. This was all bad timing, she thought as she dried herself. She should have been so pleased with herself, the triumph of her search, her recaptured fame. This was the time to boost it. Instead, she had been stuck in a besieged palace, her patron killed, his son acting weirdly and, yet, somehow, casting a spell over her. "I should have taken a cold shower," she thought amid the steam as she reached for her night cream in the cabinet. Her hand stopped short of opening it. The steam had made something bloom on the surface of the mirror—writing. Her heart stopped as she read: "YOU ARE NEXT."

13

"You did well to come to Rome," said Rafael, as they sat down in a quiet corner of the café. "I'd have preferred for you to leave with me, but now you are here, and I think you're safer out of Malta."

"Safer?" Monica wondered in her mind, trying to keep a straight face. "What does he know?" The writing on her bathroom mirror in Sebastian's palace flashed in her mind, and she shuddered. That had indeed made up her mind to leave Malta, which she had done within forty-eight hours—almost sleepless ones, as she frantically packed up her life. "Why do you say 'safer'?" she asked, confronting him bluntly at last. "What am I to fear?"

"I wish I knew. I don't know why my father was killed, nor do I know who did it. But if his murder has something to do with your search, then you'd better stay away from Malta. I have a bad feeling about the island in general."

"I figured you didn't like it one bit."

"It's not that; it's an . . . ominous feeling. You don't plan to go back now, do you?"

Monica was unwilling to be pinned down, all the more after hearing his misgivings. "Now I'm here, I might stay in Rome for a while. I don't speak the language, but I have contacts and a temporary room at the American Academy. Or I may go to the UK," she added, improvising. The less he knew about her plans—it had suddenly dawned on her—the better. "So, I guess it's time to say good-bye," she said, extending her hand tentatively.

Rafael hesitated. The results of the carbon 14 test, while highly gratifying to her, had been nothing short of earth-shattering for him. To share his knowledge with her would take a great deal of explaining on his side, and an even greater suspension of disbelief on hers. Should he try anyway? The worst that could happen would be to lose patience. No, there was more, much more, the same dilemma so many prophets had been faced with: making the esoteric exoteric, he thought, echoing unwittingly his late father's words. The fruits the pomegranate had so unexpectedly borne were forbidden to the profane—those outside the temple—and must be guarded against them. Yet it was ironic that an uninitiate, and a materialistic American of all people, would be the one fishing them out of oblivion.

His prolonged thoughts were causing an awkward silence. Finally, he looked her in the eye, took her hand and kissed it, and then kept his lips on it until she drew it brusquely away.

She was out of the café in a hurry, forcing herself not to look back.

The lecture had been advertised in the press, and a large crowd filled the *aula magna* of the American Academy's villa on the Janiculum Hill. Monica had quickly pulled together an illustrated talk on "Plants and Metallurgy in the Aurignacian: New Discoveries in Maltese Waters."

She spoke about the importance of barley for ancient civilizations and the ever-present threat of ergot, the parasitic fungus that could infest the grain and drive a whole village to madness. Precisely this substance had now been identified among the contents of the golden pomegranate, as had the spores of the notorious *Amanita muscaria* mushroom, the "fly agaric." "Both of these were known to cause insanity or even death," she explained. "To enshrine them millennia ago in this way must have been in order to ward off evil. An apotropaic act, as well as a sacralization of the most dangerous toxins as a propitiatory offering to the gods responsible for them."

Then she touched on the almost incredible metallurgic skill shown by such an artifact, yet recalled that of all metals, gold is the easiest to work. Finally, she presented the calibrated C-14 test results and showed photographs of the pomegranate, boldly claiming the same early date for it as shown by the tests: "Twenty thousand years Before Present, with a twelve-hundred-year margin of error. Smack in the middle of what we call 'prehistory!' This discovery challenges all our assumptions about when history began. Textbooks will have to be rewritten as archaeologists evaluate this and the further artifacts that will definitely come to light."

The first question put her on the spot: "Where is the golden pomegranate now? Is it accessible to other scholars?"

"I'm sorry to say that it isn't. It was in the private collection of the late Cavalier Pinto de Fonseca and has been sequestered in his residence in Mdina, Malta, pending the settlement of his estate. I'm afraid I can't tell you any more than that."

A murmur went around the room, filled to capacity by about four hundred people. Members of the press were also in attendance, both journalists and photographers. She was famous all over again, she was glad to see, reminding herself to smile often during the question period.

But it wasn't all smooth sailing. One professorial type made a long, sarcastic speech, virtually accusing Sebastian of forgery and Monica of being his dupe. There was both applause and hissing, and several people leaped to defend Monica's honor or Sebastian's. The question period degenerated into a shouting match between opposing camps, much to the delight of the photographers, until the chairman sternly called a halt and closed the proceedings.

Afterward there was a reception, and Monica was mobbed by her supporters. Among them, she noticed Rafael, looking somber and undecided as to whether he should approach her. Her heart started to race, and she hated to be so little in control of her emotions. The controversy and arguments had left her cold, being risks of the trade and good publicity anyway. But this, this was unexpected. As their eyes met for the first time since a week earlier in the café, a youngish Italian bounced up to her, full of enthusiasm and broken English.

He was heavyset, with piggy eyes, a bad haircut, and cigarette breath. After praising her lecture, he identified himself as Carlo Bono, a graduate student in archaeology. In order to spin out the conversation and avoid a confrontation with Rafael, Monica indulged him. "What are you working on?" she asked politely.

"I am on the project of the Column of Traiano. It will open to the public in two months."

"Do you mean one can go up inside Trajan's Column?"

"Exact. There was a longest restoration, now is finished."

"The more broken his English," she was thinking as he spoke, "the longer it'll take him to tell me what's on his mind; Rafael will leave, or I'll find some excuse to get out of here, accompanied by someone."

"Are you wanting to visit?" Carlo asked, interrupting her thoughts.

"What? Oh yes, of course, but in two months, you said? I will already have left Rome."

"No problem. I have access. I arrange you have a private visit, before it open to public. You must not lose it: the *vista panoramica* of the forum from the top is splendid." Some journalists were elbowing their way to her. "Look," Carlo said, raising his voice and writing on his ticket, "here it is the phone number of my office. It would be an honor to conduct you, at any time convenient."

By the time Monica freed herself from Carlo and then the journalists, for whom she put on the charm, Rafael had vanished. In spite of her own early resolve, she had somehow hoped that he would linger on for her; but now, without any further thought about him, she went to change for dinner with the academy's director and fellows. She asked them about the Trajan's Column restoration. Yes, they replied, it was due to open in the spring and was going to be the prime attraction of the coming year. But the lines would be interminable, as only ten people at a time would be allowed up it. If you have a chance at a private visit, they said, then grab it.

A few days later, Monica arrived at her rendezvous. In the Piazza Venezia the traffic circled day and night in a frantic merry-go-round, but a few yards away the little enclave around the column was almost deserted. Carlo was waiting for her, wearing a leather bomber jacket against the morning chill.

The column base was surrounded by scaffolding and shrouded in yellow plastic, but a flap was open, and the low door in the plinth was already ajar. Carlo lost no time in preceding her up the spiral staircase, but Monica paused at each of the tiny windows to study the stonework in the narrow beam of daylight. Carlo turned back with a questioning glance. "I wish I'd brought a flashlight. You don't have one, do you?" she asked.

"Excuse, no." He began to climb the stairs again.

"Perhaps I can come back another day," she continued vaguely.

At the top of the staircase, she paused in the light flooding through the open door; they were both panting from the exertion of the climb. "Tell me more about this restoration project. I can see new stones inserted here and there. Have you been involved in the actual construction, or just the planning?"

"Only the planning."

"How does such a project get approved?"

"Oh, is very *burocratico*." Carlo turned and stepped out onto the balcony that ran all around the monument, 130 feet above the ground. "Now here is the vista!"

The sun had recently risen, almost on the axis of the forum, and was peeping through the umbrella pines, casting long shadows from the scattered stones beneath. Monica scrutinized the stonework above her head. Leaning back with her hands on the iron railing, she shuffled around to the side facing the two baroque churches of Santo Nome di Maria and Santa Maria di Loreto. As she turned to glance at them, her keen eye was struck by the contrasts in their construction, as alike as two siblings but betraying in their details the two centuries that separated them. She was looking from one church to the other when she was struck from behind.

She jackknifed over the railing, breaking her loose grip but managing to grab it from lower down, on the outside. In the supernaturally slow motion of catastrophe, she heard herself let out a scream while she thought, "Now he'll grab my feet and flip me over unless . . . unless I can kick him first," and registered surprise when she was allowed the two seconds needed to straighten up and fling herself on the floor inside the railing.

A few feet away, Carlo was grappling with another man, and from the intensity of the fight, it was clearly a matter of life and death.

Still thinking in slow motion, before the shock came home to her, Monica marveled at how expertly this rather pathetic guide was dealing with her unknown assailant. The other man's back was to her, as Carlo grasped him by his hair and smashed his face against the railing.

The thought that it was disloyal not to give Carlo a hand flashed through her mind for an instant before an animal sense of

St. John the Baptist Parish Library
2920 New Hwy. 51
LaPlace, LA 70068

self-preservation swept it away. The very best thing was to leave them to it—but they were between her and the staircase door.

What if she went around the long way? Maybe she could sneak through it and escape.

She rose to her feet and started to creep around the central drum, clinging to the few handholds on the wall and looking both ways in case of another attack. She could hear the fight continuing with scuffles, heavy blows, and shouts of pain. Then a ghastly, musical shriek that was cut off as though with a guillotine.

Whatever had happened was none of her business now: she just had to get away.

Just a little farther around, the door came in sight, but so did the unknown man. His face was streaming with blood, so much blood, from a cut on his eyebrow or above it. His chest heaving, he stood leaning against the doorjamb.

"He's injured," thought Monica with a rush of adrenalin. "I *will* get past him." She paused, ready to rush at him, kick him in the stomach, and race down the stairs.

The man made no movement. Panting and hoarse, he said: "Come on, Monica, let's get out of here!" and disappeared through the door.

She gasped when she heard that voice and followed him downstairs, skipping steps in his wake.

When she reached the bottom, he was already astride a rumbling motorcycle. "Get on!" he screamed, without turning to look at her. She hesitated; he roared: "Now!"

The revving of the engine, the front wheel slightly off the ground, the acrid smell of burning oil, and they were off, speeding already. In passing, Monica caught a glimpse of a body, impaled on a piece of scaffolding just above the entrance.

She clutched his pounding chest as he slalomed in and out of the rush-hour traffic, running red lights, jumping on and off the sidewalks when the street was too congested even for a bike. Blood from his wound splattered on her face; she could feel it sting her skin as they rushed headlong.

Beyond Porta Maggiore, he suddenly screeched to a standstill beside a large tow truck that was removing parked cars. He got off the bike and hailed the workmen, pulling out a wallet and holding out a sheaf of Euro bills. A rapid exchange in Italian followed; then he turned to Monica and said "Run! This way!" He led her back through the Roman gateway, then hailed a taxi and told the driver an address.

As they sat back, exhausted in the back seat, Monica took off her neck scarf and handed it to him. "Here, Rafael, wipe your face with this."

14

"You're going to explain everything to me or I'm out of here!" Monica was shouting to Rafael. They had climbed the stairs to his apartment almost flying. She was short of breath and shuddering as she stood in the middle of his library, both their faces still peppered with his blood.

"What do you want to know first?"

Something mundane came to her mind: "Where the hell have you learned to ride a bike like that?" That certainly didn't fit her image of him.

"When I was younger, I used to like to kick around in the dirt, motocross and that kind of stuff."

"Motocross? You?"

He smiled.

"Very well. That doesn't even begin to answer my questions; you've got a lot of explaining to do, my dear."

He hesitated, but her piercing stare was enough to persuade him to say something.

"Where shall I begin?" he finally replied. "Oh, I have a rather rare blood type: Tc(a-). In fact, it's so rare, there are no donors. So when you wipe it off your face, think about it: you're wiping away a rarity and—"

Her slap landed violently on his cheek and echoed in the large room. Rafael started bleeding again from his eyebrow. "I'm sorry,

I'm so sorry!" she ejaculated and then hugged him tightly. "I'm sorry," she repeated, whispering in his ear. She then took her neck scarf from his hand and pressed it against his forehead. They sat on the sofa.

"Listen," Rafael said at last, "I deliberately set up the Penelope incident. I would make love to my stepmother right before your eyes, and did."

She shuddered and let go of him. Rafael went on calmly, pressing the scarf against his cut. "Penelope had been after me. Every time she came to Rome, she would drop in, recently unannounced. She was flirtatious, but I didn't encourage her in any way. Human bondage leaves me on the run, so I assumed she'd give that nonsense up. I must have piqued her vanity when she came to the conclusion that I was not gay, after all. So she stepped up her efforts to seduce me. She could not believe a capable man her age could resist her. I must have been the exception and represented a challenge to her vanity. I hate to say this about her, mind you. I don't think she's a bad person. I'm not passing judgment, heaven forbid! It's one thing I hate to do. I also hated doing what I eventually did with Penelope, but I had to. It was the first and last time; you must believe me, Monica."

She stared at him incredulously.

"I do think," he added, "that on the whole Penelope made Father happy. It was just a weakness of hers, and who doesn't have weaknesses? But the point is, she was willing. I never expected that I should—how shall I put it?—take her up on her invitation. I swear to this, you must believe me. But then I heard Father's new plans—he announced them at the dinner party, remember?—and realized that I now had to save him and you."

"Save? Why save? Save from whom?"

"The same people who killed him and just tried to kill you, I guess. I don't know for sure, but it must be the same people.

We do know they wanted you dead and almost managed it."

She swallowed the indisputable reality, at least about the attempt on her own life. Her heart was still racing.

"Oh, I also flirted at the dinner party with Giorgio, the fashion designer. And I was pretty sure that Father would mention to you my heroin addiction, didn't he?"

She nodded.

"So there you had it," he continued: "the heroin-addicted bisexual profligate who, maybe, first has sex with Giorgio Stilnovo, and then, certainly, with his stepmother, while his father—her husband—was just feet away.

"Father had revealed weird things about himself and had treated you horribly ever since you two found the forbidden fruit; and then, you got to peep at the soirée's juicy finale. I was hoping that by thoroughly disgusting you, you'd be fed up with aristocrats once and for all and leave Malta."

Monica did not break the heavy silence.

"I had talked to you," Rafael went on; "I knew you were hesitant about getting the results about the 'garden dirt' found inside the golden pomegranate; I sensed you'd been disappointed by the ones from the University of Malta. So I also hoped you were looking for a pretext to leave. Maybe you were, but you didn't. And I failed to save my father. It happened too soon. I hadn't even warned him yet. That's why . . ." he paused for a while and then added, "that's why I wrote, 'You are next.'"

"*You* wrote it?" Monica shouted. She jumped to her feet and walked over to the window, overwhelmed by emotions and mixed feelings. "But why?" she asked herself. As a warning, it was obvious, not a threat, but—what did he know? And what if it was all an elaborate trap, involving the death of a man? But why, why? Why all this trouble to cage *her*? She didn't know what to think anymore, and came close to dashing out of the library, out of the apartment, back into Rome's chaotic streets.

Rafael really wasn't familiar with human bondage, as he had put it. Yes, at the dinner party he had managed to shock and disgust her, yet what had bothered her the most that night, or rather stung her, was jealousy—that Rafael would find perhaps a man, and certainly Penelope, more attractive than herself. Never in her life had she experienced anything like this, but then, never before had she been competing with a woman like Penelope. Yet when she and Rafael had held hands, that repudiated female sixth sense had made her sense that he felt otherwise, that it was she that he felt something for, and no one else. And then she had lied to Inspector Soldanis to protect him. Had that been wise? She didn't dare ask that one question, but there were others.

"What did you have to warn your father of?" she said and added: "But why? Why kill him?" The turmoil inside her was not subsiding. All she knew was that Rafael had saved her from certain death. Everything else might well be a fabrication. She didn't know what to think, whom to trust.

"Why? I don't know for sure; in fact, I don't know at all."

"Who wanted to kill me? And why?" She screamed these questions.

"I don't know that either. But obviously the threat has followed you to Rome. Forgive me. This isn't a safe place for you either. I should have known better. But what could 'they' know that I don't?"

"The dogs," she thought but didn't say. "The dogs that went missing. 'They' killed them and made them disappear. But why?" What was she thinking? And who were "they"? Suddenly a terrifying question welled up, unbidden: What if this was an incredibly elaborate scheme to make her believe that the same people who had killed Sebastian were now out to get her? Why would he do this? The inheritance? That would go to him directly, half of it anyway. Then it dawned on her: Penelope and Rafael had had Sebastian murdered and put the blame on the skinheads; yet now Rafael was going out of his way to persuade her that a mysterious party had killed his father and now was trying to kill her. Her blood curdled: he had just killed a man to make their scheme look more credible. Why?

But of course—to persuade her! Once properly indoctrinated, she would testify, tell the investigators what had happened. They'd link this to Sebastian's death, and the investigation would eventually come to a standstill, incapable of ever finding the murderer.

So much for logic, conjectures, and unspoken fears. Another, more intuitive side of her felt only warmth for this frail man who had just lost his father and had become, by self-appointment, her protector and, just now, her savior.

As she kept quiet, Rafael resumed. "I'm groping in the dark. So far, I have a few very vague suspicions and an ominous feeling about Malta. Maybe there's something *you* should tell me about what's going on? You must know something I don't. Enough for them to want you dead."

Monica thought about the incidents at the bay in Malta. The dogs, the bottle. Still, she wouldn't tell him. "He's saved me once," she thought, now at least leaning toward this straightforward interpretation, "but he's such a lunatic; true, he got me out of Malta, but straight into an assassination attempt." Instead of replying, Monica felt uncertainty again, puzzlement, and primeval fear. Then she asked the strangest of questions: "What just happened, does that make me an accomplice to a murder?"

"What? No! For heaven's sake, what sort of a thought is that?"

She pressed on: "Are you going to tell the police what happened at the column?"

"What for? The guide was an impostor, out to kill you. He's dead now, impaled: let him burn in hell; *that* he's earned."

She thought back on how it had been set up. She had called the number Bono had given her and had never quite managed to speak to anybody in that office. She got a couple of recorded messages, and then Bono called her back and set up the appointment with her.

"Let me call the office again, just out of curiosity," she said, taking out her cell phone.

"No! Don't leave a trace; forget that cell phone; never use it again. Give it to me; you may use it without thinking."

Suspicion crept up inside her, again. What he said made sense—if he really was on her side. If not, he was thwarting her possibilities of escape. And what he said next curdled her blood, once more: "You're not leaving here, Monica; you're not going back to the academy. I'm abducting you."

"What?"

"For your own safety. You're a dead woman now. Please make it a little difficult for these people!"

She snatched the cell from his hands, got up, and dashed to the door. It'd be a few seconds, and she'd be out and away. Should he try to stop her, she would fight, jump from the window if needed and run for her life

Rafael didn't follow her.

That took her by surprise.

She looked back at him for what might be the last time.

He was on his knees, blood flowing anew from his cut, streaming down the right side of his face.

She dithered now, by the door. Her resolve waned, then waxed, then waned, then waxed again, in a flash. "Is that how you 'abduct' me?" she asked, "by begging me on your knees not to leave?" Rafael was either the most cunning of impostors or the sweetest of men. He was still on his knees, silent, his left eye imploring her not to leave, his right one probably, too, but she couldn't tell; it was covered in blood. "Rafael," she said in the most sensible tone she could muster, "You must understand—"

She was cut short by the ringing of the doorbell. "Eusebio," Rafael quietly called out as he sprang back on his feet. "Are you expecting any deliveries?"

"Yes," he replied sotto voce and out of sight, "but that wasn't the bell from the tradesmen's entrance."

Rafael didn't want to jump to conclusions but at the same time wouldn't rule anything out. He looked this way and that, then at Monica, frozen by the doorsill. He smiled at her, reassuringly.

Another ringing.

Rafael punched his fist into his open hand and ran out into the hallway, just in time to forestall Eusebio, who was on his way to open the front door.

"Wait, Eusebio," said Rafael in an urgent undertone. "I've left town, and you don't know when I'm due back. I'll be in the lab. Tell me when they've gone."

He came back into the room, grabbed Monica by the arm, and dragged her through the hallway and into a storage room beneath the stairs. She didn't resist him.

In the flurry of opening and closing doors that followed, she lost her orientation. They ran through a labyrinth of dark, disused closets, one opening into another, going up a few stairs and down again.

They emerged into a largish room, paneled, as far as she could tell in the semidarkness, with mythological scenes. With one hand

Rafael pushed on a detail in the carving, while with the other, he pulled on another one. A hidden door swiveled silently on its hinges. They crossed its threshold, and it closed behind them. Rafael bolted it and switched on a low light.

Panting, he drew her to a sofa, then collapsed beside her and lolled back with his eyes closed.

"Well," she thought, "this is the point of no return. If he and Eusebio are psychos out to torture and kill me, I've done myself in."

15

Monica turned her head and looked at Rafael. He was resting his head on the top of the sofa, his closed eyes turned toward the ceiling, his long hair caked with his very rare blood. He couldn't be playing cat and mouse with her, could he? An insanely elaborate variant of the game, involving an impaled man just to make it more believable?

Why was she still doubting him when she had just made her choice and taken her chance? Was it because she had never trusted anyone in her life? Wasn't this the lesson her parents had imparted to her? Having lost so many relatives and friends to the Holocaust, they knew better. Trusting strangers can be self-destructive.

After perhaps five minutes, Rafael spoke, without opening his eyes. "Eusebio ought to be here by now."

There was another long silence. Monica was trying to assemble the pieces of recent events in her mind. "I don't understand," she said out loud.

The sofa was nothing but a single bed, heaped with shabby cushions. Monica sat forward with her chin on her hands, her elbows on her knees. She continued, trying to keep a rational tone: "For reasons unknown, but presumably connected to Sebastian's murder, someone sets out to kill me." What was she doing? Reasoning it all out with him? What if *he* was. . . . What if—

"Thanks for trusting me," he said. "It was about time." Just what she needed to hear.

She swallowed and pressed on, throwing caution to the wind: "You've been lurking around the American Academy, following me wherever I go in Rome."

"No, I haven't been 'lurking around,' thank you. I've been watching you ever since you came to Rome. What else could I do? You didn't want to see me anymore, remember?"

Monica ignored the question and continued, her voice rising: "So you arrive at Trajan's Column in the nick of time to save my life, and this so-called postgraduate gets himself killed instead." Her tone changed as she turned to him, sincerity breaking through: "Don't think I'm ungrateful for that; I'm not. I'm just trying to make sense of it all. After your fight, we vanished from the scene on your bike, you made it vanish, and we came here. So who are we hiding from now?"

"There must have been someone else operating with your guide," said Rafael wearily. He opened his eyes and met hers. "I did see a man sitting on a bench, facing the forum, smoking a cigarette, but he didn't see me sneak inside the column. I hope not, anyway. He might have been the lookout man, waiting for you to fall, as you were supposed to do, and then letting his accomplice know that the way was clear to escape unnoticed."

"Why didn't you warn me beforehand?"

"You wouldn't have believed me. On the contrary, you might have informed the police, telling them I was stalking you."

He did not emphasize her silence with a long pause, but rather went on. "After your death, there'd be an investigation, but they'd never track down the guide. Nobody knew you were with him, see? They'd assume it was suicide but officially declare it an unfortunate accident. And that'd be that."

"Point taken. But still, how do they trace you to your apartment, here? Do we even know it's 'them?'"

Rafael didn't answer. He rose, crossed the room, and unbolted the door. Then he turned back to Monica. "I'm very worried. Eusebio should be here by now. And by the way, that's as good a proof that it's 'them.' If he doesn't come in another five minutes, I'm going back to see what's going on. But you must bolt this door behind me and not open it unless you hear Eusebio's voice, or mine."

"Great," said Monica. "Instead of falling off a column, I get to rot away in a dungeon."

"Five minutes," said Rafael, discouraging any further reply, and busied himself with something on the other side of the room.

Now Monica began to take stock of her surroundings. It was a large, square room, once quite grand, as she could see coats of arms, white crosses on red, decorating the heavy beams, and a painted frieze of grotesques. But beneath that, what a contrast!

The only furniture was a few chairs and stools and the daybed on which she was sitting. Someone had once papered the walls with a sprawling pattern of brown roses; someone else had started to strip the paper, then given up. Running around two of the walls were plain kitchen cabinets. The wall in between had no fewer than three cooking stoves of various types and an iron stove whose pipe exited through a hole in one of the shuttered windows. A half-empty coal bin stood next to it. The fourth wall held a broad fireplace, surmounted with a carved coat of arms: the bees of the papal Barberini family. Kitchen stuff was everywhere, piled on the counters and in the sinks, heaped in the corners, mixed up with books and papers. Or was it kitchen stuff? Such things played little part in Monica's lifestyle, but even she could tell that this "stuff" was abnormal. She had seen those huge bottles before, in chemistry labs—carboys she thought they were called. But what of the apparatus sitting on a stove that had first registered as an espresso machine? It was more like something in a moonshiner's distillery, with its spiral copper tubing and coupled glass retorts. And all those other glass vessels shaped like footballs, squids, crookneck squashes? As her eyes roved around, a cockroach ran across the floor and vanished under the counter.

Rafael had turned on two of the electric ovens, leaving the doors open, and a little warmth was spreading through the damp chilly air. Monica got up and went over to sit on a stool closer to the source of heat. "What the hell *is* this place?" she asked.

Rafael seemed distracted, taking refuge in banalities. "I'm sorry it's such a mess. I've let things deteriorate. No one ever comes in here normally—no one knows it exists, apart from Eusebio—and it's the last place I'd want to take you. All I can say is that it's safe."

"Safe?"

"Yes. The windows open onto a disused garden, only they don't open any more. That door over there leads to a subterranean vault which in turn leads . . . somewhere else."

Monica was full of questions, but the door by which they entered swiveled on itself, cutting her short.

Eusebio stepped inside the room, a kitchen towel tied around his head. "Excuse me, Sir," he said, breathing heavily, "I must sit down."

Rafael hurried over to him: "Eusebio! What happened?" He helped him to a chair.

"They knocked me out." Eusebio pointed to the towel. "Don't worry: it's just a bruise and a bit of blood. I'll be all right. You know how headstrong I am. . . ." He attempted a smile.

"Are you absolutely sure they've gone?"

"When I came to, it was silent. I checked all the rooms. The doors were all open, but they haven't stolen a thing, as far as I could see. I'm afraid they were looking for you."

"I'm certain of it," said Rafael. "Don't do anything more now. You must take care of yourself, after a shock like that. Are you sure your skull's still in one piece?"

"Yes, yes, thank you. I feel in control of my faculties." Eusebio was trying to be gallant, but it was plain to see that he was shaken and getting too old for such adventures.

"Bravo, Eusebio, my old friend! You're not that ancient!" Rafael spoke with a warmth Monica didn't know he could express. He then turned to her: "We must get out of here. That lookout man must have seen us leave on the bike and figured out who I was. So much for getting rid of it. I may be reclusive, but I'm not hard to find."

"In that case it'd be best to go back to the main apartment, and—"

"Out of the question!" Rafael snapped. "For all we know, this place may be watched. No, we mustn't go back there at all. Nothing must stir in it. Let them think we've never come back. Obviously, it wasn't watched before we did, or else they'd have insisted. Eusebio," he asked, changing tone, "is there something we can eat right in here?"

Monica looked at him inquiringly.

"We'd better eat something now that we can. I don't know how long it'll be before we can eat again, and we need energy." This was directed to Monica, but Eusebio responded.

"There may be something to eat in the small fridge," said Eusebio.

It held a few hearty sandwiches that Eusebio had prepared at Lady Pinto's behest, who with her every visit urged him to feed his master more food.

Rafael picked one up and turned it over in his hands. "My, Eusebio, this is peasant's fare! Heaven bless you," he exclaimed and took the first bite.

Eusebio's head was aching too much for him to take notice of two almost prodigious things: his master with an appetite and emoting away. "If you don't mind, I'll go and rest now," he said.

"Of course, do that," replied Rafael and then whispered something in his ear.

Monica had deferred breakfast, intending to enjoy it in a café after seeing Trajan's Column, and now, despite her trepidation, she was more than ready. A moldy sandwich was no threat; she'd had far riskier food in the jungles of Central and South America. With a knife she scraped the mildew off both sides and then took her first bite.

As they ate, she asked Rafael again what the "kitchen" was all about.

"Of course, it's not a kitchen," he said at last, adding in a different tone: "though they say that what goes on in there is women's work and child's play."

Monica looked puzzled. He didn't elaborate. "Will you tell me what the hell this is?"

"Have you noticed there are no saucepans, dishes, a proper refrigerator, even running water? I'm glad to say that nothing ever gets eaten in there—we're breaking a cardinal rule!"

"So why all those ovens?"

Strange how his instincts still told him to refrain from answering. Years of closely guarded secrecy were hard to discard, above all with an uninitiate. He must get over that if he wanted to gain her trust.

"It's for alchemy," he heard himself say. Now the dam was broached.

"What? Come on, you've gotta be kidding. Do you mean, what?—that you turn lead into gold?"

"I can't explain the whole thing now, but that's the reason for the various stoves—keeping different temperatures for long periods, even months on end—and all the distilling apparatus."

"These weird bottles?"

"Cucurbits and alembics, made in Zurich. Although the place looks a mess, we have first-rate glassware."

"'We' meaning you and Eusebio?"

"Yes. That's a long story, too, but briefly, although he works as my 'gentleman's gentleman' as the English call it, he was once my master in alchemy."

"Why does he work as a servant, then?"

"Yet another long story. Monica dear, you're the first person I've ever shared this with, and even I don't know why." Well, he did: her trust was at stake.

"You know, Rafael, this 'long story' mantra just won't do. You've got a hell of a lot of explaining to do, and you'd better start now."

"All right, all right. It's a delicate subject, that's all. And please, never tell anyone. The thing is, some years ago Eusebio dabbled in the occult. He'd been doing that forever, but unfortunately he finally made a few big mistakes."

"What sort of mistakes?"

"I myself don't know that, and I wouldn't dare ask. But they were such big mistakes, tragic mistakes, I should say, that he found it difficult to live with himself. He was on the verge of committing suicide, but my father, an old friend of his, came up with a proposal. To make amends for his errors, he should take care of me, just out of my second rehab. I don't know if this has redeemed him, but I do know that thanks to him I've been clean ever since. He insists on being my servant, even if he comes from an older and nobler family than ours. This is the plain truth."

Rafael's appetite had vanished as soon as he began to answer her questions. She, for her part, saw him transform from the vibrant man who'd just saved her life and whisked her to safety, back to the spectral déjà vu of his former self.

"Eat up," she said, "finish your sandwich!" It sounded comical, she knew, but she had much preferred the new Rafael and would do anything to prevent him from relapsing into the old one, even forgo her questions.

"What?" he wondered, as if coming back from another dimension.

"Your sandwich, Rafael," she repeated, "you should fin—"

"I feel I have to initiate you, Monica. There's no point in holding back anymore, and I really have no choice. Even though right now you think the whole thing is medieval lunacy."

"Well, I wouldn't go that far . . ."

"No? But you're a rational creature, aren't you? It's one of your charms." He smiled.

"Thank you?" said Monica, then Rafael cut her short.

"Are you done eating? Drink some water, use the bathroom, then we've got to leave; the sooner the better. Now, where's that flashlight?"

Somewhere in the labyrinth of windowless closets leading to the laboratory, Rafael lifted the lid of a wide bench, giving access to a short ladder. "We've come down a former toilet," he said as they reached the small chamber at the bottom.

"We're not going into the cloacae, are we?" said Monica.

"It's centuries since they've been used for sewage." He shone the flashlight on a massive iron grille and unbolted it, saying: "I've only been along here a few times. I hate going into caves, or anything underground; I had an accident spelunking in Malta when I was a kid. Still, we need to leave, and we can't use the front door, can we?"

The vaulted chambers of the cloaca were immense, the tunnels wide enough for a car. The bricks and blocks of the floor were uneven but dry, and the smell, to Monica's relief, nothing worse than damp earth. Another short staircase brought them to an overgrown courtyard, which was truly disgusting. It seemed to be a much-used toilet for the homeless, both people and cats. Rafael elbowed the bushes aside, Monica stepping gingerly between the messes. He ducked into a narrow passage, which had brought them out into the world of rushing traffic beside the Tiber. Before hailing a taxi, Rafael wrapped Monica's neck scarf tightly around his forehead, like a bandanna. That should cover his cut and prevent it from bleeding.

Then followed a very long taxi drive, three hours or more, with Rafael silent and absorbed in thought, clenching her hand. She tried to talk, to ask one of the many questions crowding her mind, but he gestured her to be quiet, looking at the driver.

Halfway through, Rafael asked him to stop, got out, and made a phone call from a booth in the middle of nowhere, leaving her to the driver's lascivious leer.

Finally, they came to a long dirt road in the hills, drenched in rain and peppered with puddles, which culminated in what looked like a medieval fortified settlement. As they approached, Monica could see the proud mass of the castle, standing on high ground and encircled by towers, battlements, and bastions. Once their arrival might have been hindered by drawbridges and portcullises. Now, there was only a man standing by the entrance gate, water gushing from his black hat all over his long overcoat. Rafael rolled down the window and exchanged a few words. When the man handed over a set of keys, Monica noticed that two of his fingers were missing, the middle and ring fingers.

They passed beneath the turret standing over the gate and drove along an inner street flanked by low stone houses. Every window was shuttered: the man in the overcoat might have been the sole survivor of some plague. The street widened before a Romanesque church, then climbed on uneven cobbles to the castle itself.

Rafael paid the taxi driver and took Monica by the hand. The square tower, whose leaning outline she had noticed from far away, loomed over a dank courtyard with Gothic arcades. Crossing this and entering an open vestibule, Rafael applied the key, then his shoulder, to an ironbound door and led her up a broad circular staircase. They passed the open doors of a weapons room and a bleak banquet hall, then entered a vaulted dormitory.

"Have you been here before?" she had asked, perched on the carved "matrimonial" bed that was almost the only furniture.

"Yes." That was all he had said to her since Rome. Raindrops, mixed with blood, coursed down his cheek.

Monica's practical side came to the fore. "We can't let it bleed forever, can we?"

Had she sewn before? his eyes seemed to ask.

Not exactly skin, but could it be so different from cloth?

16

By rummaging through drawers, Monica had come across a give-away from a hotel in Umbria: a sewing kit. It wasn't so much Rafael's cut on the eyebrow that worried her, although it had bled on and off since the morning. What she needed was the relief of activity. So far, she had narrowly escaped an assassination attempt, only to be rescued and whisked away to safety—hopefully; the total passivity of her last hours was getting to her.

Grappa doubled as a disinfectant. At least daubing his cut got an "ouch" out of Rafael, and the sight of the needle restored the gift of speech. "I'm not much of a stoic," he said. "Sorry if I disappoint you."

"I won't tell anyone," she replied as she pierced his skin for the first time. He grimaced but held himself still and didn't let out a sound.

"So far, so good," she thought. With a steady hand, she quickly sewed up his cut: five stitches in all. Then something came over her that she could not explain: an urge to lean forward, breathe in his breath and lick his wound, ever so lightly.

"Is this part of the procedure?" he wondered aloud.

"Not really; I just wanted to taste that very rare blood of yours."

"I see. And how is it?"

"Pretty good," she answered, smiling and licking her own lips.

"Monica," he said, looking her in the eye, "I think there's some blood left, here." He touched his own upper lip.

"Let me see," she said, and went scouting with her tongue.

And here she was, in the middle of a damp, cold room in a castle somewhere in Tuscany, in the arms of a man who, until shortly before, she had feared might be out to use her to his advantage in some sort of elaborate and devious scheme.

They made love with abandon and didn't stop until exhaustion set in. Rafael fell asleep immediately after. It took her longer to do as much, cuddled up against him, the only source of warmth in the unheated room. The December rain pelted on the tiled roof, and she could see water oozing from the walls in growing patches. She blew out the candle, ready to withstand the attack of her intellect.

Reason had always warned her to be wary of him, but her heart, ever since she first saw him in the palace's library, had told her otherwise. She felt him now sleeping beside her, seemingly peaceful and breathing regularly. Rather than Mantegna's *Dead Christ*, Botticelli's *Venus and Mars* came to mind: the goddess sitting up and calmly smiling; her lover, with his wavy black hair, sprawled in postcoital slumber, while a clutch of putti, the fruit of their union, played with his lance and helmet.

Piero had been kind in getting them some food, but he might have spared them his supervision: he stood like a sentinel, a grin on his face, dribbling at the mouth and picking his nose with the fingers he had left.

Unlike Monica, Rafael didn't seem to care. He had devoured the soup and cold cuts that Piero had provided and helped himself to wine. With relief, she could see no infection on his cut. Suddenly, he got up and spoke to Piero. She had no idea what he was saying. The custodian's house was small and damp, made of stone, as everything else pertaining to the castle. He seemed to live alone in it. Whatever Rafael had said to him, Piero seemed to consent, albeit begrudgingly.

Soon they were back in their quarters, laden with food and drink and the day's local newspaper. Rafael fussed over the fireplace and soon produced a roaring fire. "It'll be a while before it warms up the room," which was huge, "but it's something."

Monica replied with a pleasantry and a subtle hint at other ways of warming up. But he paid no attention as he searched anxiously through *La Nazione*. The first page was mostly about the Rome Conference, by now well under way, and the naval blockade. The extreme temporary measure advocated by Commissioner Altieri had come into force: all members of the European Union had dispatched their fleets south of Malta, effectively blocking access to southern Europe. Moreover, a law had been quickly passed in most southern European countries that punished scafisti with life imprisonment.

Was this the evil the little girl, Honoria, had felt during that séance, Rafael wondered to himself? The new form of slavery taking place in the twenty-first century, now infecting Malta, too, because of its admission into the European Union? Then perhaps she had had a point, though it didn't take a seer to see what was evident. Europe, at any rate, was finally responding.

A loud knocking on the door interrupted his thoughts.

Monica looked at him, then at the door. Once more she was assailed by doubts. She couldn't believe it, yet there she was, wondering, wrestling with her mistrust, and feeling scared. Who could it be? Why was Rafael so calm? Was he expecting someone? Why hadn't she demanded an explanation? What of all the questions she hadn't asked him?

He walked to the door and opened it before she could say a word.

It was Piero, panting, delivering firewood and a copy of *Il Messaggero*, Rome's main newspaper.

"Well, here it is," he said, after having scanned the article he had feared. "Foul Play at Trajan's Column."

Monica came over and looked at the headlines and photographs in the fading daylight. "Oh my God; am I mentioned in it?"

"No, no mention of you—yet. But nobody's buying the suicide idea. The man who pushed you had a long criminal record."

"That idiot?" She let out a short laugh. "Who would have thought?"

"Yeah, well, you know how it is, appearances, and so on."

"Right," she said, a shudder of unease traveling through her spine. She suppressed it, and the nagging doubts it had brought about. It was getting dark. The fire crackled, steadily burning the dry holm oak. They sat by it, wrapped in blankets, basking in its warmth. "What shall we do now?" she asked at length.

Rafael got up and looked directly at her. "Do you remember what I said about initiating you?"

"Yes?"

"We can't stand on ceremony. I hate to rush it, but here it is. You've had your hand on the doorknob, and now you're going to have to go through that door."

"What doorknob?"

"The one shaped like a golden pomegranate. One twist and the door opened, but you didn't know what you'd found."

"I thought what I found was pretty amazing. So did your friend at the Sapienza. And the audience at the Academy."

"They had no notion of it. They weren't initiated, you see." He turned toward the fire and fussed with the irons, rearranging the logs. "Oh, God, your profession is such an enemy of truth."

"Hold on, Rafael!"

"No offense to you; it's not your fault. But false notions get put about, and before you know it everyone's repeating them, then they get into the textbooks and become like sacred scripture. Nothing's harder to budge than an academically consecrated error."

"I'll agree with that. My whole career has been about budging them."

"Well, there's one more you need to put your shoulder to."

"And that is?"

"In one word: ergot."

"But I explained that already. Surely you know about the mass frenzies of the Middle Ages, caused by eating rye infested by ergot."

"Surely you know about the kykeon," Rafael countered, coming back to the sofa. "How much do you know about the Eleusinian Mysteries?"

"About what any educated person knows, which isn't much, since no initiate ever broke the vow of silence."

Rafael spelled it out. "The kykeon was the sacred drink taken before the ceremony. It contained barley, and I'm certain it was ergot-infested barley. That was what gave the initiates their unforgettable experience."

"Come off it, Rafael, the stuff is deadly. They'd have been raving mad and dropping dead," said Monica with a smile, trying to keep the conversation normal.

"You don't understand." Rafael seemed to be speaking to the fire once again. "They had some method of turning the toxic alkaloids into ergine, one of the lysergic acids. It could have been done using wood ash, or even the ashes from burnt sacrifices. I can't get into the chemistry now—by the way, we are pressed for time, you realize that; I don't feel we're safe just about anywhere—you have to accept that there's an entirely feasible way to turn ergot-infested grain into a harmless drink."

"So you're saying the initiates were really on an LSD trip?" Monica retorted, opting for being polemical so as not to listen, for the moment, to the very alarming admission he had dropped incidentally.

Rafael shook his head. "No, that's not what I'm saying at all. You scholars keep hitting a brick wall. All you can think of is Haight Ashbury in the 1960s, "Lucy in the Sky with Diamonds," college students freaking out on acid, right?"

"So what are *you* thinking of?"

"Two things. The freedom of early man from our laws and paranoid prohibitions. The so-called War on Drugs has blocked the subject; no research chemist today dares to say that he's even tried these things. Second, and this is the important one, I'm talking about a *sacred* science of drugs."

"Oh, that sounds great," said Monica, trying to curb her impatience at the course the conversation was taking. "Like 'Turn on, tune in, drop out'; Timothy Leary as psychedelic guru to spoiled Harvard brats."

"Just as I said. Monica, you're trapped in these automatic reactions. Try watching yourself, try to catch them before they catch you. Socrates, Plato, Aristotle, Cicero were all initiates of the Eleusinian Mysteries. Socrates himself was put to death for profaning the Mysteries by mixing the kykeon with his disciples."

"That's not what I read!"

"Yes, well, that doesn't surprise me. Now listen." He took her hand.

"People in the past lived in a sacred world, a world filled with meaning, saturated by their mythology. Their whole lives had a sacred dimension. Now, thanks to Christianity, and I suppose Judaism, too, you think I'm saying they were very holy people. Wrong. They were no better than anyone else, but their lives had this extra dimension. The gods and goddesses were *real* to them. And you know the gods don't follow Christian morality, either, not in the least! Please get over this idea that the sacred is about being good. Even people we call evil can be in touch with it. Think of Hecate, the Furies, the Indian goddess Kali, the Egyptian god Set. They all had their devotees. But I'm getting off the point. What I'm trying to say is that, given a world full of gods, when someone had a strange experience, he'd attribute it to a god, without question. An entheogenic substance—"

"Entheogenic?"

"It means containing a god. That's the definition, and that's the whole point. The substance would be sacred to him, because of the god's presence inside it. Think of how Catholics believe that Jesus is in the bread and wine."

"So what about Eleusis . . . the kykeon?"

"For someone living a mythological life, always expecting the sacred to break through, his responses to entheogens would be totally different from yours. For the Eleusinian Mysteries, they prepared for months psychologically, then for days with rituals, fasting, processions, sleep deprivation, and the contagion of hundreds of other initiates. Then they drank the sacramental drink, entered the Telesterion, a vast dark hall filled with columns, full of expectation that something tremendous was going to happen to them. And it *did!*"

"Zap!" said Monica irreverently. "I'll take sex any day. Go on, move the earth for me."

A little later, Rafael spoke again, staring at the ceiling. "I haven't finished your initiation, haven't even begun."

"Go on, then," said Monica lazily, looking at him sideways.

"First I have to tell you about my own—into alchemy. It runs in the family; Uncle Sophocles is deeply into it, but it was Eusebio who initiated me.

"He got me excited about alchemy, and we set up that lab together, what you thought was a kitchen. We worked with antimony, a sort of brittle white metal. It's dangerous to handle because it's poisonous, but some say it was the true 'first matter.' After a month we knew we were on the right track because an iridescent star appeared on its surface as we melted it. Eusebio said that the Virgin Mary was giving her blessing to our work, and he sang that beautiful hymn, "Ave maris stella," 'Hail, Star of the Sea'!"

"Right there, in that lab?"

"Yes. The alchemists had a motto, *ora et labora*, 'pray and work.' It was an oratory, a place of prayer as well as a laboratory. I've never quite bought the Christian myth, and Eusebio's never pushed it on me. He said if I had a visitation from the goddess Isis, that would be just the same."

"And how about transmutation? The Philosopher's Stone?"

"That's a distant goal. Eusebio warned me not to desire it, not even to think of it, before I was worthy. But the ambition's always there. We both felt it, after the albedo seemed complete. The raven had given way to the white dove—"

"Rafael, please, don't speak in riddles. Make me understand."

"You're right, sorry about that. In alchemy, the first stage is the *nigredo*, the blackness; that's where the work begins. That's the raven I was referring to. Then, if there is progress, the alchemist graduates to the albedo, the white stage; so, the dove. And when we got there with this perfectly white powder, we turned up the heat."

"What do you mean, exactly?"

"We turned it up literally, on the stove. But that alone is not enough. You also need the 'secret fire,' generated by the alchemist himself: a state of intense concentration that feels like being roasted alive."

"Then what?"

"The alembic blew up, showering us with boiling matter and broken glass. Perhaps thanks to the Virgin's protection, we were both facing the other way. After that, we closed down our operation. Eusebio said it was a sign. He took the blame himself, saying that he'd miscalculated the position of the planets, and we must try again next year. We never did, though. But I blame my own thoughts. At the moment of the explosion, I was having a fantasy about how I'd go down in history with two of the greatest alchemists, Nicolas Flamel and Fulcanelli, as one of those who'd achieved the Great Work.

"I should have known better; an initiatic axiom warns that 'you must not seek power; it is power that must seek you.'"

They were silent a while, then Rafael resumed.

"I can't describe it in rational terms. Call them a trick of the light, a Jungian projection, or whatnot, but I've seen things in those glass vessels."

"What sort of things?"

"Well," he paused, "creatures."

"Creatures?"

"Things like heraldic dragons. Birds, too. Believe me, the work puts you in a very strange state of mind. But there's another theory about alchemy that makes the whole thing much simpler, and much more real. It comes back to entheogens. The alchemy I did was real enough, but you can also read the old texts as allegories, and when you do, the correspondences are amazing. The laboratory work is just a ritual that focuses the mind when it's under their influence. . . ."

"I don't follow you."

"Just as you enclose the matter in an alembic, so the ritual encloses the imagination and prevents it from flying off in all directions, like a drug trip. The entheogen then achieves its true nature as the Philosopher's Stone. It does turn lead into gold, in the sense that the person who takes it in the right spirit has an experience that transmutes the whole of reality into pure divinity."

Rafael was speaking with a conviction that commanded, finally, Monica's respect. "So did you try that, too?" she asked.

He paused and straightened out some pillows. The zeal seemed to have gone out of his voice as he replied: "No. Eusebio was strictly against any drug use, for obvious reasons. I never heard of this interpretation of alchemy until after we were finished."

"But what does this have to do with *my* initiation?" said Monica.

The energy was back again as he exclaimed: "Everything! Don't you see that all the pieces are in position now?"

"Honestly, I'm trying, but I'm even more confused."

"All right, to simplify things, start by forgetting the golden pomegranate as the forbidden fruit."

"Forget it? How could I possibly do that?"

"What you've brought up from the depths of the sea are the *original* forbidden fruits of European civilization. They'd become the kykeon of the Mysteries and the Golden Fleece of the Argonauts, to say nothing of all the other cults that used them, like Vedic Arianism, Zoroastrianism, Jewish Prophetism, and possibly even . . ."

"Even what?"

"Never mind; no more of that for now. The point is, here they are, preserved in a golden shrine for twenty thousand years. It shows that well before what history textbooks call the dawn of culture, people knew about these things, and revered them. They're fundamental to humanity. They're literally a gift from the gods. Look, I don't know if the golden pomegranate itself belongs to the same period, as you stated so boldly; in fact, it seems inconceivable. I don't know if my father produced it out of frustration from somewhere and planted it where you fished it out; we'll never know."

"Then how did twenty-thousand-year-old 'garden dirt' end up inside it, if it was made much later?" she asked.

"Someone must have placed the forbidden fruits in there—let's call them by their true name—perhaps from another kind of reliquary; it detracts nothing from the fruits themselves. But not even my father knew what was inside it. That is *your* discovery—accidental or not, it doesn't matter—and it's earth-shattering. I'm not a Jungian type, who thinks alchemy was just psychological, but I do know a synchronicity when I see one. You brought this stuff up from the underworld—fittingly, since it was the pomegranate that Persephone ate that kept her in Hades—just when I was thinking about entheogens, both curious about them and dreading them. Curious about them because they could unblock years and years of alchemical and esoteric explorations, mostly fruitless; dreaded them because with my past as an addict I cringe at the idea of taking *any* drug."

She came closer and gently stroked his hair. "Why, are they addictive?"

"Not in principle. But what if they did throw open the doors of perception? Why would I ever want to stop taking them? Who am I, an ex-junkie, to tinker with stuff so much more enormous than a numbing painkiller like heroin? That is, assuming they really do contain God.

"But what if they didn't? You see, I never quite believed the theory. After all, there was no physical evidence, just the conclusions of a pretty far-out group of scholars. And I had no one to confide in, until you, of all people, proved that these entheogens were venerated already twenty thousand years ago! There's no confuting that now."

She smiled, but then said in all seriousness: "I don't think I'm a very good confidante. This is all so weird to me."

"You *are*!" cried Rafael, springing up and looking down at her. "You are my *soror mystica*. You don't have to *know*; you only have to *be*!"

"What, hold your hand while you go on a bad trip? No, thanks."

"This isn't self-indulgence, Monica. Oh, it's so complicated, I can hardly keep all the pieces together myself. I'm not just looking for a transcendent experience. What I seek is *sapientia,* knowledge."

"Knowledge?"

"The sort that no human being can give me. Look at us now. My father has been killed; who did it? The police don't have a clue, nor do we. Then somebody tried to kill *you*; I hate to say it, but it's safe to assume that it's the same people. Unless there's something shady you want to tell me from your past."

"No, nothing!" she hastened to say, feeling suddenly uncomfortable.

Rafael threw another log in the fire, then paused for what seemed an eternity to Monica. It had started raining again, and the tile roof echoed the sound of every drop. He closed the shutters over the four tall windows.

"All right," he finally said, "let's say in your past you haven't stirred up enough rancor or hatred for someone to want to kill you. Where does that leave us? With 'they,' again.

"The same 'they' who killed my father, failed to kill you, and then came to my apartment and knocked Eusebio unconscious. 'They' probably assumed we've escaped together, which is likely to make their task a little more difficult, or a lot easier, depending on how well I get on with this. Needless to say, I'm a dead man, too, now. So we're both fugitives from the same 'them,' and we don't have a clue about who they are—or do you?"

She didn't either, she said.

"Now, why have I picked this place? I assumed 'they' had done a background check on me and probably come up with a few of my favorite spots. They may be looking for us there as I speak. So before entering Tuscany, I called the monsignor who owns this castle, or rather, his family owns it. I had his number on the cell but used a pay phone, as you saw. He also belongs to the Order of Malta.

"I came here a few times when I was a kid. We don't see each other much at all, so he must have been surprised to hear from me, but in deference to my father's memory he consented to hosting us without asking questions. Anyway, this isn't a place that would figure in my background. So far, so good, it seems, though I believe one's better concealed by a crowd than in total isolation. I mean, if 'they' discover we're here, we're finished.

"Another thing I can safely assume is that 'they' don't know about my secret laboratory, nor the underground passage we took down to the river. And that's about all I know. Do you know anything else?"

No, she was obliged to reply. The fire at last had begun to warm the room, but the wind seemed to find many ports of entry, guttering the candles in their iron sconces. She wrapped another blanket around them.

Rafael continued, speaking into the middle distance: "So we're fugitives groping in the dark. Soon your absence will be noticed and reported in the papers; probably the Italian police will investigate your disappearance. More urgently, Inspector Soldanis, back in Malta, might try to get in touch with us, certainly after hearing you've vanished. He'll fail, assume we're guilty and on the run, and, at the very least, have an arrest warrant issued." He turned to her, despondency in his eyes. "So you see, we're wanted by everyone."

"OK, our predicament is grim; what else can I say?" She reached out a hand and touched his lips gently.

"That's good, facing one's demons. It's a start, anyway. We need to know why they want you dead, who is it that wants this, and how to stop it. This is knowledge, too, and we need it desperately." He took a deep breath. "When you came along, Monica," he added with a new tone in his voice, "I knew from the first moment."

"So did I, Rafael." She drew his face to hers, and they kissed, lingeringly; then she leaned her head on his shoulder as he continued. "And then, my father died. My eccentric, exasperating, beloved father. Now I'll never really know him, and he'll never really know me."

After a pause, he went on: "This is why I need sapientia, Sophia, knowledge—in short, I need *you*. We're in terrible danger, Monica, you do realize that, don't you?"

"What can I do, Rafael?"

"Would you do something that terrifies me, too?"

She hesitated.

"Don't think for a moment that trusting me was your big leap of faith."

She stiffened and sat up on the sofa.

"So much more is asked of you," he continued, "and of me. You might think you're about to die, without knowing that, in fact, you're about to be born. That's what being initiated is."

"But Rafael, that's nonsense!" She might have been speaking to a presumptuous student.

"Really? Isn't that what we all experience when we go through our mother's birth canal as we're being delivered? The contractions are constricting us, strangling us; surely, we're going to die any time soon, and then—to be born again, breathing the air for the first time, alive and out of her womb, another identity, another life, another dimension altogether. Life as we know it 'initiates' then."

She didn't know what to think anymore. She heard his words, perceived the strangeness of their meaning, but it wasn't the words that spoke to her; rather, the way he was now, so immensely human while explaining and overexplaining by the fire. He had been a specter every time she'd seen him, until he had saved her life. From that moment on, he had been—

"Tell me, Rafael: what can I do?"

He suddenly changed expression and whispered in her ear: "Did you hear that?"

17

For a moment, Monica and Rafael were frozen, and all they could register was that noise, the rain, and their own heartbeats. Rafael was up and dressed within seconds. "Get dressed, too," he quietly urged her, taking a candlestick. As he guarded the wavering flame, Monica could see the crimson light through his hand.

The noises came louder through the open door, and the candle was instantly snuffed out.

"Where's the flashlight?" asked Monica in a whisper, fumbling for it in the firelight.

"Monica," he said, still very quietly, "I . . . I don't have a plan for an escape. I'm sorry, I'm so sorry. Take the poker and hide behind the door. If they kill me, they'll rush in here. They'll fumble for the light and won't go searching behind the door. That's your chance: sneak away and run for your life. If it comes to this, I'm the greatest failure that ever lived. But promise me you'll do as I said."

Swallowing a lump in her throat, she felt herself nodding, and then he was gone.

His pocket lamp cast a brown, distorted oval on the blackened stones. The pounding rain was muted here, but the vortex of the staircase magnified the wind as it swept and swirled up. It was as though the castle had been abandoned to become a playground for the sylphs and wind gods.

Rafael descended one floor and checked the banqueting hall,

the blood throbbing now in his temples. The pale beam was lost in its immensity, and a whole battalion could have been lurking in the shadows, holding their breath. He continued to the armory on the floor beneath. Here the wind was soughing in a new key, higher and louder, while the rain served as its percussion.

The standing suits of armor gleamed dully when the lamplight caught them, like sinister presences arrested in midmotion. As he stole around the periphery of the room, something crunched under his foot, and he jumped back in revulsion. An image of spiders and scorpions flashed on his mental screen, while a sudden gust of wet wind buffeted his head. An instant later something whizzed past it, followed by the sharp impact of metal against stone. Terror seized him. He made for the door, tripped, and fell sprawled on the threshold, while something metallic rolled past him and clanked down the stairs, one by one.

As it reached the bottom, the storm, too, lulled, and in the comparative quiet, Rafael's reason returned with his breath. He had hung on to the flashlight, and now, as he hauled himself up, it revealed the details of the scene. One of the massive inside shutters had come loose, and so had the window beyond it. The wind gods had been having their way with both of them. The flapping shutter had knocked over a suit of armor, whose helmet probably lay at the bottom of the stairs. The only remarkable thing was that his recoil, after stepping on the broken glass, had probably saved him from being knocked out.

The wind was still sweeping up the staircase, and Rafael, now quite relieved, needed only to go down and shut the outside door. But before he took the first step, a different sort of drumming came from below: not the side-drum roll of the rain, but a heavy rhythmical tread and a quicker pattering sound. Someone was there, and making no effort to disguise his or her presence.

A faint light suffused the stairwell and grew more powerful as the intruder started to mount the stairs. Rafael could hear the scrape of hobnailed boots, but what was that faster pattering?

His question was answered by the deep growl of a dog, and the silencing grunt of its master. He switched off his flashlight and crept higher up. At worst, he thought, he could get to the dormitory first and barricade the door. Would that be better or worse for Monica's chances of escape? Worse. No, he must stand his ground and fight—but with what? He cursed his addled mind: with a whole armory of medieval weapons, why the hell hadn't he grabbed one of them first? Now it was too late, and it could be the intruder who would drive him up the stairs at pike point, to skewer him against the door and then—

Rafael climbed out of sight as the torchlight grew to a brilliant white and ventured out just as two large, backlit forms vanished into the armory. He heard the crunch of broken glass, a yelp of pain from the dog, and a string of curses. Then the iron tread resumed more urgently, together with a clangor as if armor were being kicked around at random, rusty weapons wrenched from their holders, and another cascade of glass.

Monica was caught in a mesh of unfamiliar feelings. Never before had she felt the tang of sheer physical terror. She loathed being the helpless woman, waiting for her man to protect and defend her. She relit the candle, struggled into her unwashed clothes, and made a few preparations for a sudden flight. Then she listened at the door, half-opened, trying to hear through the noise of the rain.

Yes, someone was rushing up the stairs.

She blew out the candle and hid behind the door. Now she understood what hysterics meant and only with a supreme effort held them at bay.

The footsteps came closer.

Did this mean that Rafael was dead? She nearly lost it, but somehow managed to hold steady, ready to leap noiselessly out and away from the room.

The first thing the intruder did after he entered was to turn on his heels and slam the massive door behind him. Then she was caught in his arms, trying to fight back, and—

"It's OK, it's OK!" Rafael said in her ear. "We're safe for now."

"What was it?" asked Monica, still shaking, but taking comfort in his embrace. "I heard all sorts of noises."

"Just a loose window in the armory," he replied with an effort at nonchalance, "and Piero—good old Piero!—came up to see about it. That's all; it wasn't 'them' this time." His head was drenched, and he rubbed his hair with his shirt.

"You must be frozen. Come back to bed," said Monica, a small voice inside her observing that here she went again, acting out the archetypal—or stereotypical?—female. Her male had put the enemy to flight, and she was his reward. But that was a cliché, unworthy of the new sense that she felt dawning inside her: that of loving someone more than her own self.

18

Rafael left the castle early the next morning to use a pay phone. He called the headquarters of the Order of Malta in Rome and asked that a message be conveyed to Eusebio. Back at the castle, he also spoke to Piero, to whom he gave a large tip. On his return to their quarters, he seemed more relaxed, as though the storm had cleared his mind. Monica had been washing her hair in tepid water and, wrapped in a blanket, was despondently facing a blurred mirror. He took the brush from her hand, kissed her on the lips, and said, "Don't worry, Monica. You're beautiful." As he gently brushed her hair, he touched upon childhood memories in Malta and Sicily. Then he continued in a different and more hesitant tone.

"I told you that my uncle Sophocles is a sort of alchemist. He belongs to a secret society that's based in Valletta, along with the same monsignor who's hosting us. When I came to Malta in late September, I attended one of their sessions as a guest. You see," he seemed embarrassed, but finally explained to her about the séance. His recollection was a vivid one and made Monica cringe.

"My God, the things that go on in Malta!" she said; "I don't think I ever scratched the surface."

"The island has a long tradition of this sort of thing. So does my family. Anyway, I told my great-uncle that I didn't believe in any of this because I didn't want him or any of his friends to investigate it any further."

"Why?"

"For their own safety: what the girl was saying was that there was some terrible evil in Malta. Somehow, I felt that she was telling the truth. But there wasn't much sense in it. She spoke of killings, mutilations, blood, and guts, and kept saying the words 'Tas-Santi, Tas-Santi.'"

"Something about saints?" said Monica. The words seemed vaguely familiar, though she could not place them.

"Apparently." Rafael put the brush down and ran his fingers through her thick black hair, now almost dry. "And then," he added, "there was the inexplicable murder of the most prominent Maltese citizen; I began to wonder if there was any connection."

That was his own father, for heaven's sake, thought Monica; curious how cold logic could be. She dropped the blanket and accepted the clean man's shirt and underpants that Rafael handed her. "And so?"

"Since the message came, as you might say, from the other side, I think that would be the place to seek an explanation."

"Do you mean . . ."

A long pause ensued. Rafael was looking for the words, feverishly, but not replying yet. She was waiting, not pressing for an answer.

"Yes," he said at last. "There's no choice in the matter." And there's no way of sweetening the pill, he added to himself. "I'm terrified, but now that I have my *soror mystica*, I can't let my fear deter me." He came over to stand behind her, reached his hands over her shoulders, and started doing up the buttons of the heavy silk shirt. "I'm going to knock at the portal of initiation and demand an answer. *And I need you to come with me.*"

He turned Monica around and looked at her with an expression that went to the depths of her heart. She knew with a mixture of thrill and terror that she had reached a one-time parting of the ways, something that would determine forever the course of her future life. If this wounded, tortured, neurotic, but infinitely precious and tender being could summon up the courage, then how could she refuse to lend him the vigor of body and mind of which she felt in full possession? But it was an adventure for which she had no preparation, and perhaps no talent.

This, for Monica, was terra incognita. This world of ancient rites, initiations, alchemy was the sort of thing that Freud had notoriously called "the black tide of mud of occultism." She had been taught that it was utter nonsense, not worth the time of any educated person, let alone of a scholar. Everything she had learned and cherished, she realized, would be challenged; her entire worldview would no longer apply. If she accepted to accompany Rafael "to knock at the portal of initiation and demand an answer," as he had put it, she would renounce everything that was rational and familiar to her. This was more than placing her trust in him, more than a leap of faith: this was tantamount to an annihilation of her former self. She would have to surrender herself to something that she could not comprehend rationally but for which Rafael seemed to need her desperately. She, the "archaeologist extraordinaire," would become an unknowing novice, passively following the teacher's every instruction. It was preposterous, absurd. This was the last time, she perceived, that she could say no; her intellect was fighting for her to answer in the only rational way: "No, Rafael, I won't come with you." She heard herself say: "I'll come."

He kissed her solemnly on each cheek, on each shoulder, then on her left breast, where her shirt was now marked by a proprietary coronet and the embroidered initials RPdF, adding with affected casualness: "We have to stop eating, then."

Monica's tenderness turned to remonstration. "Why that? Don't we need all our strength?"

"You have to fast for the kykeon to have its proper effects. Everyone in the Eleusinian Mysteries did so. All we can allow ourselves is water, with a little red wine mixed in. The local wine is ideal for this."

"Oh yeah? How convenient," she snapped back, mixing sarcasm with skepticism.

"Please," said Rafael, disarmingly, "let's be together in this; it won't work if you doubt it from the start."

"I'm sorry, Rafael. I didn't mean to. It's just that—"

"The local wine is the Sangiovese; it goes back to the Etruscan age. The name—Sanguis Jovis—literally means 'blood of Jove.' So, every time a priest here in Tuscany drinks the Eucharistic wine during mass, he's not really drinking the blood of Christ, as is intended, but of Jupiter. And it's these gods that we must turn to now as we prepare for the kykeon."

"I see," said Monica, puzzled by the contradiction. "And how long must we fast?" she added, still suspicious. From somewhere in her memory came the phrase "forty days and forty nights."

"Say, three days? That's all we can allow. I really don't feel very safe here, but it should be longer." He did not wait for further objections but went on: "Eusebio is expecting us in two days' time. We have to use the laboratory in Rome, and once we're there we have to keep strictly out of sight."

"And until then?"

Their bodies overflowing with endorphins and adrenaline, they made love with the wild abandon of revelers in a pagan festivity. Then they collapsed into uneasy dreams, then made love again.

On the third day, a taxi arrived and took them to Rome. Monica had to stop the driver twice on the way, to be sick. The strict regimen did not agree with her. Once again, the drive was made in silence, leaving her thoughts to wander from food fantasies to the overwhelming anxiety and foreboding that had begun with Sebastian's murder, only to intensify since. When the taxi dropped them at the Bocca della Verità—the mouth of truth—she burst out:

"Oh no, tell me we don't have to go through that shitty yard again!"

Apparently, they had arrived at feeding time. A colony of imploring cats surrounded an old lady, who was feeding them small fishes. A few bums loitering around were trying to catch them as she threw them. Rafael strode ahead, looking neither left nor right. Monica glanced around at the passersby and back again at the woman, the cats, and the bums; she remembered Trajan's Column, the knock on the apartment door, Eusebio gallantly making light of his assault; she followed.

This time she took notice of the cloaca's details as she walked along. It was built in different sections as it branched out into different conduits: some entirely of gray volcanic tufa, vaulted, and paved with blocks of lava; one, in travertine; others in brick-faced concrete dating back to the Roman Empire. Where the conduits emptied into the main sewer, a chamber had been built to accommodate the increased flow. She didn't pay too much attention to the course they were taking, as she just followed Rafael, but it seemed to her that he kept choosing the conduit to the right, four of them in all. Finally, they reached a vaulted chamber she recognized, with an iron gate in the wall. Rafael, hoisting himself up with his foot on the bars, reached up inside it and felt for the heavy bolt securing it at the top. The gate swung open, and Rafael bolted it again while Monica started up the ladder to the former toilet.

Eusebio was relieved to see them back. Behind his façade of serenity and even warmth, Monica could sense his unease. Neither one said a word about it, though, and he hastened to show her to another windowless chamber, adjacent to the laboratory, now equipped with a camp bed and a reading lamp. Along the corridor was a bathroom with an ancient copper tub, bleak but clean. He had brought some newspapers, and when Monica apologized for her lack of Italian, he summarized the essential news. *Il Messaggero* reported that the American Academy in Rome was seeking news of one of its members who had disappeared. It said nothing about her research or discoveries but suggestively linked her name with Sebastian Pinto de Fonseca, recent victim of an unsolved murder in Malta. "So I'm afraid there are many people looking for you at this moment," Eusebio added. "Ring this bell if you have the slightest need or worry." He withdrew with a bow.

It was midday, and Monica was already exhausted. She poured a glass of water, added some wine from the carafe provided, and drank it. Then she ran a hot bath and lay in it for a long time. When she got out, she nearly fainted and virtually crawled back to rest on the bed. After the fit had passed, to distract her from her complaining stomach, she looked through the English papers.

The *International Herald Tribune* devoted a whole page to the scafisti outrage, with tables of statistics and opinion pieces by Eurocrats. That's not my problem, she said to herself, and turned to the *Sunday Times Magazine,* which had an editorial about the golden pomegranate, the forbidden fruit. The journalist prided himself on being a skeptic and made much of the "courage to disbelieve." Funny: to her mind, it was believing that took courage, and it was taking every bit of it to keep believing in Rafael.

At midafternoon, Eusebio summoned her to the laboratory, which had been tidied up almost beyond recognition. Rafael greeted her: "How are you feeling now?" He kissed her on both cheeks and looked her up and down approvingly. "I must say, my shirts suit you very well." Memories began to return, but he cut them off abruptly. "Now we must begin our work."

"I think I'll just be in the way here."

Rafael shook his head as vigorously as his energies would allow after days of fasting.

"No!" he said. "You must have a part in making the kykeon. It's not enough just to take it like a medicine. It's a living thing." He held up a glass vial with contents of purplish brown. "Eusebio, my familiar genius—or do you say genie?—has procured this. By the way, where are the fly agaric caps?"

"In the small refrigerator."

"Good; thank you, Eusebio. You see, Monica, what would I do without him? And he's going to help, too."

"But I thought he was against any sort of drug use."

"Yes, that is, until my soror mystica came along; this has changed things. Anyway, the kykeon has nothing in common with the kind of drugs you're thinking of. Uppers and downers, numbing painkillers, recreational stuff that eventually becomes habitual, then addictive. Eusebio knows that all that's behind me." He handed her the vial. "Now, please empty this into the brass mortar, and start grinding it, just like you would spices. You can sit down to do it," he added. "We must both conserve our strength."

Monica did as she was told; extreme lovemaking, fasting on diluted wine, little sleep, chronic anxiety—all had dulled her mental acuity. Yet she realized full well that the ergot, the entheogen of the kykeon, was but one of the *two* sacred fungi reluctantly yielded by the golden pomegranate. What about the other one, the fly agaric? Why not use that, or that, too, since Eusebio had managed to obtain it? She asked just that.

Rafael weighed his words, then said, "Both? Together? That's unthinkable. And I must stress that if I could, I wouldn't touch either one. Not because I'm any more of a coward than the next person. It's just that one never knows if the gods are well disposed to human tampering; from what I've read about it, it seems to be the luck of the draw. But the situation being what it is, we must go ahead, so let's try the less terrifying entheogen."

"What do you fear?"

"I can't say exactly. But why do you think God told Adam and Eve not to eat of the forbidden fruit? Physically speaking, the fly agaric can induce a coma, even death."

Monica stopped grinding.

"That shouldn't happen with the ergot. And we have a sitter who will intervene should something go wrong, won't you, Eusebio?" The old man nodded. "Anyway," Rafael resumed, trying to sound reassuring, "what we need are images, visions. That's what the kykeon supposedly offers. The fly agaric is much more unpredictable; it offers a whole range of experiences, with visions rarely among them, but various other things, such as telepathy, for example, even at great distances. I see that your skepticism is surging back again. That's a good sign: keep your wits about you, even during our . . . crossing. And now, please, will you start grinding again? Eusebio?"

Eusebio had stepped out of the laboratory but was back soon, carrying a pile of books. In deference to Monica, he spoke in English.

"Dioscorides, Pliny, Crateuas the rhizotomist, and Hildegard of Bingen's *Physica*. These are the best authorities I can find. Then, of course, there's the Latin manuscript of Johannes Gewürtzer."

"Oh yes, the most unfussy of them all," Rafael commented, "though I wonder what his real name was." He began to page through the volumes, with special attention paid to the parchment manuscript. "Very well," he continued after a while, "the first stage is, in modern chemical jargon, partial hydrolysis, to turn the ergotamine to ergine. For that, we need finely powdered wood ash." He went over to the fireplace and filled a bowl with ashes. As he stood up, he swayed and sat down heavily on a chair. "I'm sorry," he said, catching his breath, "it's the fasting."

Eusebio came over, full of concern. "You must lie down for a while. I'll do the process." He took the bowl from Rafael and emptied it into a larger mortar, pounding the ashes vigorously with the pestle.

By now Monica had reduced the purplish, spiky ergots to a powder, and Eusebio combined them with the ashes. He added distilled water and set the vessel on the stove. "Do you feel equal to watching this, Dr. Bettlheim?" As she assented, he added: "Be careful not to let it boil. Keep it just below the boiling point for one hour, adding more water whenever the level goes below that mark."

Rafael, resting on the sofa, remarked: "It's child's play and women's work, just like the old alchemists said!"

During the process, Eusebio assembled a tray of other powders and liquids. Monica tried to lighten the atmosphere. "I hope that's not dried toad or eye of newt," she said.

"Oh no," said the older man, stung by her levity. "These are mild psychoactive herbs, mostly of the Solanaceae and Convolvulaceae family; also *Cannabis sativa*. The combination comes from Gewürtzer, the sixteenth-century Bohemian apothecary, but we add them only in homeopathic doses. Their effect is not physical so much as on the etheric body."

The preparation of the kykeon took them most of the day. Eusebio was continually at work, putting each ingredient into water in a padded container, which he pounded violently against the counter for what seemed like hours on end. Each time he added two or three drops to the ergot mixture. When his arms began to fail, Monica or Rafael took over, but their stamina was very limited. Working in the blacked-out room, there was no indication of nightfall, but Monica felt a great fatigue and a pulsing headache.

"Now we must rest and try to sleep for a few hours," said Rafael. "Thank God," she said, collapsing onto the sofa without taking any notice of where he might bed down.

19

Monica was woken by Eusebio, who brought a silver salver with a bottle of mineral water and a glass. She drank thirstily, one glass and then another, and saw that Rafael was already up. "What time is it? How long have I slept?"

"Many, many hours, my dear, beloved Monica, and I have been watching to see how beautifully you sleep." He held her tightly to himself for a full minute. "And now, when you're ready, we will go on our crossing."

Eusebio poured out two glasses of water, added a measure of red wine and some lemon juice to each, and then stirred in the kykeon. The atmosphere was hushed and reverent. All three felt the tremendous import of what they were about to do. Each had a different appreciation of the dangers: Rafael, with his memories of addiction and withdrawal, hated the necessity of giving himself, ever again, to a mind-altering substance. Monica feared the sacrifice of her rationality to unknown forces, but more than that, she admitted to herself, she feared the unknown. Eusebio, as the oldest present, felt a heavy responsibility for these young voyagers whom he was helping to send into terra incognita. All three dreaded the knock on the door and the uncertain future of the hunted.

After Monica and Rafael had drunk, Eusebio turned the lights out and left them, though they knew he would not go far away. They relaxed on the sofa with their feet up. Rafael held Monica's hand for a while, then they disengaged as each seemed to be entering his or her own encapsulated fantasy.

Monica had never liked marijuana, for as a lifetime nonsmoker it was an agony to her throat and lungs. She had enjoyed a few hashish brownies in her student days, but the more powerful drugs were a closed book to her. For a long time, nothing seemed to be happening, except a gradual calming of her fears.

Her thoughts wandered here and there: to her research, her success at the American Academy, her plans for when she returned to the States. Every now and again she recalled her present situation, acknowledging it almost without interest, then moved back into the chain of associations.

She noticed that the links in the chain were becoming more and more vivid. The golden pomegranate, for instance: she could almost see it, with a clarity denied to the normal imagination. With a last comment from her observing self—"This is incredible!"—the pomegranate cracked open along its five seams. Inside, instead of black dirt, was a brilliant, crimson, faceted pattern, like a three-dimensional lattice made from rubies, only the rubies were the pomegranate seeds, each one with a core of lambent gold. Monica was awestruck by the beauty of it, as it shifted like a kaleidoscope from one fivefold symmetry to another.

Then, although she did not realize it, the physical hallucinations began.

She was no longer just a spectator, but an actor in the antics of the pomegranate seeds, feeling them as a ballet dancer feels her gestures. The senses of sight and bodily movement blended, and somehow sound seemed blended with them, too, in a rhythm if not a music. Her hunger must have played a part in it, for there was taste as well. As the dance went on, the limbs of her imagination contracted until she became nothing but a mouth, turned inside out, and the seeds were darting against her taste buds, each one exploding in an orgasm of deliciousness beyond any mortal food.

No self remained as spectator. Subject and object were in blissful union, secure from the critical eye of consciousness, the petulant claims of guilt or fear. And so it was that she came to the end of the world, where there was nothing more but ocean—not as far as the eye could see, but as far as the mind could ever reach. In a condition of perfect vacuity, she beheld the last outpost of the tangible world.

It took the form of a tower, a stone tower not unlike her recent Tuscan refuge, but which Monica knew with a certainty was not that one. Built of massive gray ashlars, it rose out of earth's last cliffs, its base surrounded by the last, mute witnesses to life: grass and yellow-blossomed shrubs that might have been gorse or broom. The tower had barred windows and battlements, just as in a fairy tale, and even a pennant flying from a flagstaff on top. A palm tree sprouted from its machicolations.

Without putting it into words, Monica knew perfectly well that it had to do with Malta. And without the slightest emotion, she registered that there was evil around it: real, objective evil. Not evil in the sense of the hurtful things people do for reasons that seem good to them, but absolute evil, which desires woe and destruction to all, and finally to itself. Her lack of self-awareness preserved her from the anguish this might otherwise have caused her. She simply knew and acknowledged it as a fact of the universe, much as God, if there is a god, must have to do.

With that thought, as far as she could remember afterward, she lost consciousness.

As Rafael let go of Monica's hand, he felt as though he was casting off from a lifeboat, alone now and at the mercy of the unfathomable deep. He did not know whether to expect the clean, crystalline flash of cocaine, raising his mind to superhuman alertness; the careless motorbike race of speed; or the deep, ursine embrace of a heroin trance in which all earthly woes would become null and void—for a while. In his years of bondage to recreational drugs, it had never occurred to him that there was anything to be gained or learned thereby beyond the thrill of pleasure or the absence of pain. For all his playing with fire, risking death from an overdose or from contaminated heroin, he had never before felt so apprehensive. How could he, an ex-addict and drug abuser, expect to cleanse the doors of his perception? How could the god whom he had absorbed with the kykeon—which he did not doubt for a moment—deem him deserving of the Mysteries? He was deeply ashamed, his greatest fear that of being judged unworthy and thrown back into his inadequate self.

The words of the Preface to the Mass, *Domine non sum dignus*, resounded in his mind. "Lord, I am not worthy," he repeated; "Lord, I am not worthy." But as the familiar mantra resounded in his inner ear, he felt a different sort of revulsion: *this* was unworthy behavior, this self-abasement. What did the Christian god and his perverse ethical system have to do with the case? Nothing! Did the aspirants to the Eleusinian Mysteries mouth such words? Unimaginable! There, *anyone* was worthy, so long as they were not a murderer. "No!" his mind added in instant exculpation, "That wasn't murder; it was his life or Monica's—and mine!"

The memory of that victory on Trajan's Column brought a new sense of his own strength. Like a classical hero, he would conquer, or else fall into nothingness. And thus armed, he faced the vision that had been held up till then at arm's length.

"My initiation began a lot differently from yours," said Rafael after Monica had finished describing her visions up to the point of the castle. They had both come to with a tormenting thirst, and the sparkling mineral water was ambrosia to them. "I think I learned more from that experience than in my whole life so far, but I can't put it into words, at least not as eloquently as you have. But in the end, I did have a vision. Let me try to describe it." He closed his eyes and leaned against the counter.

"I was by the sea, too, though there was no land in sight, only a bright yellow sky, as though the sun were filling the whole thing, and this blue sea, blue like lapis lazuli. I don't know if it was the same sea as yours, or if this is peculiar to the kykeon, but it felt as though I was looking at it for years, for eons, without a wave, without an atom in motion.

"Then came the dragon. It came out of the sea, black and scaly and dripping with slime. I could smell the foulness of it, as though all the shit and putrefaction of the world were oozing through its skin." He paused. "Excuse me, I think I have to throw up."

He turned and retched into one of the large vessels.

"Here, drink this," said Monica, pouring him another glass of water. "It's never tasted so good."

"The dragon had wings, claws, a reptile's tail, all very classic, I suppose, and multiple heads. It was full of jerky motion, tail lashing, wings flapping, heads looking this way and that. The odd thing is, I had no fear that it would see me. I think I didn't have a body in the vision, or anything that could be sensed. I could see it, but it couldn't see me. What I did feel was the greatest sense of revulsion I've ever felt in my life. It was as though all the miseries of my past were rolled into this one thing, but I was outside them, and in a way above them. Then—if you can believe this—I felt sorry for this monster, that anything so vile could exist. And that's all I can put into words. There was a whole lot more, details upon details that were absolutely clear at the time, but they've vanished. I feel somewhat cheated, though that doesn't devalue what I learned earlier on."

"So, what do we do now?" asked Monica, hoping that Rafael would suggest breaking the fast but not daring to say so.

Nothing was further from his thoughts. He was leafing through the books again, turning them over, looking at them.

"They say that the initiates of Eleusis were never the same again, and that they lost the fear of death. It may not last, but I feel like that now."

"If there *is* anything that survives," said Monica hesitantly, "it might be like the state of mind I was in."

"But that's not the purpose, at least not the immediate one," said Rafael, decisively, closing the herbal with a slam. "I went into this initiation with a specific question in mind, and so far, it hasn't been answered."

"I'm not sure of that," said Monica. "I've described my castle as well as I can, but there was one other thing I didn't mention, because it was so irrational: an absolute certainty that it was in Malta." Rafael spun around. "In Malta? It doesn't resemble any castle there that I'm aware of. But of course, it could be symbolic."

"Sure to be, just as your dragon isn't in any zoo. Did you have any sense of place to go along with it?"

"Not really. But the whole thing is *so* archetypal: castles and dragons, like the Tarot cards or the engravings in emblem books."

"Not to mention the pomegranate."

"Well, that seems to be a case of entheogeny if there ever was one. You became possessed by the goddess—you turned into Persephone, didn't you?"

"Why?"

Rafael began to pace about the room. "She wasn't supposed to eat anything in the underworld, but Pluto sneaked some pomegranate seeds into her mouth, and that meant she had to go back to Hades for six months of the year. And of course, he was her lover. But no god seems to have possessed me. Getting back to the dragon: doesn't my vision resonate with what that child medium was saying? A great evil in Malta?"

"Yes, maybe, but we're no closer to locating it," said Monica. "I'm feeling an awful hangover, Rafael, and before I can discuss any more, especially making decisions, I simply have to eat something, even if I throw it up again."

"I'm so sorry. I've only been thinking of myself. And it's true, I feel vile inside. But I don't think I'll break my fast just yet. Let's call Eusebio, and you tell him what you feel like eating. And no," he went on, anticipating Monica's words, "you can't wander around the apartment. You're *safe* in here and in your room, but only so long as they don't suspect that we've come back to Rome. I'm certain that they're watching the apartment, and all of Eusebio's comings and goings. If they see any clue, any irregularity, they'll be back, and this time they won't be so easily satisfied. You don't want Eusebio to be tortured, for instance, now do you?"

"That never occurred to me," she said, chastened. "But I really am starving."

After Monica had eaten very lightly and drunk some fruit juice, she went to her room and slept. But Rafael, exhausted as he was, could not relax. When he was certain that she was asleep, he stole out of the laboratory and sought out his mentor in his quarters. He talked for nearly an hour, while Eusebio silently prepared some bland soup and made him eat it. At the end, he said: "Whatever your doubts, Rafael, you have knocked on the portal of initiation, and the gods have let you in. It's more than they have ever done for me, because I've never had your courage, or your need. Don't underestimate it: they *have* given you what you asked for, but it's up to you to use it. Think of the Delphic Oracle! Its responses were never straightforward; they had to be deciphered. You have your materia prima, and now you have to work with it."

Rafael was pensive for a moment. "I have to use the library. I suppose the lights haven't been on there since I left."

"No, I haven't been in there at all."

"Are the curtains still drawn?"

"Yes."

"Then I must risk it. I have an intuition that I can only follow up in there. I need to look through the books."

"Should I just bring them down to the laboratory?"

"No. I may well need to range around the whole library. I'd like some panini for when my appetite returns, and if you could bring me an espresso every now and then, it'll help me keep awake. But whatever you do, don't turn the main lights on in there."

"Certainly. And Rafael, whatever else is going on, I'm very relieved to see you and your lady. You have been much in my prayers of late."

"Thank you, Eusebio. I owe a great deal to your prayers."

Tears in his eyes, the older man embraced the younger one.

20

Alone in the library, Rafael took a shaded desk lamp and placed it on the floor. He glanced at his shelves heaped with ancient alchemical tomes. Once these books had been his chief obsession: first hunting out and buying them from rare book dealers, then studying them under Eusebio's guidance to separate the sense from the obscuring verbiage. The engraved illustrations, often clearer than the Latin or German texts, had led them to specific chemical processes. Careless of the expense, they had dissolved gold 20-lire coins in concentrated hydrochloric and sulphuric acid, thereby enabling the "Green Lion" of vitriol to "devour the Sun." And many more such experiments, always accompanied by intense visualization of the symbols as the retorts bubbled away.

But things were different now. The alchemical process, he realized, had never ceased, but through the gift of the kykeon it had become internalized. The image had been revealed to the eye of his imagination, and its meaning might well reside in the most cryptic and symbolic commentary. Where should he begin? Save for some educated guessing, he would have to leave it to chance, as most of these books were illustrated with mysterious engravings. He lifted a stack down from the shelves and sat with them on the Turkish carpet, holding each in turn in the pool of light as he leafed through its pages. Occasionally he looked up, but with his pupils contracted, the rest of the room was in absolute blackness.

His heart had been racing since he'd entered the library, but now it was calmer, as he began to concentrate on the matter at hand. "Dragons, winged and many-headed," he said to himself, reaching for the folios of Ulisse Aldrovandi, the voracious collector of every beast, bird, and plant in creation, the stranger the better. He opened the *Historia serpentum et draconum,* then the posthumous *Monstrorum historia.* His father had given him the books for his eleventh birthday—he remembered that distinctly—and although he had never read much of the Latin text, the illustrations had haunted his waking and sleeping hours. Winged and wingless; two,- four-, six-, and even eight-legged; crested, horned, arrow-tongued and -tailed; Wyvern and Basilisk, Hippogriff and Cockatrice, Manticore and Kraken. Every conceivable species was there, but none of them had multiple heads except the Amphisboena and the Hydra, and those had the body of a serpent.

He thought he had heard some subdued noises, soft fluttering and crackling sounds. He held perfectly still, without breathing. Silence, but for the faint howling of a very distant siren.

Steadied, he went on to the *Natural History of Monsters.* There were the hydrocephalic baby and the elephant-headed boy, Siamese twins and hermaphrodites, all displayed in shameless nudity, that had once held his horrified fascination.

A different noise in the walnut shelves broke his concentration, and as his eyes adjusted to the darkness, a gleam shone through a chink in the shutters. It came and went, came and went again, like a lighthouse or a signal. Suddenly, his mind conjured up the incongruous vision of a large tree in the wind as he heard the distinct noise of rustling leaves.

Rafael shuddered. The rustling sound faded as quickly as it had come. He slowly unwrapped his cramped legs and stole over to the window. He put his eye to the chink and saw in the street below, opposite the palazzo, two black vans parked. One of them was flashing its lights, without apparent cause. It continued for a few more cycles, then drove away, leaving the unlit van behind.

Rafael returned to his books and evaluated the situation. The rustling sound: he had no idea where that might come from, and it was better for his purposes *not* to dwell on that at the moment. The scuttering in the walls, on the other hand, was probably mice or rats. As for the behavior of the vans, that certainly troubled him.

He flipped distractedly through Topsell's *History of Four-Footed Beasts and Serpents,* then through Kircher's *Mundus Subterraneus,* both rich in dragon lore but no more fruitful. Perhaps the alchemical emblem books would be a better source, he thought, and collected a stack of these small, exquisite books, which he brought into the lamplight. The works of Mylius, Maier, and Lambsprinck were all packed with visionary engravings suggestive of entheogenic states. These very suggestions he had systematically refused to follow, as he had vowed never to ingest mind-altering substances again. Well, things had changed now.

Again, the rustling noise emerged from the silence, accompanied, this time, by a breeze in the room. Oblivious to his own goose bumps, Rafael carried on, leafing through the ancient tomes.

The breeze turned into wind.

It couldn't be a draft, as all doors and windows were shut. Rafael now had to hold down the pages of his open book. His mind refused to contemplate the obvious question: What on earth? Perhaps to ignore it was the best course of action.

The wind eventually subsided, then the breeze, finally the sound itself. As he continued to pore over the engravings, hopelessness began to creep in, more insidiously than the breeze, imagined or otherwise.

Deadly tired, his eyes and mind saturated by several hundred images, Rafael decided to give up for the time being. He took one more look through the shutter. While he was at the window, Eusebio came in with a fourth sugared espresso.

He put the tray down and came over to where Rafael was standing. "What are you looking at?"

"Sh! The vans; they're gone now, but they've been coming and going. I don't like it."

"Neither do I," whispered Eusebio. "Do you want me to go down and investigate?" The whole ensuing conversation was carried on sotto voce so it became, now and then, barely audible.

"No! Much too dangerous. Make sure all the doors are double-locked, and take the keys to bed with you. I . . . I guess I'm going to sleep."

Both withheld comment on what looked like a fruitless night: their first experience with the kykeon had been of no use; either they had not prepared or taken it correctly, or the gods had refused to help.

Rafael made as if to turn the lamp out. "By the way, *you* aren't familiar with many-headed dragons, are you?"

"The kind with seven heads and ten horns?" said Eusebio.

Rafael paused in mid-stoop. "Maybe, though I didn't notice the horns, or count the heads."

"Try the Apocalypse."

"The Apocalypse? Seriously? All right, one more try," said Rafael. He drank the demitasse in one gulp. "Can you fetch me a Bible, please?"

Eusebio went to the shelves. "Will the old English one do?"

"Fine, bring the King James."

Eusebio found his place in the leather-bound quarto and read in a low voice: "And there appeared another wonder in heaven, and behold, a great red dragon, having seven heads, and ten horns, and seven crowns upon his heads."

"That's not it. The one I saw definitely came from the sea, not the sky. And it was black, not red."

"Aha," said Eusebio, "there's a second one in Chapter XIII, though it's called a beast rather than a dragon. Listen: 'And I stood upon the sand of the sea, and saw a beast rise up out of the sea, having seven heads, and ten horns, and upon his horns ten crowns, and upon his heads the name of blasphemy. And the beast which I saw was like unto a leopard, and his feet were as the feet of a bear, and his mouth as the mouth of a lion." He handed the book to Rafael, pointing at the passage.

"The closest I've got all night; but what I can't understand," Rafael said thoughtfully, "is why those pagan gods and goddesses of the kykeon should send us to the Bible."

"It makes no difference to them," said Eusebio. "Religions are contingent on time and place; it's the symbolism that's universal."

"So do you think the seven and the ten are significant, I mean in the present context?"

"They could be," said Eusebio hesitantly. Then he added: "It's too late to speculate now. I'll go and check all the doors," and left the room.

Rafael, kneeling on the floor, reread the passages in the old black-letter type. He was absorbed in the epic of the Apocalypse, yet aware of the rustling sound, rising once more out of nowhere, and gradually turning into a breeze. "And they worshipped the dragon which gave power unto the beast." Then something touched him on the shoulder.

21

It hit Rafael like an electric shock. He turned in terror, white as a sheet.

"Sorry! I didn't mean to scare you," said Monica.

Rafael gasped for air. He smiled and signaled to her to speak quietly.

"I woke up nauseous," she whispered, "and then couldn't fall asleep anymore. I don't know: could the kykeon still be active?"

Come to think of it, wondered Rafael in his mind, the kykeon might well be still active, which could explain the rustling sound and then the breeze. He very much wanted to believe that.

"But the truth is," Monica went on, "I can't stand being away from you. And I feel that you need me still." She looked beautiful, Rafael thought, and in an instant forgot alchemical engravings, multiheaded monsters, and odd sounds and occurrences. They were in each other's arms, kissing tenderly. Their lovemaking in the castle, it was now clear to him, had been much closer to ecstasy than his first experience with the kykeon. He closed his eyes and let himself go.

She was the one withdrawing the lips. "What have you found so far?" she asked as he encircled her waist with his arm.

"You know, you shouldn't be here at all; you're running an unnecessary risk; it's you 'they' want, I'm just an accessory."

"Now you tell me? If we'd made love right here on the carpet, you wouldn't have said a word!"

"Touché," he admitted, "but let's be quiet. What I found is the source of my vision, or something very like it. It was in the Bible all along. Listen." He quoted the passage.

"That does sound like it. Is my castle in there, too?"

"In the Bible? I doubt it. But you're right!" Something only too evident hit him then: "I need to take another look through these emblem books. I'm sorry, I was so obsessed with my own vision, I didn't think of it."

Monica's glance spoke volumes: he did need her; how could he not realize it? That they should be searching together was the natural way about it.

Foremost in his mind was her safety, he rebutted, and she was a lot safer in the secret laboratory, but it was plain to see that he, too, realized that four eyes would be better than two.

Monica joined him on the carpet and started leafing through the books. Being less familiar with them, she dwelled longer on each picture.

"Goodness, these things are weird. Look at this one!" She pointed to a creature with a scaly body, three tails twisted around the sun and moon, a human face on its chest, and elegant boots on its feet.

"Ah, yes, Nazari's monster. A close relation of my dragon, I think."

"Look, here's a castle, but it's in a garden, not a bit like the one I saw. It's one by the ocean we need to find."

Gingerly and quietly, Rafael brought stack after stack down from the shelves until the two of them were sitting inside a round wall of piled-up and rejected books. Eusebio came in punctually every hour with coffee and, on and off, with sandwiches.

Monica's eyes fell on an emblem which, surprisingly, she could probably interpret correctly. A planet made of irregular geometrical shapes and human eyes was rising under the zodiacal sign of Gemini, her own. On the left upper corner stood out the word "Aurora," which she knew meant "dawn" in Spanish and in Latin, too. "Well, that's timely," she said in a whisper, showing Rafael the image.

It was dawning in the world outside: bird cries and traffic noises were coming from the street.

Rafael looked at the image and then at the walls of rejected books around them, while she kept leafing through the book. He yawned and said, "Ah, you've found Gichtel's illustrations, often attributed to Boehme himself. D'you know, he, too, had a soror mystica, Antoinette Bourignon. Back in the 1670s, they must have been a regular New Age duo. . . . Well, nobody can say we haven't tried, but I think it's time to—"

"No, Rafael," Monica insisted. "Look at this!"

She held the book in the lamplight for him to see. "That's like my dragon all right," he conceded. "I'd forgotten the dark clouds around it."

"*That's my castle!*" Monica had trouble keeping her voice down in her excitement.

Rafael rubbed his eyes and took the book from her. "What? Both in the same picture?"

"Definitely. Look, here's the cliff, the pennant; and the palm tree clinches it."

The engraving showed a dragon emerging from the sea to attack the castle. Rays of light from the heavens were reflected from a polished shield and struck the dragon's eyes.

"What are the letters around it?" asked Monica, "Hebrew and Greek?"

"So they are. Alternating. Let me see. Hebrew reads right to left. That's an aleph at the beginning. Then Greek nu, theta; I know the Hebrew yod, it's the first letter of Jahweh; Greek chi, a Roman R. It must be 'Antichrist!' I can't make out the other word. Can you?"

"Half of it's blanked out by those rays. There's a B or an R, I'm not sure which, then—oh, I used to know a bit of Hebrew, I had uncles who did the Seder."

"No problem," said Rafael, going to another shelf. "Here's the Hebrew alphabet."

"Thanks. So it's ayin and kaf, then this last letter's from neither alphabet, unless it's a sideways V."

"Or an S."

"R-Ay-K-E-S," Monica sounded the word out slowly. "Hey, this is a German book, isn't it? It says *Antichristi Reiches,* of the Empire of the Antichrist!"

It couldn't have been more ominous, but they preferred not to think of that.

"Now how about these words on the castle?"

"I think they're references to Psalms and Proverbs," he answered.

Rafael searched through the Bible again. "Psalm 18 starts: 'The Lord is my rock, and my fortress, and my deliverer: my God, my strength in whom I will trust, my buckler, and the horn of my salvation, and my high tower.' Pretty run-of-the-mill, I'd say. Now Proverbs 18—wait." He leafed through the Bible. "Aha, this must be the verse: 'The name of the Lord is a strong tower: the righteous runneth into it, and is safe.'"

Monica laid the book aside. "I've never believed in any religion, and I'm not about to start, but I must say, this shakes me up. Our two visions fit like a jigsaw, but why this book in particular?"

"Why indeed?" said Rafael, searching for the other engravings, scattered through the text. "But I don't think it can be by chance. Nothing in this matter happens by chance."

"You mean there's an assignable cause? Two inebriated lovers dabble with ancient psychotropic drugs, then leaf through outlandish old books authored by a collection of world-class weirdos, and come up with something that cannot be attributed to chance?" She spoke on, caressing him with fondness, in a smilingly ironic tone that she thought might lighten up the atmosphere. It had been a long night.

Enjoying the caress more than he appreciated the irony, Rafael heard her out, then picked up Gichtel's Boehme again and slowly leafed through it, thinking as he did so.

"Were we ever told at school that Sir Isaac Newton was a great alchemist? So was the Honorable Robert Boyle, the 'father of chemistry.' Even after them, alchemy fascinated perfectly sane people, like the royal librarian Pernety, the mine director von Welling, Mozart's patron Graf Thun, to say nothing of Goethe. Hardly world-class weirdos, my dear Monica. And as for Boehme, he's a hard nut to crack, but he was probably the first significant Christian to have appeared since Saint Francis. I know you have no time for the Christian tradition, but it's a vehicle for universal truths that have been around since long before Christ."

Persuaded though he was by his own apologia of the odd thinkers to whom he had dedicated more than a decade of his life, he was happy that circumstances made it unwise to speak at length. Who was he to lecture his soror mystica? Accidentally or not, she seemed to be the one coming up with the discoveries and intuitions. And there had been no rustling sound or breeze since she had come to him. He smiled, turned another page, and stopped at another illustration; he looked closer and drew in his breath. "My God," he said after a few minutes, "but of course!"

"What?"

What could he tell her? That perhaps he was finally making the connection? That billions of people around the world believed in a distortion of the truth? That in fact it might have been worse than a distortion: a deliberate imposture? That there was no choice left to him but to—

The front doorbell rang and rang, then rang again.

22

Eusebio had taken his time to reach the entrance door, as he should have, given the ungodly hour. He was afraid, yet serene. If it was "them" again, it'd be unpleasant, or worse. But thanks to his soror mystica, his protégé now stood a chance. As for himself, his task was completed.

The bell rang again.

Eusebio lingered for a while longer, took a deep breath, unbolted the door, and opened it.

"What the fuck took you so long?" asked a *maresciallo* of the carabinieri. Without waiting for an answer, he signaled to his men, five of them, to storm into the apartment, brandishing their machine guns.

The marshal himself slammed the entrance door behind them and then said to Eusebio: "We're looking for an American, Dottoressa Bettlheim, and also the owner of the apartment, Signor Pinto. Who are you?"

Eusebio explained and added: "What exactly was the name of the American lady doctor?"

The marshal consulted his notebook. "Bettle-e-ime."

Eusebio shook his head. "No, I'm sorry, but that name means nothing to me. Anyway, Signor Pinto de Fonseca has a male doctor."

"Really?"

Eusebio nodded, smiling all the while.

"Wake Signor Pinto, will you?"

"I'm sorry, marshal. The Signor is not at home."

"Where is he, then?"

"I don't know. He only told me that he was going out of town."

"When will he be back?"

"He said in a week or so."

"When did he leave?"

"Two days ago."

"That's not good enough," the marshal said with a patronizing glance. "I've come across mercenaries like you before, lying for a tip. Let me warn you: if I find out that you've lied to me, I'll make sure you end your days in the can. And I know the warden in Regina Coeli: you can expect a very special treatment there."

"I wish I could be of more help, marshal," Eusebio replied calmly, adding: "Would you and your men like some coffee?"

"No," the marshal retorted brusquely. A stout man pushing sixty, he hadn't expected courtesy and was surprised to find it in the face of his scare tactics. "Both persons are urgently wanted by the police of Malta in a murder investigation. Did you hear that? *Murder.* The magistrate in Malta had ordered your employer to stay available to the investigation. Instead, he's made himself scarce. How does this look to you? What's he hiding? Why's he a fugitive?"

"I'm sure the opinion of a servant would mean nothing. But hopefully there's a simple explanation, and I'm sure my employer will provide it as soon as he gets back." Eusebio looked embarrassed.

"Is there something else you want to tell me, old man?" asked the marshal, only a few years younger than he.

Eusebio spread his hands: "Well, I can't answer for the whereabouts of a young unmarried gentleman."

The questioner frowned while his men suppressed a smile. "I see what you mean. All right, we'll now search the place."

"I'm sorry, marshal," said Eusebio, taken aback, "but may I see your search warrant?"

"What's the hurry? We'll send you a copy in the mail." The other carabinieri cast a furtive glance at the butler. Obviously, with no search warrant to speak of, the abuse of power was plain; the apartment looked elegant, its owner was probably rich, so, eventually, there might be lawyers involved and consequences for the marshal. Not for them, though, so they just stood on, awaiting orders.

"Fair enough, there's no point in making a fuss," said Eusebio, once more taking the marshal by surprise, "feel free to search the apartment. I'll stay here in the hall, should you need me."

The carabinieri searched the place thoroughly, room by room.

"Hey, you!" Eusebio was being called. He reached them in the library.

"What the fuck is this?" asked the marshal, pointing at the ring of books in the middle of the room.

"Ah, that," said Eusebio. "Signor Pinto asked me to dust the shelves during his absence, and to rearrange some of the books."

"Some arrangement," said the marshal, dubiously. "We'll be back in a few days. If you hear from Pinto, tell him to get in touch with us at once." He handed over a card.

The carabinieri left through the hall, with the marshal exiting last. He paused by the doorsill and whispered, addressing Eusebio: "I don't like you, and I don't believe a word you've said. And you're no butler, either. I'll be back."

23

Once more they were walking—briskly—along the cloaca. Monica was ahead; Rafael, carrying a briefcase, was following, speaking quietly to Eusebio in Italian.

The three of them reached the Bocca della Verità with no glitches, surreptitiously emerging amid the overgrown garden. The stray cats were trying to warm themselves under the lukewarm December sun. A few bums were about, too drunk even to notice the newcomers.

Rafael hailed a taxi, and moments later they were speeding away along the Tiber. Rafael sat in the front. Eventually, he said to the driver:

"Tenga questo," he handed over two 500-euro bills. "E ora m'ascolti bene: fra poco parlerò alla signorina, in inglese. Non appena avrò finito, lei pianta una frenata, mi fa scendere, e poi riparte a razzo. Non si fermi, non lasci che la signorina esca e li porti tutti e due alla sede generale dei Cavalieri di Malta, la Villa Magistrale, sull'Aventino. È una questione di vita o di morte. Siamo intesi?"

"Come vuole," the driver answered.

"What did you tell him?" asked Monica.

Rafael didn't reply.

"Rafael? What did you tell him?" she insisted.

No reply.

"What's this," she pressed on, "some sort of a game?"

Rafael sighed and she gave up.

A couple of minutes elapsed, then he turned to face her, grabbed her hand, and said: "Monica, you've got to trust me. There's something I need to do now, and I want you to be safe. Everything will be all right; I'll be back in ten days or so. I leave you in good hands; you'll be fine. Remember, love: you've got to trust me!"

As soon as he finished, the driver slammed on the brakes, and the car screeched to a halt. Rafael sprang out, slammed the door, and the taxi dashed off, its rear tires squealing.

It had been all so sudden and quick, Monica had remained petrified. Now, she was screaming, both at the driver and at Eusebio. She tried to get out, but the driver had locked all doors. She then turned to Eusebio and slapped him on the cheek, only to be stung by instant remorse. He held still and said, coolly and in English: "This is for the best; do trust Rafael."

"Enchanted, Frau Doktor," said the count, taking her hand and clicking his heels. "I understand that you were a colleague of the late Cavalier Pinto de Fonseca. A very fine man. Tragic affair." He shook his head. "I'm sorry that our Grand Master cannot receive you. He is abroad, and so is our Grand Chancellor. However, as the member of the Sovereign Council in residence, I can do what is needed."

Hans-Jürgen Graf von und zu Hoensbroech was a tall gentleman with a smear of white hair and a thin moustache, immaculately dressed in a pinstripe suit. "One of those," said Monica to herself, determined not to be patronized or awed. Warily, she replied: "Danke vielmals, Herr Graf."

His next words surprised her. "May I see your passport, please?" Seeing her expression as she dug for it in a hidden pocket, he explained: "It's nothing but a formality that I must ask of any foreigner. This villa, and the Palazzo Malta on Via Condotti, are extra-territorial enclaves of the Sovereign Order of Malta. The Italian state has no jurisdiction over them: the police and carabinieri may not enter." He attempted a feeble smile. "In coming through our postern, Frau Doktor, you have crossed a frontier!"

During her residence on the island, Monica had heard Sebastian mention some of the peculiarities of the Sovereign Order of Malta. She knew that it kept up the appearances of an independent state, somewhat like the Vatican, with its own stamps and coinage. "We knights used to have a marvelous time ramming Turkish vessels," Sebastian had said, "but now, for better or worse, we mainly run hospitals."

"You can't expect a U.S. citizen to take this charade seriously," she thought as she handed over her passport but said, "I see, and I appreciate it. I've learned a good deal about the Order's history after living in Mdina for two years."

The count nodded and took a seat at a small desk, while Eusebio, embarrassed on her behalf, pretended to study the view through the window. Monica remained standing while the count wrote the details of her passport in a notebook and returned it to her. He did not waste time on further small talk. "Cavalier Guttadauro will show you around while accommodation is being prepared for you; then he and I will talk. This is quite sudden, you understand. I'm charmed to have met you, Frau Doktor." He rose, shook her hand, and left the room.

Monica waited until his footsteps died away, then turned to Eusebio: "Cavalier who?"

"Guttadauro. Myself," said Eusebio.

"You're a knight, too?"

Eusebio replied with an ease she had not known before, as though he had finally dropped his butler's role and was speaking as an equal. "A small number of us—we're called Knights of Justice—have taken monastic vows, and some live here or in the

Order's other house on Via Condotti. Others, like myself, live in the world."

"I never thought of Sebastian Pinto as given to poverty, chastity, *or* obedience!"

"That wasn't necessary for him, God rest his soul. He was a Knight of Honor and Devotion, like thousands of others around the world."

"And Rafael?"

"Membership isn't hereditary. The Order may invite him to join one day, and if so, he may accept. That's not my business."

"But *he* seems to be your business."

"Yes, and I'm very concerned for him. All the more so, now that his father is dead. I'm also concerned for you."

Monica was touched by the sincerity in his dark brown eyes. Fearful as she was for herself, and furious with Rafael, Eusebio's calm presence kept her in check. In this whole mess, he seemed the one man she could trust. "Thank you," she said.

They left the reception room and went into the gardens. At another time, she might have admired the fantastic obelisks and carved trophies on the walls, the sublime architecture of Piranesi's chapel, and the spectacular views from the Aventine to the six other hills of Rome. Now all this beauty was like ashes on her tongue. Her heart was aching because of Rafael's sudden departure, while her pride had been wounded. She missed him viscerally, yet at the same time resented him. Or his hubris, anyway. Having found God knows what in that dusty old book, he'd felt free to dump her, as if he no longer needed his soror mystica after making such a fuss about that!

Promising to return soon, Eusebio handed her over to an elderly maidservant, who showed her upstairs to a guest suite of two high-ceilinged chambers, a crucifix conspicuous above the canopied bed. The furnishings had the look of antiques that no one had bothered, or dared, to restore. In the other room was a television and a shelf of illustrated books. She turned on the TV, surfing through the channels to find an English-language one.

Meanwhile, Eusebio was in the smaller reception room that served as office to the Council member in residence.

"You're well aware of the support that Cavalier Pinto had given to the Order these many years."

"He's been one of our most generous donors," said Hoensbroech. "Three million euros to the leper hospital already this year. May we expect a legacy?"

"Nothing beyond the contents of his Wunderkammer, which may be more of a burden than a benefit, unless the Order decides to liquidate it," said Eusebio, "but there is the matter of his son, Signor Rafael Pinto, who has been my special charge, as you know."

"I know it; we all do, here, and admire your selflessness."

"Signor Rafael is in extreme danger, and so is his friend Dr. Bettlheim, the late cavalier's protégée. There have been attempts on their lives. I myself have been attacked." The Graf knotted his eyebrows. Eusebio continued: "Whoever was responsible for the cavalier's murder is seeking them, or at least so we suspect. Please don't ask me why: I don't know, and the police seem to be useless. Signor Rafael will be trying to find out who, and why."

"By himself? This is no time to joke, Cavalier!"

"And with respect, this is no joke, Graf."

The two men stared into each other's eyes, the German enjoying the psychological advantage of being a full foot taller. Eventually, Eusebio added:

"I believe that once this is over, Signor Rafael will continue in the generous spirit of his father. In the latter's case, if I may say so, the benefits went entirely one way, from him to the Order. Now perhaps the Order can do a small reciprocal favor."

"Please, explain yourself," said the Graf.

"I'll put it plainly. I'm asking for a passport for Dr. Bettlheim, so that she can travel without any hindrance."

The count's blue eyes froze. "This is a *most* irregular request, Cavalier!"

Eusebio smiled. "Perhaps. And yet barter is the oldest form of exchange and, between gentlemen, still the most honorable."

Hoensbroech offered a cigarette to Eusebio; after the latter politely declined, he took out an amber holder and lit one for himself. "It's been awfully rude of me not to notice that we've been standing all along, Cavalier. Do have a seat." He waved Eusebio to a majestic armchair of gilded wood, then took his own seat on an upholstered walnut settle, putting a silver ashtray bowl beside him.

The two men sat down, the count puffing away and seemingly riveted by a painting of the martyrdom of Saint John the Baptist above the mantel. His facial expression let little if anything transpire, but Eusebio knew how furiously he was evaluating the proposed barter's every pro and con. Would Rafael's hasty escape plan for Monica succeed? Or would it be nipped in the bud? What then? What would become of Monica? What could he do to help her escape?

The count put out his cigarette with a fussiness that betrayed his suppressed emotions, busying himself with the ashtray for too long. Finally, he pocketed his holder, brushed a fleck of ash from his lapel, and turned to Eusebio.

"I think we have an agreement, Cavalier," and as if on cue, the two men stood up and shook hands.

On the way out of the reception room, the count conveyed some technicalities about how they would obtain the passport for the Frau Doktor. Eusebio listened carefully and contributed some essential details.

Shortly after, he was knocking on the door of Monica's suite.

She was still in a state; that was plain to see. Perhaps practicalities would force her to concentrate on something other than Rafael, or rather on his absence. "Somebody will come around soon to take a photo of you. Would you like some time on your own to touch up your makeup?"

"My makeup? Eusebio, please!"

"As you like. Well, here it is," he added, clearing his voice: "Once you receive your passport, in a matter of days, a limousine will take you to the airport, with a bodyguard. Once there, both chauffeur and bodyguard will escort you all the way to security. You will fly to New York under an assumed name, which will be on your Maltese passport. Make sure you memorize all the details, including your date of birth. Once you arrive at JFK, a limousine, with a bodyguard, will take you to a certain hotel in Manhattan. Do keep your new identity for the time being. Bodyguards will guard your suite and escort you whenever you venture out."

Monica's patience was about to burst. She was being treated like a helpless child, without a say in her own life and fate.

"Please, Monica," his calling her by her first name for the first time did register and kept her quiet for a little longer, "please, do as *he* says. This is Rafael's plan. He will join you in Manhattan within a couple of weeks at the most."

"Where *is* Rafael?" she finally snapped. "Look, I guess I should be grateful for all this extra special treatment. But it sounds a lot like getting rid of me. And all I want right now is to be with Rafael. So tell me where he is, and let's leave it at that."

"He made me swear I would not tell anyone, least of all you. I gave him my word, on my honor. I know, honor means nothing nowadays, except to me." Suddenly, Eusebio did something unprecedented: he let himself go with a confession. "Monica, you must realize that I approve of you. I think you've been a godsend, not so much for

Cavalier Pinto as for his son. I cringe at the idea of Rafael's fighting demons out there, on his own. But it had to happen; it's inevitable. I pray that he will come through it unscathed, and I pray for your reunion with him. There's nothing else I can do, other than urge you to accept his instructions and go along with his plan."

Monica was taken aback by this show of soul. Once more, he spoke before she did. "It's time to say goodbye, Dr. Bettlheim." He paused and then concluded: "May all be well, and Godspeed." One last glance, a bow, and he was out of her suite and, she suddenly sensed, out of her life.

Monica was treated civilly, if not cordially, confined to a small apartment within the compound of the Order. The dour, silent maidservant brought her meals punctually and appeared at other, unpredictable times. She fussed around dusting, tidying, making the bed, and whisked away Monica's one change of borrowed clothes, to return it washed and pressed. By the end of the day, anguished and frustrated, but also bored, Monica ventured downstairs and into the formal garden that she could see beneath her windows.

She looked up and spotted the blue curtains of her room and the white-cross flag of the Order fluttering from a turret. No one was in sight but two gardeners, preparing the flower beds for spring planting. They stopped and stared as Monica waved a greeting, then followed a path to the other side of the villa. She stopped in front of the chapel, its façade decorated with towers, chained crescents, hammers, and the enigmatic word "FERT." "No wonder Sebastian liked this business," she said to herself. "It's like an outdoor Wunderkammer, a mixture of extravagance and mystery." In the opposite direction, a steep wooded slope separated the gardens from the Lungotevere, the road beside the river. As she leaned on the low wall, somebody came up behind her, his feet crunching on the gravel. The sound made her jump and spin around.

"Dr. Bettlheim," the count said, "I must explain the delay in doing what Cavalier Guttadauro has requested. Your petition has been granted, but our passports are no longer issued from Via Condotti. They contain a microchip and other modern security features, and they're now made in Vienna. That takes at least a week. For the time being, it would be better for you not to be too visible, if you understand me. I will have the English journals sent up to your rooms."

Reading? All she could think about was Rafael; more than that, she was *possessed* by her missing him; never had she known these feelings. For her own sanity, she must try to snap out of them.

Back in her suite she read the *London Times,* erratically, unable to concentrate for more than a couple of paragraphs at a time, until she chanced on an editorial about the naval blockade and the Rome Conference that was now in progress. However, she learned, Commissioner Altieri's plans had not gone unchallenged: the newspaper's own leader wrote that his measure reeked of isolationism and racism. The *Independent* had an interview with the commissioner, in which he fervently defended himself by saying that it was never meant to be a permanent solution, merely a temporary measure. In fact, he, too, was incensed at the participants in the Rome Conference who seemed to him to be temporizing, perhaps with the tacit intent of keeping the naval blockade in force indefinitely. "Yes, illegal immigration from North Africa has virtually ceased, as a man will cease talking if you gag him. If you leave him gagged, he will also starve," said Altieri.

The next day's papers brought the news that the great demonstration against the Rome Conference was set to take place as planned. Altieri himself would participate. In two days' time, up to a million participants were expected from all over Italy and Europe. Rome had been taking countermeasures, summoning extra police and carabinieri from the provinces, because a demonstration on this scale was sure to attract extremist and violent elements. The pope himself chimed in to say that, while advocating and praying for peace, he supported the demonstration, as long as it would be perfectly peaceful, in the name of the universal brotherhood of mankind.

Life at the Villa Magistrale was claustrophobic. Rafael's image would not leave Monica's mind: the grip of his hand the last time it had held hers she could still feel, with a burning sensation that traveled from her palm to her heart. The gardens were too small for jogging, and anyway she had virtually been forbidden to show herself outside. She tried the television, but all the channels were in Italian, and she had never cared for TV anyway, unless it aired a show about her. Beyond reading the papers, there was absolutely nothing to do but wait for the next meal to appear, and worry, worry, worry—little about herself, very much about Rafael. "It must be easier for people who can pray," she thought with a glance at the crucifix.

The only bright spot of the day was when the maidservant announced that Cavalier Guttadauro was awaiting her in the salon. He came bringing her fresh clothes and feminine necessities, a few of them, but all the right ones.

She hadn't expected to see Eusebio ever again and was delighted to acknowledge that her foreboding had been wrong. "Everything I own is still at the American Academy," she said. "My clothes don't matter, but I left my laptop there, with my whole life on it, and of course the contents of the golden pomegranate. I wonder what's happening to them."

"It'd be much too dangerous to find out, at this point." He opened an Italian paper. "This is bad news, Monica."

Again, that tone. Her smile vanished from her lips as she shuddered. "What is it, Eusebio?"

24

"This is utter blasphemy!" exclaimed Buttigieg, raising his plump hands in horror.

"No, Monsignor, I have to disagree," said Rafael, making a supreme effort to appear calm and weighing his words before he spoke. "Blasphemy is expressing disrespect for what people hold sacred. On the contrary, people don't hold this sacred enough: they enshroud it with words and dogma, with no notion of what an experience of the Real Presence is."

Rafael knew how much his sudden appearance in Malta disturbed these gentlemen. Their image of him was in sleek tailoring, with Jesus-style hair and beard, not this skeletal apparition in travel-worn clothes. After leaving Monica, he had taken a train to Bari, of all places, just to sidetrack potential followers, with a stop at a barbershop; then from there, his head shaved, an all-night train to Reggio Calabria; the ferry across to Messina; a bus down to Syracuse, where he had bribed a fishing boat to take him to Malta. The cash Rafael kept in his lab to buy apparatus and substances for his secret alchemical experiments was proving invaluable.

The boat had left him at Marsascala, from which a taxi brought him to the gates of the capital, and a short walk to Sophocles Pinto de Fonseca's residence near the Auberge de Castille. When he announced his name to the intercom, the manservant had willingly opened the door but on seeing him had said brusquely, "Who are you? Where's Signor Pinto?" His great-uncle had been desperately worried to know what had become of him, ever since the news had portrayed him as a fugitive from justice. For a few hellish hours he had come to wonder if Rafael could have murdered his father. But the mere fact that he had returned to Malta and placed himself in his hands had dispelled those doubts. It filled the old man with relief and remorse for ever having suspected his great-nephew of parricide.

Now they were both in the salon of the Ambini Palace—the scene, two months before, of little Honoria's catatonic trance. Adeodatus Ambini had seated them at a circular library table, staring at a silver galley filled with out-of-season blooms. Monsignor Buttigieg was the fourth person present, but Rafael had asked that none of the other members of the Society of Harmony should come to this private meeting. He had a strange request to put to them.

Sophocles's old voice trembled, as though unequal to the burden of his words. "You speak of an experience of the transcendent. I've sought it all my life through Catholic, Masonic, and Hermetic ritual; I've sought it through alchemy, both in the laboratory and in the alembic of my own soul. I've sought it through divination, and there we have been quite successful. The Sistema Megalocosmica, the System of the Greater Cosmos, has been revealed to us; but even there, I have gained only transcendent *knowledge,* not experience."

"You seem to underestimate the greatest cosmological revelation since Plato," said Buttigieg, reaching over to pick up a fallen petal, which he held to his nose.

Sophocles did not attempt to reply but went on: "I think we were wrong to send those children out into the unknown. We should have gone there ourselves. Armed with all our wisdom and maturity, and with faith in our gods, we could have come to no harm. It was cowardly of us."

"Impossible," said Ambini. "Clairvoyance requires an innocent soul. None of us could have entered the mesmeric state."

"I know, I know," said Sophocles. "But what if we had done as Rafael is proposing to do?"

"We'd all be dead by now, or in prison," said Buttigieg, dropping the petal back into the galley.

Rafael felt weak, sick, and overwhelmed with worry, above all about Monica. But he couldn't let that get in the way of his plea. He looked sympathetically at the old priest and said: "Monsignor, I know you think this is very strange, but with all your knowledge of myth and ancient history, you can see how many incomprehensible things make sense, once you apply the entheogenic key."

"Name one!"

"I'll name a dozen!" he retorted and then collected all his energies in a bid for lucidity. "The fruit of the Tree of Life in the Garden of Eden," he began, "that 'fruit that makes one wise,' but which the Elohim wanted to keep our ancestors from eating, 'lest they become as gods.' Number two: the soma of the Vedic hymns, the mystical juice pressed from an unnamed plant that's still celebrated by Hindus as the giver of immortality. Three: the haoma of Zoroastrian Persia— same word, same function. Four: the Burning Bush that spoke to Moses and gave him the experience of the transcendent 'I Am.' Too bad that he turned it into a book of restrictive laws! What next? The Song of Solomon, a paean to entheogenic ecstasy. And six, the vision of Ezekiel: that's as good a report of the experience as ever written, with the wheels, eyes, seraphs, and eating the scroll; every detail corresponds. Then in the classical world: the Mysteries surely weren't just rigmarole of words and gestures. The kykeon of the Eleusinian Mysteries was another entheogen." He didn't want to but had to stop and take breath; exhaustion was overcoming him.

"Are you all right, Rafael?" put in his great-uncle. "If you're too tired, we can go home and meet again tomorrow morning." It was late at night.

"I'm fine, thank you." This was the time to lunge and win, not to fall asleep, he said to himself. Wake up, wake up, you weakling!

"But back to the matter at hand," he resumed, finding some residual energy God knows where and drawing from it for dear life. "There's a whole mythic cycle including Perseus and the Gorgon's head, Jason's quest for the Golden Fleece, Hercules and the Apples of the Hesperides—often it's disguised as an 'apple'—and evidence of its use right up to classical times; Aristophanes almost let the secret out in his comedies."

Disbelief still loomed over the old men's faces. All Rafael could do was keep piling on evidence.

"Later there are the Grail romances, and I can't think of a better theory among the many implausible ones about what the Holy Grail really was." But he was losing them, and his strength with it. He wasn't sure whether he had laid the groundwork as convincingly as he had intended, while rehearsing it mentally on the trains, ferry, bus, and fishing boat. His rehearsal had been an incoherent hopscotch spanning erratically thousands of years, but that had been the best he could produce under the circumstances. Anyway, it was time to cut to the chase.

"The essence of the thing is that all these ancient religions and mysteries offered an *experience* that gave a *certainty* of the divine, and their followers were never the same again. They lost the fear of death, because they knew the reality that awaits us all on the other side, and they knew that it is good. Now I'll admit that mystics such as Saint Theresa or Saint John of the Cross attained ecstasy through fasting, prayer, and self-punishment. But the mystically gifted are as rare as infant prodigies. Surely the direct experience of divinity is the birthright of the whole human race."

Rafael took a deep breath, surprised, indeed impressed by his own eloquence in meeting Buttigieg's challenge. He had never articulated this so cohesively; his scattered studies of esoteric traditions were finally falling into place. Eusebio would be proud of him. Since no one was interrupting, he continued:

"When no one has experience of their own, when the Mysteries are dead and only belief is left, religions become a tool of the powerful. It suits them to have a God who denies his presence to almost everyone, so that they can dish it out themselves in a starvation diet of catechisms and prohibitions.

"Think what high promises the Church makes to children. After years of catechism they're led on to expect that First Communion will be a transcendent experience. And what happens? The Body of Christ is an insipid wafer! They aren't even allowed to drink the wine!" Ambini looked across the table to see how Sophocles was reacting and raised his eyebrows in silent query. Almost eighty years ago, they had taken their First Communion together. At the mention of the Body of Christ compared to an insipid wafer, Buttigieg had crossed himself and noticed the glance pass between his friends.

Undaunted, Rafael pressed on. "Then more years preparing for Confirmation, leading up to what? Again, a resounding anticlimax. When the bishop puts his hands on their heads, no fire comes down from heaven. The kids don't dare say so because the whole dull farce is arranged by adults who were disappointed in their turn and hence in denial about it. Like the First Communion, it has all the trimmings of an initiation but none of the essence."

Buttigieg noticed the ghost of a smile pass between his old friends. "Adeodatus, Sophocles!" he broke out. "What do you make of this? It's outrageous!"

"I'm not sure, Monsignor," said Ambini. "The Church insists

that Jesus is physically present in the bread and wine, but what if we really experienced that when we took the sacrament?"

"We do experience it," said Buttigieg, "in faith."

Rafael knew that it was hopeless to argue with faith, in his view a very clever stratagem that various religions have in common. Now was the moment to drop the first bombshell. He went on: "This hit me when I discovered that the entheogens in my father's pomegranate were twenty thousand years old."

Rejection was written on all three faces.

"Oh yes, you weren't aware of this. *Those* were the forbidden fruits borne so reluctantly by the apparent fruit, in the face of all the misguiding biblical references of the pomegranate. The entheogens were identified first and then carbon dated; their great age is a fact, not educated guessing. It showed that at the very birth of culture, entheogens were used and revered. In fact, they may have been the very thing that *gave* us culture and raised us to consciousness. They gave a sense of the sacred nature of the cosmos and the intelligent design that's evident in every atom. Religions presume to teach that, but they're secondhand substitutes for people lacking the real thing."

He took up the book that had been lying before him on the table. "What absolutely settled the matter for me was to discover this, at the other end of history. You all know Jacob Boehme."

"Of course," said Buttigieg. "Boehmenism anticipates our findings in many minor respects. But *Protestant* mysticism is heretical!"

"The true heresy," Rafael rejoined, "the distortion of truth, the true imposture is Christianity as it is practiced today!"

There was no holding back now; he had to speak the truth as he had painfully realized it. "Christianity as it is known today could have been invented by Saint Paul, who never met Christ; it's got nothing to do with what Jesus was doing."

The monsignor gasped. Rafael took no notice and went on: "Saint

Paul brutalized and persecuted the Christians, this new sect modeled after the Nazarites. Oh yes, Jesus was never 'of Nazareth,' that town came into existence centuries later; this was a misunderstanding of his cult affiliation: Galilee was a center of Nazaritism. Paul persecuted them so ruthlessly that he had to be stopped. Finally, he had his famous vision on the way to Damascus. Some clever Christian had most probably slipped the entheogen in his food, or drink, or both, to pacify him. Thanks to it, the murderous fanatic literally saw the light. He not only eased up on the Christians but, liking what he had experienced immensely without knowing what it was, converted instantly and became a proselytizer. But of what religion? He didn't have a clue and took the symbols of Christ's body and blood at face value: bread and wine, a very poor substitute for the entheogen. Christianity has been an imposture ever since."

The old men were too shocked to proffer a word.

"Please, look at this," Rafael pressed on. He held up an open page, then passed the book to his great-uncle, on his right.

The three old men took it in turns to scrutinize the engraving that announced Boehme's *Christi Testamenta,* The Testament of Christ. Ambini, when the book reached him, took a magnifier out of his pocket.

Rafael stood up and leaned on the back of his host's chair. "The heart at the bottom of the cross represents the immature mushroom, still close to the earth and unopened. The branches and the two streams show its next stage of growth, in outline, standing on its stem. The streams feed equally into two hearts, one on a dead branch, with folded wings and eye cast down; that's the negative effect of the entheogen, when one feels as though one is dying. The other heart, on a leafy branch with eye and wings raised, is the positive phase. The dove of the Holy Spirit is of course the God within the mushroom, which is what 'entheogen' means. In its next stage,

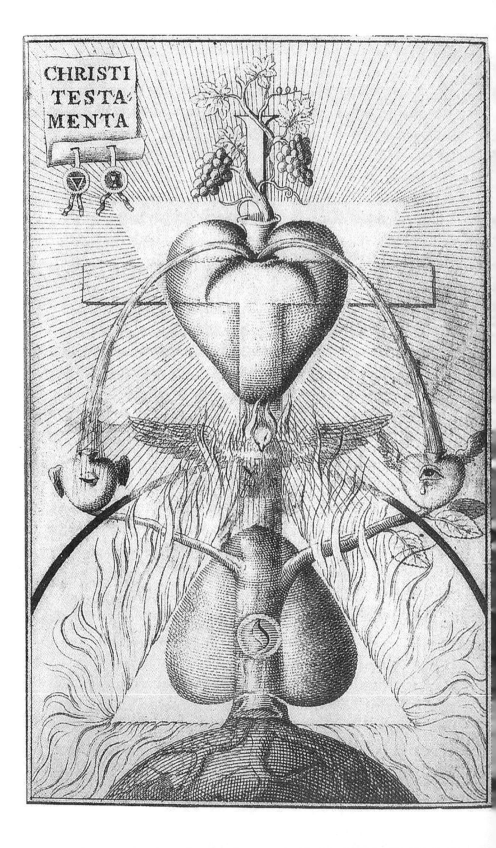

the mushroom, seen side on, takes the shape of the T-cross. Do you see it? Right there," he emphasized, pointing at it. "Then the heart at the top is its final phase, when it makes the shape of a chalice and attains its highest potency. That's represented by the grapes of the True Vine and the rays of glory."

Ambini closed the book. "That's all very clever, but can you believe that Jacob Boehme, the shoemaker of Görlitz, was involved with this nonsense?"

Why can't they see the light? Rafael asked in his mind, frustrated and angry. Why do they keep salami slices in front of their eyes? Patience, patience, he said to himself. *Make* them see the light. Aloud, he said: "To be honest, I neither know nor care. That's a question for historians to answer. I just know what I see, and the message here seems about as clear as it can be—once the key is in the lock. *Christi Testamenta,* the Testament of Christ, what he left behind, is the entheogen that gives us access to him."

Buttigieg was squirming. He reached across the table for the book and looked for the illustration again.

"But I've left out the crux of the matter," Rafael elaborated, "the one that I know upsets you. It's the idea that the use of amanita was part of the secret teaching of Jesus to his closest disciples. In fact, that it was the true Eucharistic sacrament. In simple words, the host that Jesus passed around during Communion was a round, flattened mushroom cap, that of the amanita."

"Enough, Rafael!" his great-uncle said. "That's enough. We realize you're in shock from the loss of your father, and I assure you, we feel for you with all our heart, but—"

"Everything in Jesus's life and behavior suggests a man intoxicated—in the most sacred sense. The entheogen had given him the certainty that he was divine; he knew that God was within it, so he identified himself with it, and feeding it to his disciples was symbolic of giving himself to them. What was divine in him entered into them. I don't know why you think this is blasphemy. It's God who has created a plant that can open the gates of heaven; isn't that a wonderful example of 'the exaltation of the humble and meek'?"

Ambini spoke: "Then why not just commune with it yourself, somewhere private? Why involve us?"

"Because you *are* involved, whether you like it or not! Where did we first hear about the evil in Malta? The cutting and killing? *You* let that news in. Then my father was murdered, and his assistant, Dr. Bettlheim, was very nearly murdered in Rome. Surely you don't think these things are unconnected? To me they're proof that the little girl spoke true, but of some evil worse than anything we're aware of. My father may have died because he got too close to it.

"My friends, I can't do this alone. In the past, I may not have shown much respect for the Society of Harmony, but that séance with Honoria wasn't its best moment. I know that you're the only people here with any connection to the real world, I mean the causal world that holds the secret springs of our own. And there is more.

"Eating the body of Christ and drinking his blood the way it was intended, in other words, taking God inside me, should put me in a state of near omniscience. But that's a state beyond my control, and to profit by it—believe me, this isn't recreation—I'll need direction. You must *guide* me by asking questions, as with the child mediums.

"That's why I must do this *with* you—just the three of you, who loved my father, who love Malta, and who have known me all my life. It ought to be done in a proper ritual setting, and since it involves taking a sacrament, I think you should hold a Mass."

"Oh blessed saints, what *is* he saying?" sighed Buttigieg.

Sophocles spoke: "We were all raised as pious Catholics, Rafael. Although we've come to recognize the truth in every religion, early training leaves a mark; this truly goes against the grain."

"I would agree," said Ambini, but Sophocles raised his finger and continued: "That said, I've been asking myself whether I'd consent to a Hindu soma ritual, or to something like you describe from the Greek tradition, and the answer is . . . yes, I would. But then, why not a Christian ritual? It's because I was raised, as a boy, to fear the Christian God, who was always looking over my shoulder to see if I was sinning. Watching my reactions to your plea, I find that I'm still afraid of him."

"But now that you're near the end of your life," said Rafael, "couldn't you see this as a challenge to cast away this fear?"

His great-uncle took some time to answer. The debate taking place in his soul was painfully visible.

Finally, Sophocles nodded solemnly. "I could see it as a means to exorcise my terror."

"What?" asked Buttigieg.

"I need to assure myself, once and for all," said Sophocles, "that the God I was afraid of offending was not the God I expect to meet when I die."

"Of course he's not," said Buttigieg. "But does it take an act of blasphemy to prove it to oneself?"

"My dear Monsignor," said Sophocles, "let's put these loaded words aside and face what we're up against. The dreadful evil that none of us, for all our accumulated wisdom, has a clue about. Whatever that is, and we know it includes the brutal murder of our friend, blasphemy seems a very secondary evil."

"Perhaps a necessary one," said Ambini. A deathlike silence followed his words. Nobody stirred.

Eventually, Ambini turned to Rafael and said: "The circumstances are so extraordinary that I'm inclined to think that you come here with God's grace. The Society of Harmony already performs highly irregular rituals. In the eyes of Rome, we're deeply compromised, and I'm sure the Protestants would say we're damned.

"I would have gone through fire and water for Sebastian Pinto, and I'll go through this, for his sake and for his son. Monsignor?"

"True," said Buttigieg. "I am a very compromised Christian." He turned to Rafael: "And I will make a compromise for you. I'll say the Liturgy of the Preconsecrated, which will not oblige me to pronounce Our Lord's words over an improper substance. Then you can receive it as you wish. With *my* blessing. Whether with God's blessing is a matter for your conscience."

25

"According to *Il Messaggero*," said Eusebio, smoothing out the newspaper on the table, "there was a witness to the events at Trajan's Column. He waited to tell the police until he recognized your photo in the paper, then told them that he had seen you and an unknown man kill the 'tourist guide.'"

"Oh, God, that's such a lie. I nearly died then and there!"

"This may well be one of 'them' pretending to be a casual eye-witness so that the police start looking for you in earnest and hope-fully find you for them. Anyway, today's news changes things. You'll be flying to New York via Istanbul; an indirect route is better. Same arrangement as before: as soon as your passport materializes, a limou-sine will take you to the airport, with a bodyguard, and so on. You'll be given all the details you'll need to know and the tickets on your way to the airport. Enough said for now."

Her expression was all too eloquent: why such a hush-hush? Wasn't she safe there?

Eusebio's gesture was eloquent, too, easily translated as "better safe than sorry." Then, sotto voce, he said: "Once you're back in the States, the Italian police can't touch you, not on the basis of one self-described witness. And I hope by then Rafael will have brought the truth to light."

"Have you heard from him?"

"No, he won't be in touch. I have no way of reaching him."

"Where did he go? Please tell me."

His tired smile was full of compassion. Words were redundant as he shook his head, made a bow, and left.

Monica could not sleep for worrying until about 3 a.m. When she woke, it was already nine o'clock, and breakfast had not been brought to her. "I know this isn't a hotel," she said to herself, "but still . . ."

She dressed, ready to go downstairs and make polite inquiries, but when she tried the door, it was locked. She tried again, then in increasing panic she banged on it and screamed, but to no avail. It was a thick door, probably very heavy, to judge by the four hinges, and it opened to the inside, so there was no hope of breaking it down. From being a refuge, the villa had turned into a cage! Why? The reason suddenly seemed obvious to her: how long would it be before the Order of Malta invited the Rome police to enter their territory and remove their embarrassing guest?

There was no time to be lost.

Monica filled her small backpack, hoisted it, then opened the window. The three-story drop to the garden was unthinkable. As she saw no one around, she sat on the windowsill, leaned out, and looked upward. There, there was a way, and anywhere would be better than staying put. She ventured outside the window, holding on for dear life to the thick trunk of an ancient wisteria that wrapped around that part of the villa.

As she started to climb, she discovered that a series of hand- and footholds in the chunky architecture would help her. She quickly reached a balcony, overlooked by a mighty arched door that stood ajar. Peering around it cautiously, she could see an immense room occupying the entire floor of the villa. A long table with a red cloth was set with dozens of chairs. To the left was another open door, and between her and the door, two electricians were up on a portable scaffold, working on a chandelier. Monica walked purposefully toward them.

"Ciao," she said, using the one word she could risk without betraying her accent. Still, with that one word she *had* betrayed her not being Italian: "ciao" was a bit too brazen; no respectable Italian woman would so address two unknown workmen. And they loved the confidence. "Ciao, bella!" they replied, ogling her. The youngest one thought about taking a break to get to know her. His boss said something, and he reluctantly went back to work.

Just outside the door was a mess of tools, among which she noticed a large rubber flashlight, of the sort that doubles as a blunt instrument. On impulse she grabbed it, raced down the broad ceremonial staircase, and emerged in the garden on the other side of the villa, near where she had first entered with Eusebio. Immediately she heard voices, then shouts, and saw the porter waving at her from the end of the garden path.

She turned the opposite way, jumped over the low box hedges, skirted a swimming pool, and made for the thicker growth of trees and shrubs that surrounded the formal garden. The shouts were urgent now and angry. "Dottoressa! Dottoressa! Ferma!"

She heard footsteps and scurrying, but evidently, they couldn't see her yet. The sounds retreated as she came out of the trees onto a narrow path, following a low wall. She paused to stow the flashlight in her bag, scrambled over, and dropped down.

The ground on the other side was lower, but it was soft, and she rolled over to break her fall. She stood up, panting, and looked around to orient herself: she was in another grove of holm oaks, sloping away from the villa. As she looked, two heads appeared over the wall where she had jumped. She didn't wait to see if they had spotted her but plunged on down between the trees, until with a jarring halt she saw a sheer drop ahead. Hanging on to a trunk, she peered over it.

There, twenty feet below, was a busy road. Traffic was moving in both directions, the sidewalks were full of people, and, coming from somewhere far off, there was a great noise of shouting. Fifty feet to the left, a staircase led down to street level, and Monica made for it.

A gate blocked its upper end, surrounded with iron spikes to deter intruders from climbing around it. As Monica studied the chances of getting around them without being impaled, the cries of "Dottoressa, ferma! Si fermi!" resumed close behind her. Four men were pounding down the path to the gate. She sat on the stone edge of the drop, turned on her belly, let herself down to arm's length, then let go.

An elderly couple stopped to stare as she came helter-skelter down the slope. By the time they noticed the angry men on the top of the wall, she was away.

The Via Marmorata was not usually so crowded, but today it was swarming with people, spilling from the sidewalks into the road, where the cars had no choice but to slow down and stop. People were forming into knots and groups and raising banners.

"Slowly now," she said to herself as she started to walk toward the people. Her legs kept wanting to break into a jog, but she forced them to obey her will. She must act normally and mingle. Then she heard a voice.

"Eccola! Eccola là! Dottoressa, si fermi! Stop!"

She turned for a fraction of a second and caught a glance of a few men pursuing her. No, it was worse: they were now joined by carabinieri, a whole squad of them.

She was running as she'd never run before, slaloming between knots of people, stopped cars, and crawling Vespas. She had no clue about where she was going, other than away from her pursuers. Their screams were growing louder, though.

Should she stop and confront them? Her legs replied immediately, by running even faster.

The screams behind her were growing fainter, melting with the people's slogans, shouted at the top of their voices. "Of course," she thought, "the demonstration!"

Still, she didn't slow down.

Eventually she reached a newspaper kiosk, stopped behind it, and leaned on it. Though she didn't want to, she had to stop: her heart, she felt, was about to burst. She tried to catch her breath and wiped the sweat away from her forehead.

"Ferma o sparo!"

The carabiniere was a very young recruit, thin as a plank, the only one who had managed to keep up with her. She tried to sidestep and dash off, but he closed in on her, quick as lightning. He pressed his submachine gun to her stomach and raised his voice: "Ferma o sparo, ho detto!"

She was done for. It had come to this. The police would stupidly and wrongly jail her for the death of the "tourist guide"; while she was awaiting trial, "they" would easily spot her and eliminate her. What a neat plan. They had outdone her and poor Rafael. She stood defeated.

More carabinieri caught up with their young colleague, puffing and panting. They exchanged a few words with him, and out came the handcuffs.

A middle-aged officer, probably their boss, walked up to her, handcuffs in hand, and said, "Porga le mani, signorina."

She saw it happen as she raised her hands: an object flew out of nowhere and hit him on the head. The man doubled up on himself and fell to the ground. She could see blood spout immediately from his head. She turned to the direction the stone had come from and saw a band of masked young men and women, some brandishing iron bars, others with cobblestones in their hands. "Fascisti!" they yelled, and again, "Fascisti!"

More hotheads joined them. The young recruit took aim with

his gun. Forty, maybe fifty masked demonstrators were closing in on them, uttering their war cry.

Another carabiniere let out a burst of fire—in the air, but nobody had noticed, their eyes fixed on the recruit. This took them by surprise, enough time for the carabinieri to scram, leaving their injured—or dead?—marshal on the ground.

"So much for the peaceful demonstration," Monica thought, scared to death yet relieved at the same time.

"Compagna, vieni con noi!"

The hotheads. They were speaking to her.

"No Italian," she said, "I'm . . . English." God forbid she should confess that she was an American!

"English? Aspetta," said the closest one to her. "Marco, vieni qua."

Marco, masked, tall, and muscular, approached her. "I speak English," he said from behind his mask. "Here," he continued, "take this."

A ski mask.

She put it on.

"Let's go!" Marco said, and she joined them.

Parco della Resistenza dell'8 settembre was the staging place for the demonstrators. How many people were there, Monica wondered? The large square was crammed with demonstrators and, as far as she could see, so were the streets leading up to it. The crowd's roar was deafening.

Marco didn't let her out of his sight. "We'll be up in the first ranks, with the Black Bloc kids. It's gonna be fun. Just stay near me; you'll be all right."

The situation, Monica felt, was surreal. The demonstration and ski mask were a godsend. But the idea of parading with the Black Bloc chanting anarchist slogans was hard to digest, particularly if they proved to be as loose-handed as their Italian counterpart who had flung the cobblestone at the carabiniere.

Well, they were, and how.

As the huge mass of demonstrators paraded along the Lungotevere Aventino, her trained eye had classified various types of cobblestones: of porphyry, granite, and tufa, no doubt torn from Rome's ancient streets. She also saw slingshots with iron balls as projectiles, bars, clubs, knives, and sundry tools such as sledgehammers and huge wrenches.

As the stream of angry demonstrators poured along the river, the police and carabinieri readied themselves to receive them with armored units and trucks carrying riot-control forces, equipped with shields, full-face helmets, clubs, and teargas guns. The demonstrators came to a standstill, a very eerie calm before the storm.

A police megaphone blared out some incredibly loud warning.

The demonstrators' immediate response was a bloodcurdling primal scream, and then all hell broke loose.

Amid the deafening din, Monica saw everything rain down from the sky: cobblestones, slingshot projectiles, iron bars, rubber bullets, and God knows what else.

Marco was beside her, busy flinging cobblestones over great distances and shouting insults. "Here, watch me!" he said as he arched himself to propel his stone as far and as violently as possible. "Take one! You do it!"

Willy-nilly, Monica too began to fling cobblestones, hoping to avoid anyone in their trajectory, but doubting it very much. The density was that of an anthill: everybody, sooner or later, was bound to be hit by something.

Teargas was now enveloping the scene. Some of the demonstrators had gas masks; most didn't.

Monica's eyes were starting to tear up. Then she began to cough. It was time to leave. As Marco busied himself with a particularly massive cobblestone, she darted off to the side and quickly lost him.

Or did she? Visibility was scarce; for all she knew he could be running after her.

In the haze and amid the deafening hullabaloo, she felt that she might have gotten her bearings at last.

No, it all looked the same, she was lost in the middle of a violent demonstration with too many people on her tail even to run down the list, with Marco having just joined the club.

Yes, she'd been here before.

Had she?

Of course, that was the Bocca della Verità, by the river.

God, she'd been so close to "home" all along!

The usual overgrown garden was deserted, for once. The bums must have joined the demonstration, maybe turning into pickpockets for one day by mingling with the nonviolent rear guard, well behind the hotheads.

With no hesitation, but looking behind her back and all around her as keenly as she could, Monica discarded her ski mask, pulled out the rubber flashlight, and entered the cloaca, trying to visualize exactly how Rafael would go about it.

"Just keep to the right," she reminded herself as she gingerly paced along the uneven stones. Conduits, she noticed for the first time, intersected it at about every twenty paces, and she hoped that keeping to the right would be enough to locate the access to the secret laboratory.

What else could she do? she asked herself as she slowed her pace, careful not to miss any right turn. Her only chance was to reach Eusebio, confront him, and reconsider the situation.

Now more than ever, she wanted to be by Rafael's side. Far better to risk her life helping him than lose it anonymously, killed in jail by some faceless hired assassin. She was a force to be reckoned with, she declared to herself with a sudden surge of self-confidence, and "they" were going to realize it soon. She took the fourth conduit to the right.

The flashlight died on her.

"Not now, goddamn it!" she let out, "not now!"

Her words echoed in the underground maze, then slowly faded. She could now hear drops falling here and there, their impact on the lava blocks amplified by the cloaca.

In utter darkness, she fidgeted with the flashlight.

What if that was it?

What now?

Would she ever find her way out, groping in the dark in that underground maze?

She knew before she tried to deny it that the answer was no.

The flashlight flickered back to life; then a beam came on, steadily.

"It was just partly unscrewed!" she said out loud, "silly me!"

Taking a deep breath, she paced along for a few more yards, her footsteps echoing loudly. As she slowed down to a snail crawl, she recognized the vaulted chamber with the iron gate in the wall.

She rattled the gate, but it was securely bolted. She remembered how Rafael had opened it from the outside by raising himself up somehow and reaching inside, but she lacked his height and his reach. To search for the bolt, she had to heave herself up, wedge her feet painfully between two of the vertical bars, and then feel around with one hand inside the gate. It took her several attempts before she could even find the bolt, and then it had to be pushed upward. In the end she managed it by fastening her backpack to the bars to give her feet extra purchase, then using the long flashlight to extend her reach and push the bolt up.

The gate lurched open, banging her against the wall. She lost her footing and dropped to the ground.

She could not bolt the gate behind her, but she found the iron ladder in the wall and climbed up into the former toilet. As she raised the lid, she was relieved to see a faint light filtering through a dirt-encrusted window. But it was little use. She had not taken note of the directions from there and was unsure of the way to the laboratory and her old Spartan living quarters.

It took her another quarter of an hour of frustration, trying one door after another, before she met with any familiar landmark. It was in a windowless room, where the flashlight revealed a paneled wall decorated with classical heads. She remembered how Rafael had easily opened one of the panels by pressing it at some point. Then it had led straight into the laboratory.

"Why didn't I pay attention?" she asked herself. Well, how could she have noticed every detail in this crazy sequence of events? It was sheer genius to have remembered the turns in the cloaca, then gotten through that iron door.

"I must be rational, or I'm going to die in this hole," she said to herself. "I'll start at one corner and try to find a hollow panel." She worked around slowly, tapping each panel in turn, working in the dark to conserve the batteries. When one of them gave a hollow sound, she tapped all around it again, comparing its tone to the others. Yes, this was definitely different. She turned on the flashlight and saw a bearded head with a half open mouth—the *Mouth of Truth*! As her finger slipped in between the teeth, she knew that these pagan gods were on her side. For there was the latch, and with a click the panel swung open before her.

She instantly recognized the smell of the lab, a blend of dust and chemicals. She was home—if one could call that dismal haven home.

Hungry, thirsty, exhausted, and terribly frightened, she knew that she had made it to the one safe place and, she hoped, the one friend she could still count on. She found her way to the light switch, then after washing herself and drinking some water, she went through the dark passageways into the apartment. The noise of the demonstration was audible through the windows, but she took care not to be visible from outside.

She first tried Eusebio's own quarters, knocking gently at the door. When there was no reply, she tried Rafael's: the bedrooms, the sitting and dining rooms, the study, the kitchen, and finally the library.

Here the shutters were still closed, and she hesitated to switch on the light. The last time she had been there, Rafael had been so insistent on not letting any light betray their presence. As her eyes became accustomed to the gloaming, she saw the books they had read together on the floor, but not in an orderly circle. They were scattered everywhere; and there was something else dark on the floor.

It was a body. Eusebio's.

His shirt had come off, his hands and feet were tied together, and his torso was a mass of blood. She forced herself to look closer.

His nipples had been ripped off; some of his ribs were visible through the broken skin; finally, she saw the gaping wound in his neck.

She recoiled back in horror, tears streaking down her face.

This was worse, far worse than anything. Gentle Eusebio, the secret knight who for some obscure reason chose the path of service; Eusebio, who had talked the Order of Malta into protecting her but could not keep her safe there, though, heaven knows, he must have tried. Eusebio, the one person who knew where Rafael had gone on his mission; of course—that must have been the cause of his agony and death: "they" had tortured him to know just that and then killed him. Had he spoken?

She went into the adjacent bedroom, tugged a blanket off the bed, and returned to the library to spread it over the body. Then she threw herself on Rafael's bed and cried until she could cry no longer.

The noises outside the window made her sit up, and the danger of her own situation came home to her. The apartment had already been invaded; the murderers could return at any time. She hurried downstairs and took refuge back in the secret lab.

An hour must have gone by; hunger and nausea competed all along, then hunger won out. She wouldn't go back to the apartment for any reason, nor did she have a plan to venture back out, yet she opened the small fridge and found two sandwiches and some orange juice. She ate and drank.

Now she forced herself to think. Who could have done that? The carabinieri? They could be crude and brutal, but they would have been able to take Eusebio away and deal with him on their own turf. Also, they would more likely have kept him in custody. There was no gain in killing him, but if they had gone so far, a bullet in his back "while he was trying to escape" would have made more sense than this mess.

Was it "them," those faceless creatures from hell who had sent the assassin to Trajan's Column, then planted that story in the newspaper that set the police on her trail? They had come to the apartment that very day and knocked Eusebio out. Whoever "they" were must have something to do with Sebastian's death, too. For all her two years in the rarefied surroundings of Mdina, Monica wondered if it could be some atavistic Maltese vendetta. On that overpopulated island with its bizarre history, who knows what family rivalries and hatreds may have festered for centuries. Did someone have it in for the Pintos altogether? Perhaps it was a delayed fallout from the Second World War. Or those hunters, the ones who had defaced the prehistoric temples in defense of their supposed rights. Which side was Sebastian on in all of that? He was a hunter himself, yet a lover of antiquity. How had he become so very rich? There was much about him that she had been too polite to ask, too incurious to pry.

How about the fired factotum, Joe Dagenham? Monica had put up with him because he was part of Sebastian's entourage, but among people of her own age, a less appealing one would have been hard to imagine. She had immediately given him the "hands off," and he had managed to respect that. But there was a quality in his eyes that made her wonder what he might dare to do. He was, after all, an ex-Royal Marine, a trained killer, but could he possibly have organized things with such skill? In any case, why go for her, when it was the Pintos whom he had reason to hate? Reason? What reason? Could it be that he had assisted Sebastian with the staging of the "discovery" of the forbidden fruit, but then Sebastian had failed to reward him, and in fact dismissed him brusquely? Had Joe tried to blackmail Sebastian? What was she thinking? It couldn't be Joe, could it?

Wait: could he have been involved with that nymphomaniac Penelope? He might have been plotting with her to do away with father and son, then enjoy the fortune. The tourist guide could simply have been a friend of his, and that would explain why he had no trouble tracking her to Rafael's apartment. Monica tried to walk calmly through the imaginary stages: a couple of pals, perhaps ex-Marines turned soldiers of fortune, backed by Penelope's money? That would have sufficed. And herself? Much too close to the family, perhaps privy to some clue that hadn't even dawned on her yet, and better out of the way.

What if she had been the target all along? Was it conceivable that Sebastian's murder was incidental, her own the real goal? Who had cause to hate her?

What else? The Russian skinheads? Sebastian had ridiculed them. Whether they'd had their vendetta or not, he was dead. Why would they take it out on her now? And would they be able to? Would they follow her to Rome and try to kill her there so very deftly? They seemed too brash for that. Of course, they might have called some friends from Russia, perhaps wilier than they were.

Oh, it was all too confusing, too absurd. Nothing about her could be important enough for murder.

It had to be something larger, some great issue in which she, for all her purported celebrity, was a mere pawn. Ah, the Order of Malta! Years before there had been that business about the P2 Lodge, the Italian banker who hanged himself in London under the bridge on the Thames, the scandals around the Vatican bank. She had never understood nor cared what it was about, but those people had almost unlimited power, and what a front it was for corruption, money laundering, false passports—such as the one they'd cooked up for her! With their extraterritoriality, their reputation for charity, chumminess with the Pope and the whole Catholic aristocracy of Europe, they could get away with anything.

Sebastian, she was sure, would not have been part of such corruption; he was too eccentric and impolitic. Nor would Eusebio. And that might explain both murders. As for that German count, he had looked the very image of an old Nazi, even though he'd apparently helped her. Or had he captured her, letting her gently into his web, only to hold her as a trump card in some dark plot against Rafael?

Thinking again of Rafael, Monica felt an intolerable longing, and her fear for him surged up again. The only thing worse than finding Eusebio like that would have been to find Rafael. In all this thinking in circles, she had left out the clues to be drawn from his own behavior. He had not mentioned a single one of these suspicions, though he was as capable as she of thinking them all through. He must have done so days ago, in a cooler frame of mind; and yet his solution had been, frankly, beyond the bounds of logic and reason. He had knocked on the door of the unknown, and she with him. How could she forget their dual vision, the castle on Malta and the dragon threatening it? Could that be a clue to any of the possibilities, or to others again?

Something was missing from her harrowing list; something, she felt, was escaping her.

Then it hit her.

Eusebio must have made a fatal mistake: returning to the palace not via the cloaca but through its street door. Of course: it was watched day and night; "they"—and by now "they" implied any one of the people and groups she suspected—would have been astounded to see him come back without having seen him leave the place. How could it be? Obviously, there must be a secret passage. Hence, they had stormed into the apartment, overwhelmed him, and tried to extort the truth from him through torture. Judging from his butchered torso, he probably had resisted and not spoken, his stoicism being rewarded with a death blow. But what if he *had* told them about the secret passage, the laboratory, and how to access it from the apartment? Would they burst into the lab at any moment?

26

It did not take long to prepare the chapel for the ceremony. The musical glasses were moved aside, and behind them a pair of doors opened to reveal a small altar with candles, a cloth, a chalice and paten, and a Roman missal. Rafael, who had slept for the whole day the deep sleep of the exhausted, acted as server, a duty he had often fulfilled as a boy.

At the Offertory, he placed the six dry mushroom caps—identical in shape and size to the Host—on the paten and filled the chalice with the water in which they had been steeped. To the astonishment of the monsignor, the water had turned red like wine.

The dose was immoderate, but it was no accident. Rafael ought to have made friends with the entheogen gradually, little by little, finding eventually a dose neither too strong nor too weak for optimal mutual communion. But there was no time for caution, and this one chance could not be wasted. Communication *must* be established; God *must* be stirred inside him, or else all would be lost. Yes, poisoning, coma, death—all were possible, but nothing, nothing would hold him back now.

Monsignor hesitated, beads of sweat standing on his forehead. Eventually, he began.

As always, he said the Mass in Latin. At Rafael's urging, he read from the First Epistle of Peter and, for the Gospel, Saint John's scene of the Last Supper.

The priest's voice broke several times as he read those infinitely moving words. Then came the moment to administer the preconsecrated sacrament.

He looked nonplussed, uncertain of how to proceed in these bizarre circumstances. He made a conscious effort to keep the word "heretical" out of his mind. It was, as it turned out, a supreme effort of will. He also made a supreme effort to keep the word "dangerous" at bay.

Rafael waited, kneeling, but still the priest did not turn to him. He was leaning on the altar, breathing heavily.

"Monsignor," said Rafael quietly, "are you all right?"

Buttigieg turned around. With an ashen face, he made the sign of the cross. "Ite, missa est," he said, using the traditional closing formula, "Go, it is the dismissal." With that, he staggered to a chair and sat, crumpled in his vestments, his eyes closed but his lips silently moving.

But the Mass—if it ever was a Mass—was not over. Its most crucial part, the very reason for the Mass to exist, had been skipped.

Rafael felt abandoned. Sophocles and Ambini were staring from him to the priest and back again. Was this what it had come to? he asked himself. Was this what was asked of him? This, too, this much?

With painful resolve he stood up and went to the altar. His great-uncle and Ambini watched, unable to say a word. He took stock of the ritual objects: the chalice, the paten, the book. Feeling that he was hazarding his very being, but carried along by an all too animal instinct—do or die—mixed with an all too human mood of solemn exaltation, he took the silver dish into his hands.

In a loud yet reverent voice he said the words of consecration over it:

"Hoc est enim corpus meum," (for this is my body).

Holding reverently the Host with two joined hands above his head for all to adore, he ate the first amanita cap. Then the second and all the remaining ones, slowly, with awe and trepidation on his face.

Ignoring the sounds from Buttigieg, who had now begun to weep, Rafael continued to read from the open missal:

"Hic est enim calyx sanguinis mei," (for this is the chalice of my blood); and then, "of the new and eternal Testament."

He reverently raised the chalice in front of himself with his two joined hands, holding it for all to adore, and then drank the steeped amanita wine.

He stood almost petrified and observed a long silence.

This done, he turned from the altar and again spoke the words of dismissal.

Buttigieg had already left the chapel. Sophocles and Ambini, dumbstruck, managed to murmur the traditional response: "Deo gratias."

As Rafael waited in the salon for the effects of the entheogen to make themselves felt, he read once again the words from Saint Peter's Epistle: "Beloved, think it not strange concerning the fiery trial, which is to try you, as though some strange thing happened unto you. But rejoice in as much as ye are partakers of Christ's sufferings, that when his glory shall be revealed, ye may be glad also with exceeding joy."

Whatever form the fiery trial would take, he felt that he was ready for it. Against all probability the Mass had been celebrated, and that alone seemed to indicate some divine approval.

For an hour he drifted in and out of sleep, then got up from the sofa on which he was lying and went to relieve his bladder in a perfectly normal way.

He was still in the bathroom when he felt the Real Presence.

Unlike the ergot experience, no visions were summoned, but a sound, loud and frightening, like white noise or a rushing waterfall.

It was as though he had woken up on the brink of Niagara Falls to hear a thunderous roar that had always been there, but which he had never noticed. Yet when he ran the bathroom tap, he clearly heard the trickle of water in the basin.

As instructed, the old men came back as soon as they heard him stirring. They were worried, and Sophocles asked how he felt.

"I'm all right," answered Rafael quietly, while the sound grew ever louder within him.

"Do you need anything to eat or drink?"

"Some water." Sophocles hastened to bring a carafe and poured him a glass.

Rafael drank it, set the glass down carefully, then lay back on the sofa. The others drew up three chairs facing him. Buttigieg, his face set in an inscrutable expression, held a pencil and writing block.

It was time.

Ambini hesitated, exchanging glances with his friends, and finally put the ritual question: "Guiding spirits, what news of evil and of good?"

Rafael felt the words penetrate his ears and plunge into the maelstrom of the Real Presence that was surging within and around him with undiminished energy. His rational mind, still operating in its own small sphere, realized the absurdity of asking questions of Omniscience. Every question would open the door to an infinity of answers, spreading into complexities beyond human imagining. What were "evil" and "good"? Those human concepts alone would take a billion years to define in all their shadings and consequences.

Now the maelstrom seemed to be churning away, doing precisely that. Words and images flew by in their myriads, too fast to catch or be brought down to the level of human comprehension. Rafael realized that he must resist this infinitude to which the entheogen had given him access and keep a foothold in his own smallness.

"Rafael, can you hear or see anything?" asked Sophocles, worried by the silence.

The question was so redundant that Rafael at first did not answer. Then he spoke from that precarious foothold: "Not quite yet, but I'm on the way. Ask precise questions."

That had taken an effort, and he gratefully sank back into infinitude. Eons later, as it seemed, another question summoned him back to his little self.

"What is this evil in Malta, of which the spirits spoke?"

The maelstrom whirled again, but this time as though the titanic energy were focusing itself into a narrow funnel. The answer came out through his lips, as mild and clear as the water from the bathroom tap:

"Mutilation; murder."

"How is this connected with the death of Sebastian Pinto?"

"He would have found out."

Ambini hesitated before asking the next question:

"Was he innocent of it?"

No reply.

Ambini asked again: "Was your father innocent of it?"

Rafael was having trouble hearing outer sounds, or rather: he found them intruding. The inner sound was turning into light, a yellow radiance coming down through the crown of his head and filling his whole being. It was the most blissful sensation imaginable. Yet as with the sound, the small personality of Rafael was struggling to remain present. He was still conscious of the answers coming to him from the light, and of the brief delay as he found the words for them, as though translating from a concatenation of foreign languages.

"Who killed your father?"

Rafael felt a sudden pain in the chest, as if he had been stabbed, followed by a fleeting glimpse of his father's murderers. He could have tried to describe their faces to the old men but held back. He was gasping for air, as if the stab in his chest had been real, through his lungs.

"This is going too far!" Buttigieg said; "he can hardly breathe."

"Shall we stop?" Ambini was quick to put in.

"Don't stop!" Rafael roared. His voice, cavernous and so incredibly loud, hit them in all its brutality. "Don't stop now!" he repeated, beyond himself, his eyes still closed.

Sophocles turned to him, trembling. He didn't dare ask another question but still asked it in his mind: "Is this evil still going on?"

"Yes, the evil is still going on."

His great-uncle realized that his question had been answered without being asked aloud. Trembling, he cleared his throat and spoke loudly: "Where is it happening?"

Rafael no longer felt any pain. On the contrary, he had never felt so well. Waves of bliss carried him, as though on angels' wings, into the presence of the Father. Whether it was his own father, distilled from the most primal and cherished memories of a lifetime, or God the Father in whom he no longer believed, it made no difference. He was the Son, the beloved and chosen one, and he was united in the most perfect love.

But a question had been asked concerning evil, a concept absurdly remote and quite unreal, and of course the answer was there even before it was spoken. A clear concept formulated itself out of the infinitude of bliss and presented itself to Rafael's verbal mind for translation. It was a real place, and he knew exactly where it was, but he was aware simultaneously of the need to withhold the information. He must not tell the old men what they asked, for then they would have to go and find it. And that would be too much for them. Their guardian angels, not seen but sensed as presences more real and palpable than bodies, appealed to him to spare them the knowledge, and Rafael was silent.

"Rafael, can you hear me?"

He made no reply. The answers were coming thick and fast out of the light, and at last he saw it all: what the great evil was, who had killed his father, and the endless tentacles that stretched out from that primal abhorrence to fasten on himself, on Monica, on Eusebio, on these powerless old gentlemen, and beyond them on Malta, on Europe, on Africa, and finally on the whole groaning world. The realization was appalling, yet still the bliss was present, radiant, and pure in enjoyment of its own infinitude.

"Rafael, it's Sophocles. Are you there?"

Rafael opened his eyes, and as he did so, the bliss vanished and something else came on him like a tornado, ripping through the fabric of everyday reality. The elegant room crumbled, as though the separate atoms of flesh, wood, silk, oil paint, and porcelain were returning to their prime matter. What was left was a void—or had he gone blind? He passed his hand in front of his open eyes: nothing was to be seen, neither hand nor room. Instead, the void was taking on the indescribable dark flame that one sees when looking at the sun with eyelids closed. The flame grew both brighter and darker at the same time, and then it was in his belly, the sharpest pain imaginable. He doubled up on the sofa, squirming like a pinioned insect. Yes, he *was* an insect, something many legged, soft bodied, squirming inside the black light that was also his pain. Or was he full of insects, obscene millipedes, and poisonous caterpillars, clamping their jaws onto the sensitive lining of his guts and eating him away from the inside? He suffered like an insect, without reason, language, or hope.

In the midst of his misery, a thought flew up to him from far away and long ago, from when he used to be human. "Don't throw up in here," it said primly. As soon as Rafael heard it, the pain diminished. It struck him as tragicomic, the polite voice of conscience, concerned that he not vomit on the Oriental rug like a cat with a hairball, while he was suffering the torments of the damned. As language came back, formulating this phrase in his mind, he began to laugh and laugh, until he gasped for breath.

His laughter had kept the terrors at bay, but when it faded into sobs and hiccups, they came back. Not the insects this time, but something worse yet: impersonal shadows of old fears and a hopeless depression. Flung back from indescribable bliss into his own self, he felt like a man broken on a wheel, like Prometheus, or Christ, with physical and mental pain blended in a single agony.

Only one hope remained, only one friend loyal enough to come down and kill the pain. And her name was Heroin. He desired the drug as he had never desired her before. He opened his eyes, intent on finding a dose somewhere to hand. But the room was still all in fragments, like a scattered jigsaw. Unable to fit one piece to the next, he fell back on the sofa, back into the pit.

For a few minutes the old men simply stared at him, too shocked to speak and even to think straight. Buttigieg was the first to break the silence.

"Is he breathing?" he asked, a lump in his throat.

"I don't know—I can't tell," sobbed out Sophocles, heaving his old body over to the sofa and kneeling by Rafael's side. He took Rafael's wrist and searched for a pulse. "I can't feel his pulse."

"Oh, no, not another catatonic trance!" said Ambini.

"Rafael, say something!"

"Rafael! Rafael!"

"Is he in a coma? Is he breathing?"

Grabbing Rafael's other hand, the monsignor kneeled by him and whispered in his ear, "Surge, Rafael, et ambula": arise, and walk!

The three old men, all on their knees, continued to repeat, "Surge, Rafael, et ambula."

27

For two nights and two days Monica had remained inside the lab. Were "they" looking for the secret passage? If they were, and if they should find it, then she was dead. Why hadn't she escaped, then? What if "they" had been watching, even patrolling the whole area around the palazzo, all the way to the river? Then she would be caught as she was trying to escape.

She had tried to think rationally: waiting in there was her best option at the moment.

Her faint hope was that Rafael would come back to the lab. Her reasoning was not entirely unsound: failing to contact Eusebio, he might worry about him and her and rush back to Rome, assuming he had left it.

Rafael, where had he gone? Why had he left her behind? What for? Was he better off now, on his own? Was she?

Again came the novel realization that she cared much more about someone else than about herself. To the point that she would give her life to save him, if only she could.

She had lost count of how many times she had been startled by a noise, a creaking in the wood, or a vague smell in the air. All she had been able to do was bolt both entrances and hope that "they" would not come back.

The thought of Eusebio putrefying in the apartment next door made her sick. Weeping was not useful, but somehow it helped her from time to time.

Was she being paranoid? No, there was a tortured and dead body in the library; "they" had tried to kill her. But still: who would be waiting in ambush in the overgrown garden? The usual bums, who else? With its four million inhabitants and all the other hundreds of thousands of demonstrators who had invaded Rome recently, she should hardly be noticed.

Still, she was not ready to get up and leave. It wasn't only anguish and mental strain. She was hungry. She had gone through the sandwiches and the orange juice. Had found half a bottle of red wine, and drunk that too. Wandering into the apartment's kitchen was out of the question. Although she was still hesitant to venture outside through the cloaca, it seemed as though the choice was being forced upon her: leave the lab or starve to death.

She knew the small fridge was empty by now, but she opened it once more. For the first time, it occurred to her to look in the small ice compartment.

In it she found a few ice cube trays, and a bag, half full. She unpacked it: it contained some frozen . . . vegetables? No, they weren't vegetables; they looked like . . . mushroom caps. Then she remembered.

"Where are the fly agaric caps?" Rafael had asked Eusebio when they had returned to the lab from the castle in Tuscany.

"In the small refrigerator."

She concentrated as keenly as she could, calling back to mind her time in the lab right before they took the kykeon. Rafael had said that they would start with that because the fly agaric was much more unpredictable. It was unpredictable in that it offered a range of experiences. Not quite visions, he had explained, but various other things.

She thought she'd heard some noises. Yes, noises coming from the apartment. "Oh my God!" she said to herself, "they're back!"

The noises were muffled and faint, but they were there, her mind was not toying with her.

She cast a quick glance at the entrance into the lab from the apartment: it was bolted, she knew that already, and they could never figure out how to open the door through the panel.

Unless Eusebio had told them.

But why would they have waited a couple of days instead of entering right away?

To let her come back into the lair.

"Such as telepathy, for example, even at great distances." Rafael's words had intruded in her thoughts. Telepathy, a potential gift of the entheogen.

The noises had not gone away. She took a deep breath and grabbed the frozen mass of the fly agaric, then headed very quietly toward the cloaca's entrance.

Back in the cloaca, she found a conduit perpendicular to the way out, and then another one, both to her left. She must remember this.

Some fifty yards in, there was a widening, paved in volcanic stone. She sat on the floor, cold and damp.

There was no going back now. Her options were almost exhausted.

She broke a chunk of the ice on the stone by her feet and placed it in her mouth.

It melted slowly.

Then she started to chew the mushroom caps.

She repeated this process three, four, five times.

Feeling serene, she turned off the flashlight, laid it down to her right, and waited for the effects in utter silence and darkness.

28

The wind felt comforting on his face. Comforting, too, were the open spaces around him and the fresh air after the traffic fug of Valletta. His great-uncle and the other old men had hardly had time to rejoice; he had asked them immediately for a motorcycle. Yes, he had awoken at last, enfeebled but with perfect recollection of what he had learned and was now speeding toward the evil place.

He took the Mdina road and within ten minutes was skirting the old capital to the north. A surge of emotion made his eyes tear as he thought of the family palace, of his father, and of his difficult but not entirely unloved stepmother. How was she handling events, he wondered. If he came out of this alive, perhaps they could be friends, of a sort, though the depths and heights of his recent experiences were something he could never share with her. Indeed, they made almost every human encounter seem two-dimensional. The exceptions were Sophocles, vacillating between wise old man and credulous fool; Eusebio, dear Eusebio, worth so much more than anybody suspected; and, of course, Monica, the most three-dimensional of them all. He shouted out loud, as the bike buzzed between his knees like a giant hornet: "Monica, Monica, I love you!"

As if in response, two other motorcycles came up behind him. One flashed its headlight, then gave voice to an ear-splitting siren. There was no ignoring the message. They were powerful motorcycles, and their riders knew their way around much better than he did. He drew off the road.

A uniformed policewoman dismounted and walked up to him. "You were speeding and are riding without a helmet," she said in Maltese. "May I see your identification, registration, and insurance document?"

Rafael had his Maltese passport in his pocket. Producing it would have meant turning himself in: he was wanted in Malta in connection with his father's murder. Time to improvise. "I'm afraid I left my ID behind," he said.

"Oh really?" she retorted, staring at his shiny bald head. The other policeman was young and wiry and seemed glued to his motorcycle as if he had been born on it. He would be a terrific chaser, Rafael considered. "Well, what's your name?"

"Hierophant Misraïm."

"What?"

"Hierophant Misraïm. I could spell it for you."

He did while she wrote it down.

"Your registration and insurance."

"I don't have the other documents. The bike isn't mine," he said. That didn't register well.

"Whose is the bike?" she asked.

"Somebody lent it to me."

"Who?"

"A friend's grandson, in Valletta."

"I see." She was clearly doubting his story. "And this friend's grandson lets you go out on it without a helmet or papers?"

"It's my fault. I'm sorry, can I just pay the fine?"

"You'll certainly do that, but you can't go anywhere until you get a helmet."

"What am I supposed to do, then? I'm in a hurry."

"What's the hurry about?"

"I'm going to visit a relative in Mdina."

"Then you can call your relative and say that you'll be late."

"And how am I to get there?" Rafael's voice was beginning to show strain.

"You'll call a motorcycle dealer and ask them to bring a helmet to you here."

"Oh, for God's sake, that will take forever."

"Not my problem. You know the law."

"I don't even know any motorcycle dealers. And I don't have a phone."

"You can call from the police station. Get on your bike, and follow me. Slowly. And don't try any funny business."

The policewoman led him back around the Mdina bypass into Rabat, never exceeding thirty kilometers per hour. He could see her making a call on her phone. It took them a quarter of an hour to reach the police station on Victory Street.

"Leave your bike here, and follow me."

He followed her into the building.

"Wait here."

She left him on a bench, under the eye of a seasoned officer, who sat at his computer, smoking. Twenty minutes later, another officer summoned him to an interview room.

"No helmet, ha? You're, what, in your mid-thirties? Not some teenage joyrider: why do you do such a dumb thing?"

Rafael looked at the officer: his eyebrows were so bushy that they pushed his eyeglasses half way down his nose. "I was in a hurry. The motorbike was lent to me but didn't come with a helmet."

"You're telling me that the owner of this motorbike doesn't wear a helmet himself?"

"I don't know; I don't know him." Rafael's very rare aristocratic blood was boiling; he couldn't help it, but he made a supreme effort to conceal it. At least nobody seemed to recognize him.

"You don't know him, and he lends you an Aprilia RXV 4.5? This doesn't add up. I want to speak to the bike's owner. What's his name?"

"Ambini. It's his grandson's motorcycle."

"I'll check that," said the officer, reaching for the Valletta telephone directory. To Rafael's relief, Ambini was home. But would he have the necessary presence of mind?

"Good afternoon," said the officer. "Am I speaking to Mr. Ambini? I have a young man here, in the police station at Rabat, one . . ." he had trouble pronouncing the name "Hie-ro-phant Misraïm. He was riding a motorcycle without a helmet and speeding. He says the motorcycle belongs to your grandson. Is that correct?"

"This is it," thought Rafael, motionless and looking bored but ready to uncoil and dart away.

"Aha," said the officer. "Is it registered? Is it insured? You wouldn't know, but you think so? That won't do, Mr. Ambini. Well, can I speak to your grandson?"

Good old Ambini, thought Rafael. He had played along. He was safe, for the time being. But his grandson was not home. This was going to take a while. "May I use the toilet, please?" said Rafael.

The officer looked him in the eye. "Yes, you may, but just a moment." He summoned another policeman. "Bring this man a specimen bottle." Then, to Rafael, "You may be under the influence of drugs. Go to the toilet under this officer's supervision and give him a urine specimen."

The officer looked with horrified surprise at the bright orange liquid in the specimen bottle. "What the hell have you been drinking?" he asked.

"Oh, I'm on a carrot diet."

"You, on a diet?"

"I mean, a regimen, to balance the mutual correlation of yin and yang, you know."

The policeman raised his eyebrows incredulously and told him to resume his seat with the interviewing officer.

"We've cleared that up, at least. But still, you shouldn't have left without identification, the proper papers, and a helmet."

"I was in a hurry."

"Yep, and speeding to prove it. On your way to Mdina, but if you were coming from Valletta, why were you on the bypass near Mtarfa?"

"I live in Rome. I don't come here very often, and I get confused by the roads."

"You get confused, do you? Well, we'll see about the cause of your confusion. Wait here."

He was supposed to wait for the lab report on his urine. He knew from bad memories that they'd be looking for heroin, methamphetamines, cocaine, marijuana, and other stuff; certainly not for *Amanita muscaria*. Still, he was wasting time when there was no time to waste, and in the worst possible place, too.

The waiting room was right at the entrance. There was only the seasoned officer in the way, sitting behind a desk. A *corpulent* seasoned officer. Between the surprise and the difference in weight and age, he'd certainly beat him to the door. Once outside, he'd have to leap on the bike, crank it started, and dash off before they could catch him. Should he fail, they'd keep him there indefinitely. But what if the lab report came back with something they didn't like in it? He had no idea if the chemicals to be found in the mushroom were on their bad list, and this was no time to find out. And what if they discovered, after all, that he was the late Sebastian Pinto's son, wanted by the very police? All they had to do was search him, and his passport would be found, bearing that very compromising name, as well as a photo very similar to the ones they had been given to identify him.

The phone rang. As the officer picked up, Rafael was on his feet dashing to the door. He had slammed it by the time he heard the policeman scream.

Where was the bike? Where was it, damn it?

Rafael found himself running to the left and to the right. It had been removed. Where to?

Hoarse calls and insults were coming his way: several policemen had burst out of the station; all were after him.

He saw a fenced-in enclosure and darted toward it. Inside it, he didn't need to look far: the bike was there, among those of the police.

He ran faster than he thought he could till he jumped on and cranked it. But the police, some forty yards behind him, had blocked the only entrance with a car.

"Shit," he thought as he started speeding right in their direction, "I wasn't planning on this! If only I can get enough speed . . ."

He unleashed all the power he had between his knees; in no time, he had reached the police car in a cloud of fumes and dust. "Stop! Stop!" they were screaming.

Keeping the clutch squeezed, he downshifted two gears, while the momentum carried him forward. Then, a few feet away from the front of the police car, he let go of the clutch and simultaneously accelerated heavily. The front wheel lifted up and, without slowing down at all, he climbed on the car's hood, then its top, finally jumping off, clearing the fence with the front wheel, smashing its top down with the rear one, and landing on the outside without losing control.

It all had happened in a flash. The policemen were left behind, staring in amazement.

He quickly reached top speed. Only then did he look back. Two cars were chasing him. But it was rush hour. They were soon entangled in traffic, despite their sirens and flashing lights. But the policemen would certainly radio other units and tell them to stop him. He left the asphalted road with a leap.

This was his turf. No car could follow him here, and no police motorcycle either. During his holidays in Malta as a teenager he had roamed across the island, especially off-road.

He careened toward the Great Fault, uphill, downhill, over rocks, ruts, low bushes, and damp earth, with British entrenchments and towers flying past him. He skirted the precipitous slopes as it started to thunder. As the rain streaked down his face, he felt every cell in his body ragingly alive, the police and their silly antics already forgotten. "Catch me if you can!" he thought.

Thyme and rosemary, the smell of damp earth, and his own exhaust whipped up by the wind assailed his nostrils as, having reached the Victoria Lines, he entered the Tas-Santi region. "Of course!" he thought. "I heard this months ago from little Honoria's mouth. I should have known better."

He was now less than half a mile from Fommir Riħ Bay. He turned off the motor and came to a halt. He hid the motorcycle behind a rock formation and started to walk.

Cautiously now, he walked down, parallel to a watercourse piercing the cliff, swollen with rain. Careful not to slip and to be as inconspicuous as possible, he continued to scramble down the cliff path till he saw that he had the bay to himself. That was no surprise: the weather couldn't have been worse.

His plan was a simple one: enter the cave and ascertain whether what Omniscience had told him corresponded to reality. How could he doubt anything from that source? The police would, though.

So he would venture inside the cave, taking great care not to be spotted by anyone. Once vindicated, he would sneak out, scramble back to the motorcycle, and ride straight to Inspector Soldanis.

29

How long had he been there? Was it two days already? Rafael had no way of knowing. His whole body ached; his hands were tied behind his back, his mouth taped over, as well as his eyes.

He had entered the seaside cave unseen and on his guard, or so he had thought. Several minutes had gone by without his noticing anything unusual, not a sign, nothing stirring. His trepidation had slowly decreased as the cave, sheltered from the elements, provided him with a respite from the storm. Then he thought he spied a shadow to his left side and felt a sharp pain in his back, as if he'd had been kicked. He turned around and was overwhelmed from behind, struck simultaneously on the head, in the stomach, in the ribs. He must have passed out.

He had awakened with the taste of blood in his mouth, short of breath as if he were being choked, his neck in a lot of pain. He couldn't see anything until some sharp voices in a language unknown to him approached. Suddenly, the tape was ripped away from his eyes. When the pain and shock subsided, he squinted and slowly focused on two Asian men in front of him, wielding submachine guns, shouting orders at the top of their lungs. By their gestures he understood that they wanted him to look at something they must have placed in a corner of the cell—a chamber pot.

He now realized why his neck hurt so much and why he was

short of breath: there was a collar around it, hooked to a thick iron chain riveted to the wall.

One of the two men took out a long knife and went up to Rafael, but from behind. Before Rafael had time to scream, he felt his hands come loose.

Their shouting resumed instantly. Again, they were showing something with gestures, this time interspersed with some sardonic bursts of laughter. They wanted him to use the pot.

The collar pulled on his neck as he stretched to reach the pot, then he relieved himself.

As soon as he was done, they tied his hands again and placed tape on his eyes.

For a long time, he was left in there undisturbed. He could hear noises coming from behind the door, and voices, presumably in the same oriental language.

Had it been one day? Two? He had no notion.

Then he heard the door fling open again and felt hands on his body. He wriggled away, but there was nothing he could do to get away. Still, his attempts must have irked the jailers, as one more blow landed on his nose. Then another.

He felt his own blood stream from the nose down to his lips and chin as they searched him. They took all he had in his pockets and left.

Another interminable interval.

What was this? Was this what he had learned? He wanted it not to be so, but he could hardly think of another explanation. These were the Chinese thugs he had been told about. One of them had been his father's murderer.

What a fool he had been, what an unforgivable ass! He was surprised to have enough energy to be angry at himself.

What could he do now? What?

More hours elapsed. He felt the blood from his nose stop trickling from his chin. Then coagulate. Then dry.

The door was opened; the tape from his eyes ripped away. And from his mouth.

He squinted in the neon light and saw a Caucasian man in his fifties, thickset. Two Chinese thugs were beside him, armed. He displayed impressive biceps under his taut, tanned skin. A gold cross and a medal of Our Lady hung over his undershirt.

"Take a piss," he said in Italian with a distinct Sicilian accent, as one of the thugs freed Rafael's hands. He was weak by now, hungry, and, above all, so thirsty he could hardly move his tongue inside his mouth. For a while he did not stir.

"Didn't you hear me?" the Sicilian said and kicked him in the crotch.

Rafael writhed on the floor gasping and thinking, Let me die now! But the Sicilian insisted.

Eventually Rafael managed to get up and relieve himself again.

"Good," the Sicilian said, "we run a clean business here." The three men left.

Though Rafael had never seen this man before, he had been told of him, too, during his Communion.

Was it all true, then? Was it?

This cannot be true, he kept saying to himself. I must have fallen into a reverie, the aftereffects of the entheogen. Yes, this is just another bad trip.

Footsteps approached, closer and closer. Rafael, lying on the floor, squinted.

A few men entered the cell. "Ma," he heard, a new voice, "lo avete conciato per le feste!"

"Scusate, Capo; ci è scappata la mano."

"Salvatore, I disapprove of brutality!" the same smooth voice continued. "Let it not happen again, is that clear? And that goes for you, too."

Salvatore nodded, and so did the thugs.

"Sorry about that," the same new voice continued, in a different tone and addressing Rafael, "but you must understand: nobody likes intruders. I must say, I prefer your Jesus Christ look. Salvatore, untie his hands."

When the Sicilian was done, Commissioner Altieri turned to Rafael and said, "May I help you up?" extending his arm downward.

Perhaps, Rafael wondered, he was already dead. It was conceivable. The mushrooms he had eaten were poisonous; he had experienced bliss, but then agony, and never woken up again. Now he was being haunted in his afterlife by the same specters.

"Can you hear me?" Altieri asked.

Rafael, still on the floor, nodded slowly.

"Sorry about your father; he was an interesting man." He told one of the thugs to bring him a stool, on which he sat.

Rafael fixed his gaze on Commissioner Altieri. He was wearing a light gray suit over a crisp white shirt. His tie was of blue-black silk, thin, impeccably knotted. A little mud spattered his black shoes, and as he spoke, he took out a handkerchief and rubbed it off. Then he said: "Salvatore, please bring me a glass of water."

"Is he doing this on purpose?" wondered Rafael in a flash of lucidity. "He knows I'm dying of thirst."

Altieri began to speak, but Rafael was not registering anymore. He floated in ether, or in limbo, or in purgatory, but was welcoming the increasing distance between his earthly self, contained by his aching body, and his mind, unfettered and free to leave it behind. Monica, Monica! Where was she? What had become of her? Why couldn't he die, already? Altieri kept speaking, soothingly, unhurriedly. Rafael, finding a residue of energy, finally interrupted him. "I know everything," he wheezed in an undertone. These were his first words since he had spoken to the police, back in Rabat.

"What did you say?" asked Altieri, leaning forward.

Rafael did not reply. The Commissioner resumed, "Now, as far as your—

—An ear-splitting howl shook up Altieri, who nearly fell from the stool. Rafael was howling in an outburst of rage and desperation, writhing on the floor like a wounded snake.

Altieri stopped the thugs from intervening and just stared. Rafael, sprawled on the ground, half-choked by the collar and the exertion, looked at him with glazed eyes. And then hissed, barely audibly: "I already know everything."

"What did you say?"

"I already know everything, you bastard!" This time he managed to say it out loud, and Salvatore heard it, too.

Altieri was taken aback. "What exactly do you know?" he asked.

With a supreme effort, Rafael sat up until his back leaned on the wall. He was wheezing loudly.

"Take his collar off," Altieri told Salvatore.

"Now," he continued, "will you tell me what you know?"

The sudden arrival of more oxygen in his brain made Rafael feel inebriated, euphoric. He would tell him, he would shake the bastard out of his hubris, he would make him believe that many more people knew everything, too; he would be leaving a scared, fearful man. That's all he could do, but it was something. He breathed as deeply as he could and said:

"I know that you are the seven-headed dragon, out of the sea, black and scaly and dripping with slime." The words flowed out of him, but Rafael himself hardly heard them. "I can smell your stench as if all the shit and rot of the world were oozing through your skin."

Salvatore was about to cut him short with a punch in the face, but Altieri motioned to him to let him speak.

Rafael was having trouble sitting up but continued, hoarsely: "You can't hide from me. You can't hide your wings, your claws, your tail, your seven heads. You can lash your tail, flap your wings, move your heads everywhere—but you can't scare me. I know what you've done, and I know what you're capable of doing. I saw you before, but . . ."

"But?" Altieri pressed him on.

"I have no pity for you anymore. No. You must die, and I will kill you."

"All right, all right, that's enough. Very well, I shall leave you in the company of *malesuada fames*."

Salvatore stood aside as Altieri left the cell, then helped Rafael on his feet. When he managed to make him stand, unseen by anyone he hit him in the stomach with both strength and precision. Rafael doubled up on himself and fell to the ground, gasping helplessly. Salvatore lingered for a while, relishing the spectacle, then left, locking the door.

Et Metus et malesuada Fames ac turpis Egestas. Virgil's words floated back to Rafael's departing consciousness from some forgotten Latin class. "Fear, Hunger, and Want" were three of the loathsome doorkeepers of Hell. But now that he knew them, they could hold no further terrors for him. There was Salvatore, a blundering Cyclops addicted to violence as the only drug that made him feel alive. There were the Chinese guards, all personality already squeezed out of them by their oppressive regime, now reduced to automata with no desire but for mere existence.

Beyond the horrors of the cavern, he saw with clarity the fear, the hunger, and the want that kept the whole operation going, in a mutual exchange of desperation. But he also saw himself, free from it all, holding his life in his hands, raising it as he had raised the chalice as an accepted and acceptable sacrifice. He was the shaman, the wounded healer, carried by the sacramental entheogen to a state beyond pain, beyond self. He had laid his instruments on the ground and taken up a bowl made from the crown of his own skull. Its edges were wrapped with silver, and it brimmed with a fragrant golden liquid.

Being still incarnate, Rafael was able to stand a little way outside these dreamlike images, and to observe them rationally. He knew exactly what the shaman was about. Taking the sacrament, suitably prepared, was only part of the practice. No artificial preparation can rival the alchemy that takes place in the alembic of the human body, which transmutes the entheogen into something purer and more benign. It no longer carries the side effects of nausea and stomach pains, which he well recalled from his experience in the Ambini Palace. The shaman goes through the gates of hell, for that is his calling, but what he brings back is the means for an easier journey, one that he freely gives to simpler folk.

Rafael opened his eyes. He was still in the cell, the low light bulb still glowing overhead, the long chains like snakes crawling up the wall. The pains all over his body woke up with a start and resumed their assault on his sanity. Thirst was the most urgent of all.

"Enough!" he said to them. He refused to let them spoil his death, the supreme event of his existence. He would go out in a state of bliss, a painless, joyful transition to a better place.

Why are you hesitating, he said to himself? What are you waiting for? What have you got to lose? All dignity was already gone, all inhibitions dissolved in the stark relationship of murderer to murdered. He'd done much worse things in his life: shared the needle with perfect strangers, used unknown pushers, all for the promise of a few hours of comforting numbness. And the entheogen, he knew, did not bring numbness, quite the contrary. It brought union with a reality that was love, light, and the end of uncertainty.

He raised himself slowly, trying not to put pressure on any of his cuts and bruises, and crawled reptile-like across the floor of the cell. He lifted the chamber pot to his lips and drank.

Monica's whole being was concentrated on one question: Where had Rafael gone? Her experience with the kykeon had made her hopeful, as though to dispatch a question on the wings of these altered states would guarantee an answer. But part of her was not playing the game. Her mind ranged around the whole world, trying to answer the question for itself, knocking on the doors of every possibility.

What could Boehme's alchemical emblem, the last one they had seen together before being interrupted by the carabinieri, have possibly suggested to him? Had *that* been the catalyst? She thought back over the sequence of events. How much had he risked to protect her? Everything: his life, up on Trajan's Column; his liberty, making himself an outlaw; and his conscience, for, if she was beginning to understand him, he would never forgive himself when he learned what had happened to Eusebio. A final question arose from the depths of her being: *"What can I do for him?"*

As soon as she formulated those words in her mind, a maelstrom of images swirled around her. She saw Rafael without hair or beard, like a skull. "Goodbye, Monica; goodbye, my love," he whispered. She tried to answer him, but he didn't hear, or wouldn't reply. Instead, she glimpsed an Asiatic face under a baseball cap, saw a medal of the Virgin on a golden chain, and heard a smooth voice speak the word "fames." Sebastian Pinto, too, came fleetingly into sight. More irrefutable than a hard fact, the knowledge came to her then that he had been shot dead in that dingy place; she then saw him lying right beside his dying son.

Rafael? Rafael, dying?

Another voice like a raven croaked out, "Tas-Santi, Tas-Santi!" and then she saw the seaside cliff, as she had seen it in her kykeon vision, though this time it was a place she knew.

As the images flickered by, she desperately tried to catch them, to concentrate on one alone, Rafael's, but it was futile. The tornado had her in its power, and she, too, was being whirled around, her head spinning like a top on her shoulders.

The spinning sensation became faster and faster until it reached some critical speed. As an airplane propeller, once in flight, becomes a static blur, so she became locked in a state of inner vibration, a high-tension paralysis. Incapable of thought, her mind froze.

Then she felt it. Something was touching her body, something tentative and searching. It scraped her face, felt up and down her arms, and squeezed her breasts hard. The spinning sensation still deafened and blinded her, but the lower senses were more than alive. A terrible smell came to her nostrils, and instantly she knew what it was.

The Beast had come out of the sea and was forcing itself on her paralyzed body. The smell of putrefying meat came in waves as it brought one of its seven heads close to hers. Other heads were busy holding down her arms and legs, and one of them was slithering under her shirt, where she could feel its horns gouging deep furrows on her bare skin.

The horror of it had banished all sense of reality, but now, as strong claws started to pull at her jeans, some small voice of reason spoke up inside her. "Being raped by the dragon won't help Rafael."

She opened her mouth to respond, but the dragon clamped its beak to hers, pushing its forked tongue between her teeth. Its scales were grazing her chin, and it was forcing its slimy tail between her legs.

With this final outrage, her will returned, the spell of paralysis broke, and she clamped her teeth together as hard as she could. She felt her assailant tremble and try to tear its tongue free, while the other heads went into spasms, clutching at every part of her body. She bit harder, then without warning her stomach churned, and she vomited, full into its face.

The beast recoiled, and she pushed at it with all her strength. It rolled off her, and as she got to her feet, sight and hearing returned.

Her flashlight—where was it? She found it and turned it on.

In the beam it cast she could see the beast rising from the ground, roaring, but before it reached its full height she aimed a kick at its middle, then another at its head, and a third one at the white blur of its genitals. A bum, an all too human bum, had assaulted her, not the dragon!

Then she ran toward an unfamiliar exit, pausing to vomit once more and terrified that she would meet one of his companions before she could regain the light.

The gray December light could not have been more welcoming to her, as she came out of the cloaca beside the Tiber. The lights were beginning to come on; there were more bums hanging around the riverside, but they took little notice of her. She could still feel the turbine spinning inside her, but now it seemed to give her energy, and she felt an absolute confidence in herself and her own will. She knew that she could act normally on the outside, however tumultuous her inner being. With this certainty she entered a café and headed straight for the toilet.

She had kept her small backpack on when she gave herself over to the entheogen, and it was still with her. She dumped her vomit-spattered shirt and put on a clean one, doing what she could with her appearance, then walked out of the café with the same determined stride. She felt no desire whatever for food or drink, and, above all, no fear of man or beast. On passing a bank automat, she made the maximum withdrawal with her credit cards, then hailed a taxi.

30

In his office at the police headquarters, Inspector Soldanis was assessing the situation. Moscow had issued formal, piqued, and insistent requests to release all its subjects. Lady Pinto was suing everyone: Malta's whole government, the magistrate who had issued the warrant against her, as well as the inspector himself. Joe Dagenham had been found at last, but dead, killed in a hit-and-run car accident somewhere in Essex. There were no witnesses, no clues as to where he was living, and no one anxious to claim the remains. Sebastian's own son and Monica Bettlheim had become fugitives—together? To cap it all, an eyewitness had come forward accusing the archaeologist of having killed a man by shoving him off an ancient column in Rome. When he had read that, Soldanis had burst into laughter.

The temptation to seek early retirement was becoming every day more irresistible. He obviously had lost his touch, or maybe, very early on in his career, he had just gotten lucky a couple of times. Once retired, he could finally go on his honeymoon with Lady Nicotine, in Cuba; why not? He had grown tired of his cigarettes; though lately he smoked from sixty to eighty a day, he derived no pleasure from them. He was ready for a change, and Cuban cigars might well be the answer.

"Inspector Soldanis?" His assistant was on the speakerphone.

He didn't bother to reply.

"Inspector Soldanis?" Varranin repeated; "Are you there?" There was an excited tone in his voice. Was he getting a raise? Soldanis wondered as he laconically replied.

"There's a development in progress," said his assistant. "Are you ready for it?"

"What do you need next, a drum roll?" he thought, but said, "Sure."

"We'll be right up."

"I can't wait," Soldanis added in his mind as he turned off the speakerphone.

A couple of minutes later, Varranin made what must have been his version of a triumphal entrance, escorted by two officers. In between them was a woman in an anorak and jeans, with a small backpack.

"She was picked up at the airport. The Italian authorities realized she had slipped through them by the time the plane was landing in Malta, so they alerted us. Apparently, there was no need to arrest her: the moment she stepped off the plane, she demanded to be taken to you."

"Well done!" said Soldanis, suddenly sitting straight up, and then even standing up to greet the woman. "It's good to see you, Dr. Bettlheim. Please have a seat."

In addition to being surprised, now that he took a good look at her, he was disappointed. She was no longer supremely beautiful; just very beautiful, like a model. And much like a model, she looked famished.

"I hope you don't mind my asking this," Soldanis said, once Monica had sat down across from him, "but have you lost a lot of weight?"

Everyone in the office was taken aback; that wasn't exactly the first question they expected to hear from him. Monica didn't expect it either and said: "I have no idea. . . . I guess so."

"Varranin: get Dr. Bettlheim a Coke and all the junk food we have in our dispenser. Yes, the one in the hallway downstairs. Quick march! You two," pointing to the officers, "out!"

The officers looked at him, baffled. "Yes, yes: leave!" Soldanis repeated.

Monica expected to be assailed, now, by a barrage of questions. Soldanis eyed her from top to toe, but kept quiet. For a few, long moments he said nothing.

A knock on the door was followed by Varranin's return, wielding a tray with two cans of Coke, granola and candy bars, chips and sundry junk.

"Please help yourself, Dr. Bettlheim," Soldanis finally said.

This was becoming ridiculous, and there was no more time to waste.

"Inspector," she said, ignoring his invitation, "Rafael Pinto had nothing to do with his father's murder, nor did I."

"Right!" replied Soldanis, loudly. This promised to be entertaining.

Once more, Monica was taken aback. "You have no trouble believing this?" she dared to ask.

"Me? My opinion doesn't really count. The law, on the other hand, would probably have a great deal of trouble, since both you and Rafael absconded. Didn't you realize it was the worst thing you could do?"

"We couldn't help it. We were trying to save ourselves."

"Really? And who was after you?"

"I don't know yet, not exactly."

"Right." It was time for a cigarette.

"Listen," Monica said, earnestly, "I don't care what you decide to do with me. What I'm here to tell you is that I know where Sebastian was murdered, and I also know that his son, Rafael, is dying," her heart sank as she said this, "is dying as we speak, in the very same place."

"Where would this place be?"

She told him.

Aha, thought Soldanis, that would definitely be within his jurisdiction. "Can you prove what you're saying? These are strong allegations. Do you mind if I tape the rest of our exchange?"

No, she didn't mind, and no, she could not prove anything. Her mind was working furiously, trying to come up with something plausible. Ah! She could tell him about the dogs, how she'd taken them for a walk shortly after Sebastian's death.

"They picked up a scent and led me down to Fommir Riħ Bay. Then I got distracted, and they disappeared. No one's seen them again. I've come to the conclusion that they followed their master's scent into the cave and were killed in it by the same people."

"How fascinating," Soldanis said, "two bloodhounds scenting their master—how could they be wrong?"

"Exactly!"

"Have *you* entered this cave?"

"No."

"Never?"

"Never." A brief pause followed, then Soldanis reprised.

"You said you were distracted—by what?"

"I'd picked up a bottle of Ty Nant. The label had washed off, but the shape's unmistakable. It was Sebastian's favorite mineral water. He'd have it flown in from Wales; it's not imported to Malta. Now, he was religious about recycling; he never tossed anything out of the yacht, ever. So he couldn't have dropped it there. He must have been overpowered, and the bottle must have fallen away from him."

"Also fascinating, but this, too, is circumstantial evidence. You must realize that."

Soldanis was reacting just as she had feared. Feeling desperate, she finally revealed: "I heard from Rafael."

"Yes?" Soldanis was all ears.

"He's in that cave, in terrible shape. If you don't go in there and rescue him, he'll die."

"Excuse me, how have you heard from him? Did he call you on a cell phone?"

"No."

"How did he contact you? By radio?"

"No. I can't explain. Look, Inspector, you have to trust me on this one. Rafael is about to die. The same people who have killed Sebastian are killing his son. The murderers must be in the cave; that's why it'd be no use if I went. I'd have gone straight there, but I'd be captured, too, and killed. I don't care about that, I only care about Rafael, but I'd be no use to him on my own. You've got to go there with your men and rescue him. Please, Inspector, please; I'm begging you." Her voice was broken by sobs.

"Very beautiful, even under duress," thought Soldanis. And not cynically. He felt for her; she was obviously smitten with Rafael. Still, he said: "Listen, I'd like to grant you your wish, but I can't. I can't order a military blitz based on what you've told me. I'd never get the green light. Oh, and there's more. I'm afraid I'm going to have to take you into custody. You're wanted both in Malta and in Italy, remember?"

His words were not registering; she couldn't stop sobbing.

Soldanis put out his cigarette after a last, greedy puff, turned off the tape recorder, and said: "Wait for me here, I'll be right back." He walked out of the room.

Eventually Monica wiped away her tears and looked around her. She was alone in the office.

Some time went by. Soldanis was not back. He'd be right back, he'd said. How long ago? Had it been ten minutes? Fifteen?

She heard footsteps behind the door. They grew louder, louder yet, then fainter.

Monica got up and went over to the door, just barely opening it. She could see a hallway with no one in it. She closed the door and went back to the desk. Hesitating for a moment, she opened her backpack, filled it with the cans of Coke and junk food, and headed for the door.

31

"Here, drop me off here." The taxi stopped, and Monica paid the fare and got out, breathing in the salt air under the overcast December sky. It seemed to have taken forever to get to Tas-Santi, but her watch said only forty-five minutes. Sneaking out from the police headquarters had been unexpectedly easy, and here she was, above Fommir Rih Bay, scrambling down the cliff.

She still had no plan and couldn't have had one all by herself. She might have tried to sneak into the cave undetected, just to see with her own eyes what she already knew, at least in part, and then run back to Soldanis. But that had never been an option, and in fact she hadn't asked the taxi driver to wait for her. Not only because she doubted very much that "they" could be so easily fooled, but also and above all because she wanted to be reunited with Rafael. Nothing else mattered any longer. Time was unforgiving in its passing, and there wasn't any more left to waste.

Was Rafael still alive? Would she make it in time at least to comfort him, if all hope was lost?

For the first time she entered the cave, unhesitatingly.

It was dark inside; her footsteps echoed off its walls as she walked along the perimeter of the small inner lagoon, connected to the sea. Her feet splashed in the water from time to time; the noise she made this way, amplified and reverberated, was the very opposite of stealth. She didn't care.

Once she was well inside, she stopped, looked up, and yelled: "Come and get me, you assholes! You've been after me all along; here I am, now. Come and get me, do you hear?"

Nothing stirred but the wavelets in the lagoon, lapping gently against the limestone walls.

What was this? she asked herself. Had she just imagined everything? What she had learned from the entheogens, was that merely autosuggestion?

She collapsed to the ground, defeated and desolate.

How long she stayed there, her trainers sodden with the cold salt water, she didn't know.

Then she felt something behind her; yes, hands, tying up her own. She offered no resistance. On the contrary, she just made it in time to say, "Welcome, welcome!" before her mouth was taped over, and then her eyes.

With a man grabbing her by the elbow on either side of her, and one pressing what must be a gun on the nape of her neck, she was made to scramble over damp, uneven ground; then her head was pressed down, as if she were entering a low door. She was walked uphill for another minute, till she no longer heard the sound of the water. When they reached level ground, she heard a few phrases being shouted in a language she didn't know. Then she was pushed in what she thought was a straight line. She suddenly no longer felt the pressure from the gun in her nape.

"Is this it?" she wondered. "Are they going to shoot me right now?" She cringed. Her last thought was for Rafael.

Her hands were freed.

Her heart was racing madly as she heard a door, presumably, creak right in front of her. She was shoved in roughly, and the door slammed behind her. She heard it being locked.

As soon as she felt that she was alone, she ripped the tape away from her mouth and eyes. A dim light bulb provided enough light for her eyes to search frantically for . . . was that Rafael?

She rushed over and knelt down by him. What had they done to him? He was bald, skeletal, his face smeared in caked-up blood.

She leaned down and embraced him. There was a faint heartbeat.

What could she do now to revive him? How long had he been in there? She had no idea, but however long, the first thing one would die of would be dehydration.

She could see no water in the cell. There was nothing in it but long, thick chains hanging from all the walls, each with a collar at the end, and an empty chamber pot.

She frantically emptied her backpack on the floor. She snapped one of the Coke cans open, froth wetting her fingers. With one hand she managed to hold Rafael's mouth open; with the other, she poured the liquid inside it, very slowly, tiny sip by tiny sip, with pauses in between.

Please come back to me, she thought, more urgently than any scream.

She managed to pour the whole canful into his mouth. Then she tried to revive him.

Nothing, he wouldn't come to. But he kept breathing.

Don't lose it now, she said to herself, don't lose it. She could not, would not give in to panic and despair. She reached for the second can and started over.

Little by little, she managed to pour this down, too. How long had it taken her? Maybe an hour? Her watch told her more than two.

She wetted a handkerchief with her saliva and started to clean his face, wiping away the dried blood. It took her mind back a few weeks, after he had just saved her, in Rome. "Rafael, Rafael . . ."

His eyelids twitched.

She leaned down and lightly kissed his eyes. They snapped open but stared in terror. Sensing that he was about to scream, she covered his mouth with her hand and said, in an undertone: "It's all right, it's all right. It's me, Monica."

He relaxed. With an effort, he lifted his arms slowly and embraced her.

Then he closed his eyes again. She would let him sleep. He must recover. But she had saved him!

Saved him?

They were both prisoners of murderers. What chances did they have? She refused to answer the question.

For another hour or so, she did nothing, unable even to think, but somewhat content to be with Rafael and hold his hand while he slept.

He was still asleep when she heard footsteps approach. The door was flung open before she could think of what best to do, or say.

"Welcome, Dr. Bettlheim," said Altieri, looking very urbane in an impeccable blue suit. "It's wonderful to see you again—and at last. I see they haven't mistreated you. Good."

"You're Commissioner Altieri, aren't you? Are you here to rescue us?" she was finally able to articulate.

"Rescue you?" Altieri looked amused. Monica's heart sank.

"I take it you don't know," he said, looking over her shoulder. "Of course, he couldn't tell you much, could he?"

Monica kept quiet.

"How true to form: always good at finding things, never at connecting the dots." Altieri looked at his wristwatch, then at Monica. "Very well, I'll give you a few minutes of my time. Follow me."

"No, I won't leave Rafael behind," she snapped.

"Why? He won't go anywhere. But suit yourself. Goodbye."

She looked at Rafael, then at Altieri. Somehow, she needed to know. "All right, all right, I'm coming."

Altieri matter-of-factly led her out of the cell, with one of the Chinese guards close behind.

Passing through a short passage, its ceiling supported by crooked beams, they emerged in an irregular cavern, the size of a church. The lighting was garish and patchy, coming from arc lamps fixed to the walls at head height. They cast long shadows on the concrete floor from the piles of wooden crates, steel drums, plastic buckets, and other paraphernalia. Here and there were sprawling heaps of clothes and bedding. The dark yellow walls were eroded into fantastic shapes, as if carved from bone. Clefts and hollows opened in every direction onto dimly lit passages. Stocky Asians, dressed like Monica's guard in khaki, were bustling about, loading some things onto dollies and throwing others into a gaping chasm. There was an unpleasant smell in the air, of exhaust fumes, disinfectant, and mold.

Altieri took up his stance in the center. "I have the British to thank for this facility. You know that Malta is riddled like a Gruyère cheese with natural caves. During the World War the British tidied them up, enlarged them, and put in modern conveniences—quite modern, for the 1940s. They designed this bunker for military storage and small-scale repairs.

"I wish I could show you my project in full swing, but since Malta joined the European Union, it's become harder and harder to carry on. Then something else happened, and circumstances forced me to shut down this facility. Your late sponsor, Cavalier Pinto. It was at the dinner party in the palace in Mdina; he announced his new project—remember?—you were there. He mentioned that both he and you had been led by his dogs, on separate occasions, to a place along the Victoria Lines, near Fommir Riħ Bay—right here, in other words. That was bad enough. But it got worse.

"He added that here, beneath the surface, there was an 'archaeological treasure trove'; these were his exact words. The authorities had closed off the place both to the public and to researchers. He promised to fund the building of the new hospital if the government lifted the ban and allowed him to start digging here. And the prime minister was eager to say yes.

"This precipitated events. I had to do something right away while I began dismantling in a hurry. So I staged the cannibalistic shipwreck in Lampedusa. Someone else took care of the nasty details, of course. I was told they had some trouble getting the bites right."

Monica gasped.

"It worked, by diverting attention from Malta. The naval blockade was put in force, the Rome Conference started, and I gained the time I needed. As for Cavalier Pinto, I didn't wish to get rid of him. On the contrary: the last thing I wanted was an investigation on Maltese soil following his murder. But he came wandering around here, by the cave. Worse yet: he entered it. He was overpowered as you were and shot right in here. Then at night he was taken to Gozo and placed inside his hunting lodge, and my men easily furnished the police and the press with some clues against the skinheads."

Monica was speechless, hope ebbing fast.

"And then there was that other matter," Altieri continued: "you."

"After Pinto's death, you yourself came here. My guards alerted me: they were ready to make you vanish like the dogs, but I said no. Another investigation in Malta would have been disastrous, and I needed time. Still, there remained a lingering fear that you might come to the right conclusions. A clever Dottoressa was walking away with too many ideas in her head.

"And on top of that, Pinto's widow might come up with the donation, the prime minister would remove the ban, and before we knew it, you'd be digging right above our cave!

"You had to be eliminated, but away from Malta."

"My poor Rafael," thought Monica, tears in her eyes. "I would have been safe if I had stayed right here in Malta."

"Falling off Trajan's Column would have been such a fitting way out for an archaeologist," Altieri continued. "But Rafael interfered and made it all more complicated."

Monica no longer knew what to think or fear; she asked: "What is this all about? What the hell do you *do* here?"

"You must imagine yourself as an illegal immigrant," Altieri said as he motioned her to follow him, "tired, hungry, and scared, arriving by night at Fommir Riħ Bay. Your guide leads you up the beach to the cave, the same way you came in. But he doesn't lead you to the central cavern; in fact, you never suspect its existence. No, the guide brings you straight into one of these rooms." He opened a door. "More legacy from the British: a shelter on the left for men, one on the right for women and children, where you can use toilet facilities, eat a meal, and recover from your voyage."

They were largish spaces, dug out of sheer rock. At capacity, up to forty people could fit in either room, crammed like sardines into ancient iron bunks. Monica could see the walls decorated with travel posters of European cities.

"Of course," Altieri continued, "all these courtesies are unnecessary, but they do make for a quieter life for the guards.

"After you've rested, you're summoned, one by one, for immigration processing, which you believe is the magic ticket to a new life. Once inside Europe, you can earn much more money than in your homeland, or if you dislike work, you can prey on the local population." He shut the door and opened the remaining one in the same corridor. It looked like a hard-up doctor's waiting room, with anatomical posters, a sink, a chair, and a wheeled stretcher.

"Your guide brings you in here, where my medical assistants sit you down and give you a brief, reassuring examination. One taps your chest, looks inside your mouth, and takes your temperature, pressure, and so on. Then the other one gives you an injection, an "inoculation shot," or so you're told if you try to resist. In no more than five seconds, you're out cold.

"They wheel you out, and you never see the rest of my facility. It's surprising how little equipment a surgery needs when the patient's recovery is not a factor. They never wake up, of course. Within a few minutes, all the useful organs have been harvested and packed in refrigerated containers.

"I don't need to tell you of the desperate need for replacement organs. People are dying every day for want of these forbidden fruits—a heart, liver, pancreas, kidney, or lung—and many of them are children."

"These forbidden fruits . . ." repeated Monica as if in a nightmare.

"Precisely, forbidden fruits. Corneas," Altieri expanded, "are the simplest replacements: the instant gift of sight. Leukemia sufferers need bone marrow. And kidneys, liver, heart . . . there's surprisingly little left of a healthy body, and it's disposed of hygienically down one of those oubliettes." He paused at an alcove, where the Chinese guards had just opened the cover of a crevasse.

"There's my version of Lethe, the waters of oblivion. Weighted down with sinkers, it falls into a cave below sea level, so it can't be washed up on the shore. The fish deal with it, along with the effluent from the toilets," he smiled, "and that has a helpful side effect of attracting sharks that keep swimmers from the bay. I saw to it that a warning sign be placed there."

Monica was beyond shock. On the flight to Malta, she had been rehearsing in her mind all the possible evils that the dragon might symbolize. She had thought of the drug trade, but that seemed too predictable; of child prostitution and other satisfactions for wealthy perverts; of trade in arms, biological weapons, and nuclear material.

She thought also of the scafisti and the trade in human beings: she had not forgotten the cries in the night when they found the golden pomegranate. But somehow her imagination had not stretched to this.

"Where do the organs end up, you may wonder. Not in the official pipeline, to be sure. The organ transplant racket is designed by governments and the medical profession to keep the supply low and the demand high. That's where I come in: there are well-to-do patients all over the world who don't need to join a waiting list: Europeans, North and South Americans, the new Russians, and so on. They know where to go; we have a few clinics here and there in Eastern Europe, and they ask no questions. The facilities for implant at the other end are first-rate, which is what counts, together with speed. I can have organs flown out by private plane within hours."

Monica was speechless, her glazed eyes staring in horror. She had stopped, and Altieri was not pressuring her to keep walking.

"Whom do I get to do this? The surgeons, guards, and technicians are all mainland Chinese. A connection with one of the Triads—Chinese mafia—supplies them, and they come and go in the same way as the immigrants, by boat. They're efficient workers and very focused: no roaming around Malta and getting drunk for them. They know that if they make one false step, they'll become donors themselves. After a couple of years, the Triad sends them back home with a large wad of dollars. The scafisti, mainly Sicilian, all mafiosi, provide me with the raw material. And that's all: just like the Ouroboros."

He ignored the horror in Monica's blank gaze.

"You don't know what an Ouroboros is? Your dear Rafael could tell you himself, if he were . . . up to it.

"It's the serpent that holds its tail in its teeth. A symbol of eternal renewal through transmutation. Taking base matter in the nigredo, the black stage, and bringing it to a nobler state. Extracting the Elixir of Life." He met her eyes, unflinching. "Don't you see it yet? Do I have to explain it to a brain like yours?"

Monica said nothing. Altieri turned away and sighed.

"Evidently I do. Forget about your dilettante lover: you're in the presence of the only real alchemist alive, because *I* have actually succeeded in transmuting matter! Out of base lead, so to speak, I have made gold! Oh, I know what you're thinking. Always money on the brain. Yes, yes, I've made an immense personal fortune, but that's nothing but a by-product. The work is its own reward, because for every life that is sacrificed, many others are saved from certain death."

Monica found words at last: "You call it sacrificing?"

"Your God Jehovah knows all about that, doesn't he? The sacrifice of lower beings and lower races for the sake of higher and chosen ones? Didn't he create the whole system, whereby every creature preys on some other form of life? I accept it, though I call it nature. But back to alchemy. The fact that the donors are Negroes makes perfect sense, you see. From the nigredo, the prime matter is transmuted into the albedo, into whiteness."

"I'm not hearing this, I'm not: it's worse than the Nazis."

"Oh, that old jibe!" Altieri exclaimed. "What did the Nazis create? Nothing but chaos and misery for Europe. I create joy! In the premoral period of mankind, actions were judged by their consequences; sacrificing the life of an undesirable to save the lives of five or more people would have been judged favorably.

"All around the world there are thousands of transplant recipients who *bless* me every day they wake up alive. They don't know my name; they'll never know who they really have to thank for their new lease on life. But it doesn't matter. All that love and veneration touches me, in some mysterious way, and do you know what? It keeps me younger. I've given them the Elixir of Life, and it comes full circle: they're giving it back to me! I feel that I've discovered the secret of longevity."

"That's simply the most insane thing I've ever heard. You won't get away with it. Whatever you do to Rafael and me."

"It's not something one 'gets away with,' like a trespasser not getting caught," said Altieri with a pointed look at Monica. "Are you underestimating me? I've said nothing about my political career, but believe me, in my position I am literally above the law. And morally, of course, I am beyond good and evil.

"Enough! I thought you were an intelligent woman, but your reactions are petty and provincial. Guard, tie her hands and lock her up. Farewell, Antigone."

As Monica was being taken back to the cell, Altieri returned to the control room, now emptied of almost all its equipment and furniture. His admiration for his own ingenuity was fading, and an angrier mood was replacing it. Over the past month he had been obliged to wind down his operation in Malta, all because of Sebastian Pinto, a man with a sixth sense for trouble. The immigrant flow was blockaded, and Malta had become a dangerous place. The evidence had to be removed, and while the cave entrance had been ideal for working purposes, it did not make for speedy evacuation. Everything had to be done by night, and the December storms were interfering with motorboat access. Such was the case at present, as he had just read in a text message from Salvatore: he should have been going to back to Strasbourg but instead would have to rough it for the night here.

32

Inside the cell, Rafael was still sleeping. Monica squatted down on the floor beside him, then managed to sit, stretching her legs.

"Let me untie you," he whispered.

A sudden rush of joy went straight to her heart: he was awake and coherent.

He slowly sat up, and as he worked on the knots, he said, still sotto voce and somewhat haltingly, "I feel better . . . much better. Hang in there; I think I've got it."

It took a while, but finally her hands were free. They kissed. Joy overwhelmed them as they lingered, embracing each other, oblivious for a moment of their predicament. Still in an undertone, Rafael added, "I've eaten all the junk food you've brought. It's saved my life."

She began to tell him what Altieri had revealed, but he knew it already. He slowly explained how, and what he had done since he had dropped out of her life in Rome. He didn't enjoy explaining it, because it was his rash decision, taken on a whim after seeing Boehme's emblem, that had gotten them both into this. Also, he realized that he was having trouble focusing on his own words.

He's still dehydrated, Monica thought. She placed her hand on his forehead and realized that he was feverish.

For all his efforts, Rafael was lapsing again into a semi-unconscious state. It was the last thing he wanted, but he couldn't help it. Soon his eyes were closed, but his mind's eye, alert, descried in the distance the arrival of the black-winged daemons, the Oneroi.

• • •

Loud noises filled the cave. Very loud noises. Shots? First single ones, then many short bursts of what sounded like automatic fire. Monica was up immediately, listening at the door.

"My God, Rafael, what's going on?"

Rafael barely opened his eyes but did not stir. "The end of the world," he said dreamily. "But it doesn't matter to us."

"Come on, Rafael, it *does* matter. It means someone's come to the cave. There'd be no point in shooting otherwise."

"Do you think they'll shoot us?" Rafael seemed past caring, but Monica cared for the two of them.

"No, I don't. They could have done that already." Did she really believe that? Or was it merely wishful thinking? She thought it through, aloud: "They're clearing out of here, and they don't want to leave any evidence, least of all us, dead or alive."

"They could have dropped us down the oubliette," said Rafael, sitting up with great effort.

"They could," said Monica with a shudder. "But maybe . . . maybe as soon as Altieri knew that you had some sort of information, he feared a raid, and they've kept us as their last bargaining chip. As hostages, I mean."

"So this is a raid?" He barely had enough breath to speak.

"I don't know, Rafael, I don't know, but it sure sounds like it."

No, it didn't. All shooting had stopped already. They could hear no more noises, only a brooding silence.

Rafael lay down again. "There's . . . there's nothing we can do."

"Please, Rafael, please: you can't give up now; don't! You—"

He had grabbed her hand and was smiling at her.

"Don't go in, you stupid jocks!" Soldanis shouted above the slash of the waves. "You'll get shot! Come around the corner, here."

The young soldiers reluctantly turned back from the crooked passage and slouched against the cave walls, cradling their Beretta machine pistols against their flak jackets. After the sound of firing from within, there had been a long silence and no sign of their two colleagues who had spearheaded the raid.

Once inside the cave, finding the entrance had been relatively easy: some of Soldanis's men had located recent footprints up a twisting path, hidden from view by stalagmites and rock formations. It had led to a small entrance, no larger than a window. While Soldanis was trying to come up with a strategy to surmount this bottleneck, two soldiers had taken it upon themselves to sneak in.

Anyway, Soldanis considered, Dr. Bettlheim's hunch was not unfounded. Something very wrong was taking place on the other side of the entrance. A metallic scraping noise interrupted the flow of his thoughts.

"No shit!" the sergeant in charge of the platoon said and then turned to Soldanis with a look between the annoyed and the reproachful.

A steel door had slid into place, blocking the entrance.

"Now what?"

Soldanis turned to the sergeant, a gangling youth scarcely out of his twenties, demanding a solution. "What do you think?" the Inspector retorted, "we're gonna have to find another way in. Don't send any more men in until I call you. Keep this entrance plugged. If anyone tries to come out, fire some blanks. If that doesn't keep them back, you can pick them off one by one. Short bursts. Stop 'em, don't kill 'em, if you can. I want them more or less alive."

"What if it's hundreds of them, sir?" asked the sergeant. "Whoever fired in there is a good shot; flak jackets and helmets didn't help: they must be going for the head shot."

"Aiming at the face? Hundreds of them?" wondered Soldanis,

disconcerted. This was the AFM's Quick Reaction Force, trained for much larger theatres of operation than a police inspector was. "If it's hundreds of them, then hold them back whichever way you can."

The sergeant smirked, and Soldanis chose to ignore that. "Now," he continued "let's have five men come with me to look for another entrance."

The predawn rain was pelting down as they emerged from the shelter of the cave and started to clamber up the cliff path, with their flashlights as the only source of light.

The path was more than slippery: the watercourses, dry for most of the year, had not only come to life, swollen, but turned into veritable waterfalls. The soldiers had coped with them on the way down, but on the way up, encumbered by their weapons, packs, and flashlights, they were making the climb difficult and slow.

"What are we looking for?" asked one of the men.

"Wait," said Soldanis, pointing to the receiver in his left ear.

He listened a while, then spoke into the microphone: "We entered through the cave following latest intel. We didn't even know; it wasn't on the records of wartime bunkers, not the ones the police have. Call me back if you find any record of a bunker here, with another entrance to it."

After a long quarter of an hour, the AFM control center at Hal-Far called back. They had found the record of a British bunker. According to their intelligence, it didn't extend all the way to the cave below. "Cut to the chase, will you?" shouted Soldanis, a river of rain cascading off his felt hat.

There was just one original entrance.

"Where?"

Somewhere turning off the Tas-Santi road, there was a descending path to a blocked-up entrance, overgrown now. "Is that the best you can do? This place is a wilderness," said Soldanis. In reply,

Central Command asked to speak to one of the soldiers. Exact coordinates were relayed to him, and a GPS taken out of a bag. The beams of their flashlights revealed the rough path sloping down to the old entrance. Shortly after, they confirmed that it had been blocked.

"No," said Soldanis, back in communication with Central Command, "it's not a door. It's a wall of concrete blocks. Tell me all you can about this bunker, quick!"

Soldanis listened for a few, intense minutes, then said: "All right, listen carefully. We have no time to lose. We already have two men down; the people inside are armed; machine guns and deadly aim; no idea how many they are, could be a small army, for all we know. If the bunker's been extended all the way to the cave by the sea, there's certainly enough space inside.

"As for this entrance, we must assume it's been blocked with reinforced concrete and then some. We've no time to chip away at it. We need the engineers. Send them in at once."

The answer aggravated Soldanis.

"So, what if it's the Third Regiment? Call the Engineer Squadron, and tell them to come here at once, do you hear? At once! Hey, hey, I'm not done: I need extra ammo for my men: blank cartridges, pay attention, I repeat: blank cartridges, thousands of them. And also, earplugs. Yes, earplugs. How many? A hundred of them. Is that clear? Repeat my orders." They were repeated, with no mistakes. "Good," said Soldanis, "get on with it. Over and out."

The soldiers gave him a look of both bafflement and commiseration. What the hell was a cop doing with them, and giving them orders, to boot? Blank cartridges? Had he gone mad?

Inside the cavern, Altieri had quickly appraised the situation. The two intruders shot dead were wearing uniforms. It looked like a special force, presumably from the army. Malta's? He wasn't sure, but this was big trouble. He shouted a few quick orders to the guards and the technicians too: armed to the teeth and with boxes of ammo standing by, they were to keep their firearms aimed at the entrance and fire as soon as anybody attempted to get in. He went back to the control room and got in touch with Agrigento, in Sicily, by radio.

Altieri wanted an emergency pickup, with a blitz force to take care of the soldiers who were presumably besieging the bunker.

"Capo, the sea's too stormy," Salvatore replied.

"Nonsense, you must cross over at once. Salvatore, do you hear?"

"Yes, Capo."

"I said, cross over; don't waste any more time. Understood?"

"All right, all right, we are going to try."

"You do that, right away!"

Altieri was exasperated. He could have sent for a helicopter, but how could it land near the cave unseen? He could only wait out the storm, or hope for his men to manage to go right through it, arrive safely, and take care of the intruders and his escape.

He cursed the American woman, then went to the small armory, took out an HK submachine gun, and walked to the generator room.

The first explosion was almost deafening. Shortly after, all the flashlights were pointing at the entrance as the smoke slowly cleared, whipped away by the storm.

It was still obstructed, and not only by debris: evidently it had been blocked with reinforced concrete for a depth of many feet.

The engineers went to work again. In the meantime, Soldanis repeated his plan to the soldiers. More had come up from down below, and now he could count on the eighteen men still at the cave entrance, all wearing earplugs, as were the thirty who had joined him up above. Some of these had been made to recharge their automatic rifles with blanks. This was a counterintuitive decision that didn't sit at all well with the soldiers, particularly with the ones who were being effectively disarmed, save for their handguns. But Soldanis reassured them: they must trust his plan.

Once more the engineers warned everybody to take cover. Soldanis gave the order.

The second explosion, a much more powerful blast, lit up the sky.

On the inside, all the guards but one crossed the floor to meet the new threat, aiming their AK-47s at the disused ramp. Their ears were buzzing from the noise, echoed and amplified by the cavern.

There was a long pause. Altieri and Monica and Rafael, locked away in their respective rooms, were suffering the torments of hell, but for opposite reasons.

Roaring out of the smoke came a military jeep with its lights blazing, its engine whining. The guards jumped aside as the jeep traversed the main cave, splintered a pile of packing-cases, and crashed into the opposite wall. They riddled it with bullets before they realized that no one was in it. In that moment of confusion, a dozen soldiers in full body armor ran down the slope, firing with machine guns.

The noise in that enclosed space was intolerable. The guards tried to return fire, but the assault on their ears was driving them mad. Certain that the machine gun fire was filling the cave with a hail of ricocheting bullets, they ducked behind fuel drums and into alcoves, emerging to loose a quick burst more or less at random.

The moment the jeep had come in from the top, another blast had shaken the cavern, at its bottom: the steel door had been blown away, and the soldiers left down below had trickled up through the narrow defile. The one man left to guard it, one of the two technicians, had been distracted and deafened, too; trying to overcome the pain in his ears and a whirling sensation, he wheeled around and was easily taken out with a clean shot, his head exploding in a red haze.

Two guards were sheltering behind the crashed jeep, near the passage to the sea. In the general pandemonium, they had not realized that the blast behind them had opened the cavern's lower entrance and were unaware that it was now invaded from both ends. As one of them cautiously peeked over the vehicle, the sergeant shot them both in the back and smiled.

The other soldiers with live ammunition had no mercy. They couldn't afford it: there was no knowing how many more enemies this labyrinth might conceal. From opposite ends of the cavern, they took deliberate, single shots, to prevent bullets from ricocheting and hitting their own men, or the ever-present menace of the fuel drums.

Their companions, meanwhile, were discharging volley after volley of blanks. The resulting reverberated, amplified racket was literally earsplitting. Inside their cell, Rafael and Monica kept their hands pressed to their ears. The guards had no such luck. As they tried to return fire, they were visibly becoming disoriented, their ears ringing with that one persistent tone of the suddenly deafened, each one isolated, surrounded by marksmen trying to kill him. Why weren't *they* going deaf? Why?

One by one, the guards were taken out with surgical precision.

But at Soldanis's urging, the firing went on. If there were more guards hiding in that maze of alcoves, tunnels, and recesses, deafening them was the best strategy before going in after them.

Even with ear protection, the racket was beyond belief.

Eventually, he ordered his men to hold their fire.

The cavern was enveloped in smoke, pervaded by the acrid smell of gunpowder, and by a silence so deep it seemed unreal.

Several bodies lay on the ground. Still, the soldiers regrouped, sure that their work had only begun.

Altieri, seeing the master switch in his soundproofed refuge and hearing the deathly hush, considered for a moment shutting down the electrical supply. But that would have left him, too, in total darkness. Was this it, he wondered: to be trapped inside his own lair?

One guard was still alive, hiding in the passage that led to Monica and Rafael's cell. His head was spinning, his ears bleeding, his mind a turmoil of thoughts of murder, hostage taking, and escape from the noise. The decision came naturally: murder was easiest.

Unseen and wielding his machine gun, he unlocked the door of the cell and rushed in with a nasal shriek.

Something that jerked up before his feet tripped him.

Another chain, swung by Monica, hit him in the back of the neck.

He plunged forward, hitting his head on the stone floor and dropping his gun.

Monica looked cautiously around the door.

Altieri too was peering cautiously, having opened the door of the generator room just enough to glimpse the surroundings. The cave was full of soldiers, momentarily frozen, but alert for a surprise attack. All his men were down. The situation, considered coolly, was bleak.

Suddenly he stepped out of the room, his hands up. "Who's in charge here?" he said in a stentorian voice.

Still in her cell, Monica cringed as she heard this, while all the soldiers trained their weapons on him, awaiting orders. The incongruity stunned them. Who was this polished gentleman in a dark suit, appearing out of the blue and addressing them in an imperious tone? Some were beginning to wonder if they hadn't seen him somewhere before.

Soldanis was not wondering: he had recognized Commissioner Altieri from seeing him on TV often lately. The inspector stood some thirty yards away, in the center of the main space.

"Hold your fire!" he said to the soldiers, and then, looking at Altieri: "*I* am in charge, Commissioner."

Delighted to have been recognized, Altieri asked: "And you are with the Armed Forces of Malta?"

"Just this once," Soldanis replied.

"Thank God! Thank you, gentlemen; thank you for saving us. This is the end of a nightmare. There are two more prisoners, in that cell." Years of public speaking made him sound at ease in front of any audience, even this one, aiming rifles at him.

Soldanis gestured to a few soldiers to search the cell. "Careful, now; watch out!" he added.

As she heard the soldiers approach, Monica and Rafael stepped out. All the soldiers in the room stiffened at once. "Hands up!" yelled the sergeant, "hands up, *now*! And drop your weapon!"

"It's all right, it's all right!" shouted Soldanis. "I know this woman; she's Dr. Bettlheim; she's *not* an enemy." The inspector hadn't recognized Rafael.

The soldiers held their fire but kept their weapons trained on her. She had walked up briskly to Commissioner Altieri and, wielding the machine gun she had taken from the guard in the cell, was pushing him backward. Rafael was trailing behind them, unsteady on his feet.

"Inspector!" Altieri said, "Inspector: have this woman stopped! This is an outrage!"

As Soldanis and the sergeant shouted at each other, Altieri whispered to Monica, so that only she and Rafael could hear: "We were *all* prisoners; play along and you'll be fine; I'll forget our differences, I promise."

Soldanis and the sergeant were still barking at each other, the latter gnashing his teeth, or at least so it seemed to the inspector. They had distinctly different views on how to handle the situation.

"Think, woman," Altieri continued in an undertone as Monica kept forcing him to walk backward, her gun leveled at his stomach. "Just think: it's your word against mine. They'll never believe you, or him," he added, looking over her shoulder at Rafael. Slowly but surely, she was pushing him toward—

"God damn it!" bellowed Altieri. "Somebody stop this woman once and for all!"

Soldanis realized that this was going too far. "Dr. Bettlheim, put down your weapon!"

She did not.

The soldiers' fingers were wrapped around the trigger, her head and chest lined up as targets.

"Drop your weapon now!"

There was a tinge of desperation in Soldanis's voice. She perceived it, and it was as if it made her snap out of a trance. Slowly she lowered the machine gun.

"Drop your weapon," yelled the sergeant, "drop it now!"

She took a long look at Altieri. He returned it, without flinching. Finally, she laid the gun on the floor.

"Kick it away from you," the sergeant added, "now!"

Frustrated and enraged, she kicked it so strongly that it went scraping along the floor.

"Well done, gentlemen!" said Altieri, breathing with relief. "Now, I have important meetings to attend in Brussels and Strasbourg. Please take me to the airport at once. You can interview me as we go along. I'm afraid I'm pressed for time."

"Don't you move!" said Rafael.

While Monica had picked up the guard's gun, he had taken his knife and was now holding its point to Altieri's chest. Two guards moved in on him, but Soldanis motioned them to wait.

"Remember what I told you, you seven-headed beast out of the sea; you bag of pus and feces under your smooth skin?" said Rafael, as he moved forward a pace.

Altieri moved backward as Rafael went on, in fevered tones: "You can't hide from me. You can lash your tail, flap your wings, move your heads everywhere—but you can't scare me!"

He took another pace.

"We've cut off one of your heads," he continued, "but the others are still spouting lies. You're a mass murderer. It's our word against yours, right? And ours is the truth, and it shall prevail. You had my father killed, did you not?"

Altieri took another pace backward. "Inspector, this man is raving. Please disarm him."

"I won't hurt you, beast, but you must die." said Rafael, gently pushing Altieri further toward the alcove, where the oubliette gaped open. "You're just going back into the sea from which you came. The corpses of your victims are waiting for you down there."

Altieri suddenly noticed where he was, turning around in terror. "Inspector, don't let Pinto kill me!"

"But of course!" thought Soldanis, "This is Rafael Pinto! What the hell happened to him?"

Rafael now had the knife touching Altieri's throat. He made as if to jab, and Altieri staggered to within a foot of the brim.

"No, no! Help, soldiers, stop him!"

The sergeant's right index finger twitched. If it was coming to this, he himself would shoot.

Soldanis took a deep breath and came up to Rafael, thus making a clean shot impossible.

While all eyes were fixed on them, Monica quietly stepped aside.

Slowly, gently, Soldanis laid a hand on Rafael's knife arm.

Rafael resisted. Beads of sweat stood on Altieri's forehead, and his heart was racing.

Monica distanced herself farther from the scene.

Rafael's strength was fading rapidly. He lowered the arm at last. Soldanis took the knife away from his hand and quickly handed it over to one of the soldiers. He then turned to Altieri, who was trembling.

"So, Commissioner: you were a prisoner, too? I wonder why anyone would imprison you, of all people, and here, of all places?"

"I wish I knew myself," said Altieri, edging away from the hole.

"You do know yourself," said Rafael, from the depths of his delirium. "You know your own foulness and your unspeakable cruelty. You say it's your word against mine, and I say that your name is Antichrist, the father of lies."

Altieri looked at him with scorn. "Stop this babbling, will you? Inspector, this is outrageous: there is absolutely no evidence to connect me with whatever's been going on here. On the contrary: I was abducted, blindfolded, and taken here a prisoner."

"No evidence?" came Monica's voice. She had returned to the cell and was now driving the wobbling guard with his own sidearm. His eyes were wide with terror, and blood dripped from his nose and ears. "Ask this man," she added, "as soon as he gets his hearing back. He'll tell you everything."

33

Spring comes early to the southern Mediterranean, and by Easter time, the summer flowers were all in bloom. Deep pink oleanders lined the highways, and the prickly pears were already setting their fruit. Mauve bougainvillea cascaded from the balconies of the honey-collared buildings, and the yellow mimosa blossoms gilded the sidewalks. At the Pinto Palace, Dingli, in black waistcoat and shirt-sleeves, was polishing the brass dolphin that had done three centuries' duty as a doorknocker.

Monica had returned to her apartment, but most of her life was now spent with Rafael in the palace itself. An amicable settlement had sent Lady Penelope back to London and Paris, which she had always preferred, and the ancient Mdina house was Rafael's alone. In the mornings, he would make plans for the renovation of the palace and its garden, pleasantly torn between a responsibility to Maltese tradition and a taste for contemporary Italian style. After lunch, he would rest, or try to rest, for his sleep was still troubled by horrors. When he awoke, it was often in a mood of deep depression. He refused all stimulants whatever, even alcohol, having resolved that his objective, for the time being, was to attain a plateau of serenity and self-possession from within. This task would be his alone, though Monica often set her own work aside to deploy every strategy—emotional, intellectual, erotic—in support of it.

Once a week, Rafael would visit his great-uncle in Valletta.

Sophocles was now showing some early symptoms of Alzheimer's disease, and Rafael had taken on the responsibility of hiring full-time caregivers, discreet enough to stay in the background and appear only when needed. Of the other members of the Society of Harmony, Monsignor Buttigieg and Adeodatus Ambini stayed pointedly aloof, but Miss Despott, who had officiated during the fateful séance, had taken on an unexpected importance in Rafael's life. She listened to the account of his experiences and evaluated them with an absolute lack of moralizing. Still wracked by regret and self-reproach, Rafael found he could speak to her of Eusebio and find comfort in her compassionate stoicism. This new friendship went some way to filling the void left by a death that could only be termed as martyrdom.

Monica, too, though in some ways the more resilient of the pair, needed to recover. The physical traumas were more easily overcome than the trauma to her worldview, which had been shaken to its foundations. Hanging over her, too, was the threat of extradition to Italy on a charge of murdering the man who had called himself Carlo Bono. In all the high judicial proceedings that had followed the revelation of Altieri's infamy, this minor detail had been neglected, and it was not until March that the Maltese authorities had finally persuaded the Italians to drop it.

With the complicated unwinding of Sebastian's will, it appeared that he had made separate provision for "archaeological and mythological researches" in the event of his death. With that, the future began to take shape in Monica's mind. First, she found that despite, or perhaps because of, the tribulations she had suffered in Malta, she had fallen in love with its landscape, its people, its history, and prehistory. To be a citizen of a tiny, unimportant country had its attractions, compared to the imperial politics, the academic rat race, the media circus of the United States. Malta would be the center but not the circumference of her new life. However, the "mythological" part unsettled her. She too went to see Miss Despott.

"You have been through the nigredo, my dear, an alchemical process reflected in all the great mythologies, or through the Dark Night of the Soul, as Saint John of the Cross called it. You now know what that means, from the inside."

"But Sebastian . . . he seemed so worldly, and scornful of anything mystical."

"Mystical, yes, but don't you see that he himself was a mythological figure? His bulk, his wealth, his domineering personality—and I found him pretty obnoxious, I can tell you. He was a Hercules type. His whole life was hard labor, bearing the burden of that body, that wealth, and the responsibility it brought, and the terrible worry over his son. He did a tremendous amount of good for Malta. And how poetic that near the end he found the Golden Apple of the Hesperides!"

"I hadn't thought of Sebastian himself that way—I mean in mythological terms. Do you think he did?" said Monica.

"Sebastian knew that archaeology is only the servant of mythology. It's practical and earthy, of course, but what's its ultimate purpose? Not just piling up knowledge of the past, but feeding the Imagination, with a capital I. The Imagination lives and breathes on mythology; that is, on truths beyond time and space that most of us can only grasp through images. That's the reason we have Wunderkammers and museums, houses of the Muses. And the Muses inspire us to create images in turn, through the arts and, I may say, through magic, so that we can live a richer life than through these bodies alone."

Monica nodded.

"You've had labors aplenty, too, my dear. And they're surely not finished yet."

"No. Eusebio called alchemy 'women's work and child's play.' A funny way to put it . . ." Monica paused.

"Indeed. The nigredo can drag you through Hell itself."

"And I've come back alive, not like those immigrants—I still can't bear to imagine what went on there."

"Mythology is full of atrocities."

"Ugh, yes. But I'm sort of purged by it. I've had a glimpse . . . the child's play aspect . . ."

"Go on."

"No, I can't put it into words, but it's there, and it's not going to leave me."

"Bless you, dear. You'll be fine." Miss Despott leaned forward in her wheelchair to shake Monica's hand.

A week later, on this April morning, Inspector Soldanis was due to call for a visit. Dingli straightened up his old bones as the inspector arrived and greeted him.

"Mr. Rafael and Dr. Bettlheim are expecting you in the library," he said. "Please follow me."

The interiors of the palace were plainer than on Soldanis's previous visits; there was less furniture, but even more flowers in great glass vases. Some large modern paintings in figurative style had replaced the dour ancestral portraits. Light streamed from the garden windows, no longer half-shrouded by velvet curtains.

Rafael had already converted his father's Wunderkammer into a library and moved his books into it when he left his apartment in Rome, with its too-painful memories. As Soldanis shook hands with Rafael and Monica, he noticed with approval that they had both put on some weight since their privations, and that Rafael had abandoned his habitual black for white trousers and a wide-striped shirt of many colors.

"No longer a screaming skull," the inspector said to himself, remembering Rafael's ravings in the cavern. "And someone's taught her how to dress, too," he added, looking at Monica. He couldn't know that, as soon as she had been allowed by the authorities, Lady Penelope, only too eager to leave Malta once and for all, had left behind most of her wardrobe, telling Rafael and Monica that she had no intention of ever recovering it. The dress Monica was wearing happened to be a vintage Pucci silk jersey sundress. She was supremely, even achingly beautiful.

As his eyes registered this reality, the inspector breathed with relief and accepted the champagne that Dingli was now offering.

"I know you're on duty, Inspector," Monica said, "but this is a special occasion, and we all have something to celebrate."

"The very best of health to both of you," Soldanis said, raising his glass.

"Do sit down," said Rafael, indicating a deep armchair with a large ashtray beside it. "Smoking is permitted."

"In a library?" said Soldanis, lighting up with a wry smile. Not one to miss a detail, he noticed that Rafael's glass was already filled with bubbling mineral water.

Rafael smiled back. He felt a surge of affection for this gray, ordinary man, who had put his career, then his life, on the line. "I wonder whether going through that experience was an initiation for him, too," asked Rafael in his mind.

Monica sat on the arm of Rafael's chair, her hand on his shoulder. "Sorry we couldn't make it, but congratulations on the award of the Medal for Bravery."

"Oh, that! Well, it puts me in good company, doesn't it?"

"It's the very least the new government could do. After all, without your action they wouldn't have come to power." The three exchanged a worldly smile.

"As for us," Monica continued, "I've already tried to thank you for all we owe you, but words will never be sufficient. And now I also have to thank you for getting me cleared of all those charges, and free to travel again."

"I'm sorry it took so long at the Italian end. It's no fun trying to explain things to the carabinieri. Like teaching math to a herd of buffalo."

She grinned. "I don't think the Order of Malta will ever forgive me, though," she added.

"I'm not so sure," Rafael put in, looking up and putting his hand on hers. "If they could put up with my father, they must have a sense of humor somewhere."

After a few more pleasantries, Soldanis turned to Rafael: "Might I ask a question, just to wrap up a loose end in my mind?"

Rafael stiffened for a moment, then asked: "Off the record?"

"Of course, this is a courtesy visit!"

"Go ahead."

"As I reconstruct the events, you accepted Dr. Bettlheim's theory that your father had met his end in the cave, and you went there in search of further clues. Then you were captured, and we know the rest. Dr. Bettlheim knew where you were going; she got worried, and eventually went there herself. Absolute lunacy, if you'll forgive my saying so."

"You're right," said Monica. "But my life wouldn't have been in danger if you'd locked me up as soon as I arrived in Malta. Weren't you supposed to do that?"

"Yes, and no. I mean, I should have but didn't want to. So I deliberately called a meeting for the whole station personnel, saying that it was a national emergency, to clear the corridors and give you the chance to slip out."

"Well, I did, thank you. Though I was sure at the time that I'd failed to persuade you. You didn't seem to buy my story at all."

"Ha! I didn't want to let you know that I was tempted by it; that doesn't mean I didn't find it . . . suggestive. But first, may *I* ask my question? It's this: did you know what was really going on in there, with the immigrants?"

Rafael and Monica looked at each other. "We had a vague intuition," he said. Monica nodded, wondering how far he would go in revealing the truth to this hardboiled policeman. "I realized that my father had been onto something, and I pieced it together from various hints."

"Hints from your father?"

"More from friends of his, actually."

Soldanis waited an instant, expectantly, but Rafael had no more to offer, other than champagne. He refilled Soldanis's flute, and then sat down, stone-faced.

"I see," thought Soldanis as he sipped some champagne.

"And *your* intuition? What convinced you to raid the caves?" asked Monica, ending an awkward silence.

"Do you really want to know?"

"Of course I do."

"I'll tell you. During my clueless investigation of Cavalier Pinto's case, I had done a very thorough background check on you, as I had on Mr. Pinto here and on Lady Penelope. The picture that emerged was of someone very self-directed, very ambitious. Some people had used the word "self-serving" about you. Your coming to me at great risk to yourself, in fact, your turning yourself in just to save Mr. Pinto, struck a discordant note."

"I suppose I should take that as a compliment?"

"It lent verisimilitude to your story. The two pieces of circumstantial evidence that you brought up also interested me. Then, above all, the revelations about Mr. Pinto's whereabouts and the fact that he was dying.

"Still, it wasn't enough. Especially because you wouldn't tell me how you'd heard from him. By the way, would you tell me now?"

Monica looked at Rafael. "Why," he replied instantly, "didn't you get it yet? It was magic, telepathy at a great distance!"

"What else could it have been?" said Monica.

"Right!" said Soldanis, amused in spite of himself, "Magic. . . . Anyway," he continued, changing tone, "after your interview, all I had was conjecture and inference. I couldn't legally release you, nor did I want to arrest you. I'd long made up my mind that you couldn't have had anything to do with Sebastian Pinto's murder, but you would have been extradited to Italy and tried for another murder. Doubtless acquitted, but a very unpleasant experience all the same. That was when I called David Missigonzo."

Monica looked at the inspector inquiringly.

"The former prime minister. I told him that I had intelligence about Rafael Pinto's whereabouts, in dire condition, and I told him where. He pressed me for more evidence, but I pleaded conditions of strict anonymity and secrecy. What I did say was that I needed a platoon from the armed forces, right then and there. It was to raid the cave, and I was to lead it. He pulled that noncommittal face on me; I could 'see' it even over the phone. But he agreed to see me.

"Once we were face to face, a few interminable hours later, I reminded him of how Malta had lost Sebastian Pinto, how they'd lost Lady Penelope, who was now suing him and everyone else, and how if they lost Rafael Pinto, any benefits they might expect from Malta's first family—if you'll excuse me—would go down the drain.

"Wouldn't you know? That turned him. If the raid was a flop, being at night, no one would have to know about it; the only one to lose face would be me, and neither he nor I cared about that. But what I didn't expect was for you to go alone to the caves; I wouldn't have let you."

"Another out-of-character move?" said Monica.

Soldanis smiled. "None of us is as simple as all that. You know, these things are like a chess game. Mine was a gambit, and it worked. Missigonzo took what looked like a lesser risk, but it was the end of his political career. Now the Italian government's fallen, too; the European Union is in a tailspin; the UN's in an uproar."

"And the immigrants are still coming, by one route or another. Do you see any solution to it?"

"Me?" Soldanis glanced at Rafael. What a contrast to his father, the inspector thought, and then said, in reply: "I guess the only thing would be to help their economies, boost them. But that'd be ironic, a new form of colonialism, in a sense. Luckily, though, that's outside my jurisdiction. I'm not paid enough to save the world, just the two of you."

"And I," put in Rafael, "am *not* paid to save you, yet am contributing, in my small way, to your safety."

"Really?" said Soldanis, taken by surprise. "How's that?"

"I've managed to have my stepmother withdraw her lawsuit against you."

"Well, thank you! That's very good news."

"Don't mention it; it's the least she could do."

"Right," said Soldanis; he stubbed out his cigarette and looked around him. "Well, I must be going."

"Before you go," said Rafael, "I'd like you to accept this." He handed Soldanis a package.

"Aha: trying to bribe me, at last?"

Rafael smiled broadly.

"May I open it now?" the inspector pressed him.

"Certainly."

"It's a long time since anyone gave me a present," said Soldanis, cutting the string with his penknife. He opened the inner tissue paper and revealed a silver cigar box. "That will give some style to my humble abode," he said. "Thank you very much."

"You don't need to open this one now," said Rafael, handing him another, larger package. "It's something to keep it filled for a while. Cohiba Pirámides. You know, the Cuban cigars. We were told that it's a limited edition, aged for four years."

"That for me is beyond the dreams of avarice," said the inspector. "I'm really touched that you tolerate my love affair with Lady Nicotine; indeed, you aid and abet it." He shook Rafael's hand, then Monica's.

"Speaking of treasures," he said to her, "there was a golden pomegranate that figured largely in Sebastian Pinto's last days. And in your days in Rome. Have we heard the end of that?"

"Certainly not. The pomegranate has gone to the Order of Malta, with Sebastian's other treasures. It's still very much of a mystery, along with its contents. If anything definite emerges, I'll make sure you hear of it."

"I would like that. We're both in the detective business, in a manner of speaking. And you, Mr. Pinto? I hope you don't mind my asking this, just out of personal curiosity. What will you be doing?"

Rafael thought about his reply for a while, then said: "Well, there's a lot left to explore."

"Do you mean, in Malta?"

"Also."

Acknowledgments

Our gratitude to:

The late Gillon Aitken, for his friendship and his editorial advice.
To Christopher Sinclair-Stevenson, for his friendship and his help.
Giovanna Penco Salvi, for spurring us on and for her sympathetic magic.
Gardner and Charles Monks, for their timely, precise, and imaginative involvement.
Ariel and Annie for their suggestions.

The scholars who have dedicated some or much of their life to the study of the entheogens:

The pioneers: R. Gordon Wasson and his wife Valentina Pavlovna; Robert Graves; the late Albert Hofmann, Terence McKenna, and Blaise Daniel Staples. And Carl A. P. Ruck, Clark Heinrich, Peter Webster, Jonathan Ott, James Arthur, Dan Russell, Dan Merkur, Antonio Escohotado, David L. Spess, and several more, whose omission from this list does not diminish their importance.

Robert Eisenman and the late Hyam Maccoby, for their work on early Christianity.

Dulcis in fundo, everyone at Inner Traditions, namely: Jon Graham, acquisitions editor; Mindy Branstetter, project editor; Jeanie Levitan, editor in chief; Sarah Galbraith, copy editor; Patricia Rydle, editorial assistant; Aaron Davis, cover design; Erica Robinson, catalog copy; John Hays, sales and marketing director; Manzanita Carpenter Sanz, author liaison and publicist; Ehud Sperling, publisher.

About the Authors

JOSCELYN GODWIN

Joscelyn Godwin was born in 1945 in Kelmscott Manor, the historic Oxfordshire home of William Morris. He grew up in Oxford with his adopted guardians, Muriel Hodge and Mabel Cordingley, and was educated at Christ Church Cathedral Choir School, Radley College, Magdalene College, Cambridge, and Cornell University (Ph.D. in Musicology, 1969). Settling in the United States, he pursued an academic career, teaching first at Cleveland State University, then at Colgate University from 1971 until his retirement in 2016.

From the mid-1970s, Godwin concentrated his research on "speculative music," including topics such as the harmony of the planetary spheres and the effects of music on the human body and soul. He collected, edited, and translated texts from two millennia in *Harmonies of Heaven and Earth, Cosmic Music, The Harmony of the Spheres,* and *Music, Mysticism & Magic.*

In the 1980s, Godwin moved to the broader field of the humanities, aiming to bridge the gulf between the esoteric and the academic. He brought scholarly standards to the treatment of occultism, esoteric currents, and eccentric religious movements in his books *The Theosophical Enlightenment, The Golden Thread, Atlantis and the Cycles of Time, Upstate Cauldron,* and *Arktos: the Polar Myth in Science, Symbolism, and Nazi Survival.* With articles and minor writings for academic presses and journals, he joined the growing movement to validate such studies within the scholarly world and is a frequent conference speaker on both sides of the Atlantic. At Colgate University, besides teaching music history, theory, and appreciation, he offered courses in the Western Esoteric Tradition, the Atlantis Debate, and Rejected Knowledge. The latter defied academic norms by studying paranormal and anomalous phenomena, parapsychology, alternative history and prehistory, and the philosophy of Charles Fort.

Many of Joscelyn Godwin's books are generously illustrated, such as *Mystery Religions in the Ancient World, The Pagan Dream of the Renaissance, The Greater and Lesser Worlds of Robert Fludd,* and *Athanasius Kircher's Theatre of the World.* He has compiled a book about his parents: *The Starlight Years: Love and War at Kelmscott Manor, 1940–1948; The Paintings, Writings, and Drawings of Edward and Stephani Scott-Snell/Godwin.* Early schooling in languages helped him to translate and edit books from Italian, French, and German, some done in collaboration with his son, Ariel, also a multilingual translator. They included the first complete English translation of the erotic-architectural novel *Hypnerotomachia Poliphili* of 1499 and works by Julius Evola, Saint-Yves d'Alveydre, and Hans Kayser.

Godwin has been an oboist, an organist, and a keen modernist composer, but he now prefers to play the harpsichord (especially French baroque music), the clavichord, and occasionally the recorder and the viola da gamba. In 2018 the Society of Antiquaries of London elected him an Honorary Fellow. He lives with his wife, Janet, in Hamilton, New York.

GUIDO MINA DI SOSPIRO

Guido Mina di Sospiro belongs to an ancient Italian aristocratic family and was raised in Milan in a multilingual home. Since the 1980s he has been living in the United States, first in Los Angeles, then in Miami, currently near Washington, D.C. He was educated at the University of Pavia and at the University of Southern California.

He started as a filmmaker and music critic. His first feature film, *Heroes and Villains,* premiered at the Italian Cinémathèque in Milan, Italy, creating quite a stir because of its iconoclastic and irreverent stance toward the status quo. As a music critic, while still in his teens he began writing for *Ritmo,* Italy's oldest jazz periodical, founded at the end of WW II (as jazz had previously been banned by the fascist regime). As a classically trained guitarist, he gave a few concerts in Milanese auditoria.

Mentored by Miklós Rózsa—the Hungarian-American composer known for his nearly one hundred film scores and seventeen Oscar nominations, including three successes, who nevertheless continued to compose formal concert music championed by such major artists as Jascha Heifetz, Gregor Piatigorsky, and János Starker—Mina di Sospiro left Italy and, in Los Angeles, went to the USC School of Cinema-Television, now known as the School of Cinematic Arts.

In Los Angeles, he wrote and directed the short film *If I Could Do It All Over Again, I'd Do It All Over You,* which debuted at the 32nd Berlin Film Festival, and became the United States correspondent for the music and cinema magazines *Tutti Frutti* (both monthly and weekly) and *Elaste,* respectively Italian and German. *Elaste* was a culture, lifestyle, and indie magazine that achieved cult status in Europe.

As a novelist Mina di Sospiro is published around the world in thirteen languages. He debuted with the seminal *The Story of Yew,* the memoirs of a two-thousand-year old yew tree. Keen on scientific accuracy, he wrote the book collaborating with some of the greatest botanists and naturalists in the world. He then published its successor, *From the River,* the memoirs of the eons-old Po river, for which he worked closely with hydrologists, historians, engineers, and assorted scientists.

The first novel he coauthored with Joscelyn Godwin is *The Forbidden Book.* It deals with radical Islamic terrorism, with an attack first on Italian and then on Spanish soil, while trying to analyze and then put to use by harnessing its alleged powers. It is based on a book from 1603, written by Cesare Della Riviera, titled *Il Mondo magico de gli heroi* (The Magical World of the Heroes), a very mysterious treatise of alchemy that supposedly teaches how to attain the Tree of Life and make a man into a god.

Of *The Metaphysics of Ping-Pong,* a book of narrative non-fiction written in a semiserious vein, *Publishers Weekly* states that it "can constitute a perfect introduction to the vast history of humankind's quest for philosophical clarity."

His novel *Leeward and Windward* is a romance of the high seas that toys with the tropes of conventional fiction as a pretext for a daring alchemical exploration of the *coniunctio oppositorum.* In its Italian edition as *Sottovento e sopravvento* the novel garnered rave reviews: philosopher Maurizio Ferraris has likened it to Voltaire's *Candide.*

Mina di Sospiro contributes essays for a number of web and print magazines, among them *Reality Sandwich, New English Review, New Dawn, Linkiesta,* and *Pangea.*

Under normal circumstances, i.e., in virus-free times, he lives between the Washington, D.C., area and Italy with his wife, Stenie.